Grown Men Don't Cry

by

B.W. DeCaro

B.W. DeCaro

"Some come and leave, fulfilling a single purpose; others, for a time or a season to teach us by sharing their experiences; and last, a select few who participate forever with relationships that endure through eternity."

Jaren L. Davis

This book is dedicated to my childhood best friend, Ben Huff. We were pre-teens fearless and filled with testosterone. You pushed me every day to believe in myself as both a young athlete and man. Thanks for always letting me win that 10th game of one on one. We won't talk about the first nine. You were the best friend any kid could ever ask for. I regret losing touch Ben.

When I made that seemingly innocent call to your mom in an attempt to reconnect after all these years, I could never have imagined the heartbreaking news she had to again revisit. Life is so short and so many great people die young. After that call I decided to write this book. May we meet again in Heaven some day. I'll bring the baseball gear.

Acknowledgements

I would like to start by thanking Mary Hadley. Without your inspiration this would simply be an idea that collected dust. Thank you for believing in me and providing guidance.

To Chris Hadley, your candid feedback throughout this project has been vital to its success. Thank you for spending your precious free time on my work. Oh and how can I forget the light that went off during our Thai Lunch, which led to a much improved ending? Gracias!

Dr. Al Jerome and others like him, whose tireless work helps thousands of people suffering from mental illness.

Ben Carstoiu, your thoughtful comments resulted in more vibrant and life-like characters. Thank you for devoting the time to my work.

To all of my teachers at Newfound Regional High School. Thank you for believing in my creativity.

To all of my baseball coaches through the years, especially Mr. Bucklin and Mr. Marasca, thank you for instilling a sound worth ethic and will to win.

Brian and Beverly Buffini. Thank you for motivating me to pursue my dreams.

My Editor Christine LePorte. Your attention to detail made all the difference.

Thank you to Michael Barton for helping with the final uploading. Your keen eyes made some important last minute changes.

My cover designer Krista Vossen. Thank you for listening to my vision and making it come to life!

My mom and dad, thank you for all of the sacrifices you made while trying to provide for me and the girls. Oh, and my sisters for putting up with their pain in the neck brother.

Finally, to my loving family. Thanks for all of the support, especially during the times daddy locked himself in the office while engaged in deep thought. Bic, your support means the world to me.

B.W. DeCaro

1. Ben's First Hit

April 1983 Nashua, NH

Ben

"Here we go, Giants, here we go!" I shout loudly, knowing full well this is the role I'm relegated to until I get my shot. As a ten-year-old on a ten- to twelve-year-old Little League team, I guess I can't expect much more.

Even so, we've lost all four games so far this year and I've only been up once. I had lined a nice shot, but it landed right in the lucky third baseman's glove. Coach should have seen my potential from that, right?

We're losing again, this time to the hated Yankees, 4-1. It's only the third inning, so we still have time for a comeback.

Suddenly, I feel a rumble in my stomach. Must be that extra bowl of Lucky Charms that I wolfed down before running out the door this morning. I let out a nasty fart and sit back to watch how many guys take notice.

There's nothing more enjoyable for a ten-year-old than seeing your buddies gasp for air because of a deadly one you lay down. Another comes out, but this one feels a little juicier. Oh no, I think, this might not be going away anytime soon.

I try to ignore it for the remainder of the inning, as we pull closer, 4-2. I feel another fart coming, but then realize I have no way of knowing if this could turn into the runs.

Without a bathroom at the field, this is trouble. I go up to pee behind the big oak tree that everyone uses, hoping this will do the trick. After a few squirts I realize I made the wrong move. Now I can feel the bowel movement within an inch or two of coming out.

I see my dad in the stands and walk over to him. "Ben, what are you doing out here? Why aren't you focused so that when your shot comes you'll be ready?" Dad says.

"I gotta go to the bathroom, Dad, and it's not the kind I can do at the tree."

"Son, what are you asking, for me to take you home and we miss the game?"

My dad's buddy Ray is there with him. Ray is quite the character. A chain smoker in his mid-forties, Ray is single and a bit odd.

My dad's known Ray from back when he was a social worker right out of college. They both love the Pats and Sox, and my dad enjoys drinking with Ray during the off-chance he gets out of the house.

Ray looks down at me. "Can you hold it, Ben? We only have three more innings. You know Yaz would hold it." He's referring to Red Sox legend Carl Yastrzemski, affectionately known as "Yaz."

We met Yaz a month earlier during an autograph signing. Ray knows that comment will silence me quickly. "I guess I can wait."

I staggered back to the dugout, shoulders slouched and ass cheeks squeezed. As I enter the dugout, Coach Smith says, "Get ready, Ben, you're going in next inning. You'll be playing left and are on deck once we get up to bat."

Normally I'd be pumped, but the thought of taking a big dump in my pants starts to take over my brain.

A fart is coming on; I push against the dugout fence for added effect and let it rip. Before I can stop, I feel the log ooze out of my butthole and fall into the bottom left side of my baseball pants and nestle against my sock.

Another smaller one pops out and now I have two slimy logs in my pants, one on each side of my left leg. Panic sets in. Did anyone notice?

I take a step and can feel the log squish against my leg. "Are you kidding me?" I mumble. Looking down I notice my crystal-clean white pants now have a brown stain on the left leg.

At this point my team gets the third out of the inning and heads into the dugout. Quickly, I rush out to congratulate Kemp, our pitcher, and then kick up a bunch of dirt covering both cleats and some of my pants.

Nice, it blends in well with the feces. I grab my helmet and head into the on-deck circle. As I take my first practice swing, the discomfort sets in. I guess I never realized how many body parts move when I swing the bat. Now the poop is starting to smear across my entire ankle.

Billy, our second baseman, hits a blooper over the first baseman's head, and he lands on first. I'm up.

"Let's go, Ben, squeeze one out there," Coach Smith says. You have no idea. As I walk towards the batter's box I look down in horror, realizing my pant leg is now covered in brown from my ankle to the cuff of my pants. I start to smell it at this point.

Luckily for me it's normal for a hitter to pick up dirt before he jumps into the box. I kick with both feet and create a large dust cloud, then throw some additional dirt on my pant legs for good measure.

The catcher gives me a peculiar glare as if he knows I have yet to get a hit in my young baseball career. I crouch into my patented batting stance, the kind your dad shows you when you are only 5'1" and 85 pounds.

I take a wild swing at the first pitch and miss by at least a foot, as the pitch hits the dirt in front of the plate. Paranoid, I take a look back to see if the catcher's noticed the oozing poop pouring out of my uniform.

Luckily he doesn't. The ump also hasn't acted any differently, so I try to relax a bit.

I step out of the box—*tap, tap, tap*—*gently tap the bat three times on my left foot*—*tap, tap, tap*—*then three times on my right foot*. No wonder I missed the first one, I forgot my good luck ritual.

The pitch comes at me, just missing my head. I duck down and glare back at the pitcher. He gives me an apologetic look and shows some frustration for his lack of control.

Now 1-1, I settle into the box, then out again—*tap, tap, tap—then the right—tap, tap, tap.* A fastball right down the middle is coming my way.

Smack. Wow, that felt good! I stroke a line drive over the head of the shortstop into left center field. Single. My first hit! I look up and see Dad and Ray cheering. Ray's now drinking out of a brown bag. What a drunk, I laugh to myself.

Billy moves over to third base. It's now first and third, nobody out, and we're down by two. I look up at Coach Smith, who calmly taps his cap and then swipes his left leg.

Oh man, he's asking me to steal. With the elation of getting my first hit I completely forgot about the ooze running down my leg.

At this point, it appears my pants will hold everything in, so I need to roll with it. I can't let this one get away. Dad will kill me if I don't steal in this situation, first and third, nobody out; even my sisters know that is a given.

I watch the pitcher let go of the ball, and then head for second. Coach Smith knows I have speed in my little legs. As I'm about ten feet from the bag I make my head-first dive into second. The second baseman jumps up to try and snag the ball, but it pulls him too far off the bag. I'm safe and Billy is crossing home plate. We're now only down by one. Sweet!

Our best hitter, Marshall, comes up next and knocks it over the left field wall. I cross home to a crowd of teammates, poo and all. We're now up 5-4.

Our relief pitching does the job and we win our first game. Dad and Ray are pumped. I'm ready to get home and change my clothes.

As we head back to the car, I cringe, remembering we took Ray's tiny clunker. I think it's a Pinto. All I know is its rusty, loud, and has a tiny back seat that isn't meant for people to sit in.

I sit on the small hump in the back, with my legs on one side of the car and head on the other. The windows are closed and it's got to be approaching 75 degrees. I don't think Ray has AC in this car.

Then out of the blue Ray says, "Do you smell that?" At the same time Dad goes, "Ah man. That is awful. Check your shoes, everyone."

Smirking, I check my shoes and enjoy the rest of the ride home. The first of many times where my parents will have to clean up after my shit.

2. Present Day

July 2011

Ben

"Life is a great and wondrous mystery, and the only thing we know that we have for sure is what is right here right now. Don't miss it."

Leo Buscaglia (1924-1998); author, professor

It's even more spectacular than the website portrayed. Ocean as far as the eyes can see. Our own sanctuary; like a postcard moment. Inspiring, to say the least!

I plop myself on the back porch chair and let everything sink in. No streetlights, loud engines, or traffic. Just the serenity of healthy green grass and an endless ocean (well, bay) view.

The handful of tall pines gives the yard an even cozier feel. A large bird house quaintly nestled in the corner. Nothing but the sounds of light waves crashing along the rocks below and an occasional bird chirping in the wind.

Out in the distance I hear some rumbling beyond the clouds. Is that a fighter jet? Must be. We aren't too far from Norfolk, are we?

As the sound gets more dramatic, there they are. Side by side. Perhaps a drill? In this day and age, with terrorism everywhere, who knows? But I feel safer knowing they are up there, I'll tell you that.

I start to think about the guys flying that bad boy; reminds me of Jimmy. I wouldn't be here relishing this moment if it weren't for guys like him.

"Daddy! Daddy! Let's play Dora on the swing set," Isabella and Brady shout.

OK. Time to get up. It just amazes me the amount of

life they have in those little bodies. Ever since we got here, they have embraced every waking moment.

"OK," I yell back. "Am I Swiper this time or the pirate?"

"Hurry, Daddy, climb up here, the crocodiles are going to get you."

It's hard to believe this time last year I was asking Eddie to promise me he would watch out for them while I was gone. He agreed to play the disciplinary figure with Brady and walk Isabella down the aisle.

Eddie has no kids of his own, partly by choice, partly because of Janice's medical condition. Two shots of insulin per day make it way too risky to think about getting pregnant. Yet, even though they don't have any kids, I knew they wouldn't let me down.

"How about the dogs, can they play?" I ask.

"Sure," Isabella says. "Daisy can be Swiper. Chance is the stranger. Run, Daddy. The stranger is trying to get you."

I hightail it up to the swing set, coffee in hand, and climb into the lookout tower. God, why can't life always be this simple?

"Somewhere Over the Rainbow" plays on the iPod speakers. "Someday I'll wish upon a star, wakeup where the clouds are far behind me…Oooh, oooh, oooh, ooohhhh"…. Iz has such as soulful voice. What a perfect song for this place, really gets you to reflect on life. There is something about music that always hits home for me. Throughout the most influential moments of my life I can almost always point towards a song to capture the essence of my emotions. It's pretty uncanny.

Not many people get a second chance. Iz certainly didn't. I guess I'm one of the lucky few. As Jimmy would say, "Better make the most of it."

3. Jimmy's Last Day

November 2009 Bristol, NH

Jimmy

Everything is in place. Months of planning and this day is finally here. It couldn't have come any faster.

Boy, this would have been a lot easier if I didn't have to worry about staging things. One pull of the trigger from my 9mm would have done just fine by me. But I suppose my parents don't deserve things to end that way. At least to perceive things didn't end that way. I can only imagine the shame Dad would feel and the guilt Mom would take upon herself if I didn't take these extra measures.

I don't want to let them down, especially with all of the turmoil my brothers have put them through. But I need to do what's best for me now. I'm sick of doing things for everyone else.

Just a few minutes ago I carried Mrs. Gordon's three suitcases to her car. She's heading to Manchester Airport to visit her son down in Orlando. I've been here a little over a year and this is her third trip.

Her leaving is always a little bittersweet. I definitely like not having to tiptoe around at night so I won't wake her up. She goes to bed at eight o'clock sharp.

I also get a break from trash duty, shoveling, and the other miscellaneous chores that come with helping a seventy-year-old landlord.

However, things usually get a little too quiet in my tiny attic apartment when she leaves. Silence means time to think, time for my mind to wander, and that is never good.

Yet, this year peace and quiet is exactly what the doctor ordered. I can't have any witnesses in order to execute my plan.

Sipping my coffee at the kitchen table, I peer through the 1970's drapes to see another dreary day in Hicktown, USA.

What kind of an idiot picks Bristol, NH, to settle down in? Why not San Diego, CA, or Fort Myers, FL? Heck, at least in Fort Myers I could watch the Sox every year in March for Spring Training. I'll tell you why I settled here; I had no money and no job.

I served my time and came back to live with my mom, just like thousands of other ex-Marines. Hell, I bet if I lived at the beach, the nightmares would be a little easier to handle. Maybe instead of dreaming about dead friends I would be fantasizing about nude beaches. Breasts would be a little better than gaping bullet wounds.

It's weird when you know this is your last day on earth. Surprising how little if any fear I now have of dying. Five years ago I was scared shitless of taking a stray bullet that would end my life or of getting blindsided by an Iraqi in civilian clothes setting off an IED as I scavenged through abandoned buildings.

Back then the fear kept me going. Now the lack of it is making the end seem rather uneventful.

Well, today will at least be one that I choose. I guess I'm treating today as if I were an inmate on death row. My favorite meal is waiting over at Bob and Edith's Diner. A delicious Reuben Melt with extra Thousand Island dressing. Oh, and heavy on the onions, please.

As I pull into the jam-packed parking lot, I notice my favorite spot has just become available. Must be my lucky day, I laugh to myself.

By now the waitress knows me by name. Most of the time I'm so hung-over that I can barely acknowledge her.

Helen, is that her name? Pathetic, she knew mine after my second visit. I don't even take the time to pay attention to hers. At least I tip her well, 18 percent. For a poor vet, that is.

"Hi, Jimmy. What's new?" she warmly greets me.

"Same old, same old," I blandly respond. Wow, is that really all I can come up with for my last conversation alive? How weak.

Five minutes later my Rueben Melt arrives just the way I like it. Man, I'm going to miss these. It goes down great with my Stewart's Root Beer. Just about the best lunch a man could ask for. Not a bad last meal, eh!

As I finish up my mound of fries, the final details roll through my mind.

Checklist:

Case of Natty Lite
Car Jack
Full tank of gas
Oil-stained rag
Almost new muffler – 98 Pontiac Sunfire
Boston Red Sox boxer shorts

Easy enough. Everything is set. I just need to throw on my lucky boxer shorts when I get home. The plan is simple, yet ingenious, if you ask me. The marine gets boozed up while working on his car in the old lady's garage, then passes out and dies of carbon monoxide poisoning.

Everyone knows I've been working on this POS car for months and that I drink at least a 12-pack every weekend night (not to mention the 8-pack I drink on weeknights).

From what I've read on the Internet about carbon monoxide poisoning, it really is pretty painless. If I execute properly, by beer number ten things should be fairly numb.

I'll start up the car around two p.m. and estimated time of death should fall somewhere between three p.m. and five p.m. Who cares at that point, right? The main thing is that it will be a win/win. I will be put out of my misery and

Mom and Dad won't have to feel the humiliation of a suicide. Just a dumb mistake committed by a guy who was normally careful about things like that, that's all.

I'm sure Dad will be a little curious as to how I could be that much of a knucklehead, but heck, he's passed out many a time after some cold ones.

While finishing up the last few French fries I overhear an older couple sitting behind me. Normally I'm not one to eavesdrop, but I think today can be an exception.

"I can't believe he's only thirty-five, so young to have kidney disease." The woman sounds so sympathetic. It's nice to know that some people do care, even if it is for another guy.

Thirty-five, wow, we have something in common. I turned thirty-five back in September, what a wild time that night. Probably the last time I actually laughed.

"He has so much to live for," the man responds. "Do the kids know yet?"

"No, and Sarah wants to leave it that way for as long as she can. Not that they won't notice anyway with the amount of weight Ben has been losing. He's down to 125 pounds. That's about thirty pounds lighter than his high school baseball days."

Baseball. Ben. Sarah…thirty-five…? Without thinking about my manners, I do a 180 and end up practically sitting in their booth.

"Hi, I'm sorry, but I overheard your conversation. You aren't talking about Ben Chase by any chance, are you?"

"Why yes, we are, do you know him?"

I guess she figures a skanky-looking guy like me wouldn't hang out with a polished guy like Ben.

"He and I practically grew up together. Is he sick?"

"Oh, it's really sad. He was doing so well, raising a family, great career. Then about two months ago he found out he had kidney problems. Now they're giving him six months to live, unless he gets a transplant." The woman starts to distance herself, probably feeling like she's already said too much. It turns out she's one of Ben's mom's best friends.

"About done with those fries, dear?" Helen asks sarcastically.

What time is it? Man, I've been just sitting here staring at the remnants of what's supposed to be my last meal for about thirty minutes.

Sadness. Empathy. Is that really coming from me? Tough guy feels sad. Can't be. I guess sadness and guilt.

I didn't even call him after my final tour to let him know I was back in town. Heck the only time we've hung out since then was when we nearly got killed on the snowmobiles.

He seemed fine then. Sarah was pregnant with their third child and he had a thriving sales career. Wow, how fast things can change.

The guilt started to settle in. He definitely made the effort to see me more. The worst part is I could almost walk to his house. Of course, I never even told Ben I moved back to Bristol. I'm better off keeping my distance from people.

Ever since coming back, I've had the remarkable ability to shut out even the most well-intentioned and persistent friends. Soon after the honeymoon feeling wore off of returning to the States, reality set in.

The nightmares became a routine, along with feeling sorry for myself. Then the news of a few buddies that didn't make it home and all hell broke loose in my mind.

So, calling Ben back or emailing him (and I still can't understand why people don't just pick up the phone these days) was not something I wanted to pursue. He would just ask me questions and feel sorry for me. The last thing I need is for my old buddy to feel bad for me, or worse, see the weakness in my eyes.

Some of the local townies would never be able to see through the walls I put up, but Ben would see through that bullshit in about ten minutes. Now he's dying, and I would have never found out if it weren't for my pathetic last Reuben Melt.

4. The Phone Call

Jimmy

I catch Sarah just as she's heading out the door to take the kids out for a walk. I'm sure it helps take her mind off things, although I don't see how taking three little ones out in forty-degree weather can relieve stress. I've seen running snots on toddlers and it's about as nasty as the makeshift port-a-johns we had out in the desert.

When she answers the phone, she has no idea who I am, but it doesn't take long for her to figure it out after I drop a few F-bombs while talking about Ben's condition. I've always felt comfortable around Sarah. She was like a sister to me before I enlisted.

Sarah graduated two years ahead of us and grew up in Bristol. How she's managed not to go crazy living here all these years I have no idea, but she seems to have turned out OK. Heck, much better than me. Who am I to talk?

Anyhow, she gives me the full scoop. Ben started pissing blood back in August. At first he thought it was probably just a little too much booze, but then a few weeks later the sharp pains kicked in. After doing his best to conceal the pain, Sarah took control and made the call to her doctor.

Ben probably hadn't had a physical since college. Next thing you know, his doctor is telling him to drive out to Dartmouth Hitchcock Hospital for some "advanced tests."

Assuming it was probably just precautionary, Sarah and Ben didn't give it much more thought. Although, in hindsight, she should have realized there's a reason patients get sent to Dartmouth, and it's not for precautionary measures. The tests came back five days later, revealing he has stage four kidney failure.

"What's the prognosis?" I interrupt her.

"We're keeping the faith, but the doctors tell us that

he needs a new kidney in the next three to six months or else he won't make it," Sarah says rather emotionlessly.

Clearly the question's been posed to her dozens of times at this point. "Well, can't he get a kidney transplant?" I ask. I remember reading an article recently about a college basketball star who had a kidney removed and after the transplant, was back to dunking about a month later.

"I wish it were that simple. With organ transplants it gets a little complicated." She explains how there's a long list of people waiting for transplants and that Ben has 349 people in front of him.

No one can predict how long that would take, but it's safe to say it would be longer than six months. Not to mention the issues with matching his blood type, which she doesn't want to get into.

Then she invites me to Isabella's sixth birthday party next Saturday. Princess theme. She laughs. But then the tears begin to flow.

At least that's what I picture as she begins to choke up. I'm surprised she could keep it together for as long as she did. Maybe the doctor talk became a routine at this point, but planning birthday parties, and thinking this may be the last one Ben sees, is anything but routine.

Little does Sarah know I won't be around for the Princess party next week. I still accept graciously.

It hits me that I owe Ben one call before my exit.

I dial the cell number Sarah provided. "Yo, scumbag?" I blurt out.

"Who's this jerk?" he says in that all too familiar cocky tone.

"Just a messed up old Marine. Oh, and former catcher to your wild-ass arm!" I reply.

"Hah, I thought you headed back to the desert. Where are you?"

Once I tell him I'm in Bristol, he immediately takes charge and says, "Salty Dog, five p.m., happy hour. On me."

Normally I would have pushed back, especially since by then I should have been breathing carbon monoxide with a nice buzz.

However, I guess I have one final decent decision left in me and figure one more day won't kill me. Kill me, get it? Anyway, the old lady doesn't get back in town for another three days.

5. Sarah's Perspective

Sarah

I can't believe Jimmy just called me. Wow, Ben will sure be glad to see him. Even if he can't get hammered like in the old days. I wonder if he'll go into detail about what's happened over the past few years. Yeah right, he'd rather donate his testicles to science.

Whenever someone finds out about Ben's condition, they instantly start to patronize us. I know its awkward learning someone so young is dying. Heck, I'd probably act weird too.

It's not that I don't appreciate the warm comments, cards, cookies, and other random sympathy stuff. But he's not dead yet, and I'm trying whatever I can to keep his mind in a positive state.

The thought of losing him right now is just too much to handle, especially after he's come so far this past year. And to think, about a week before his kidney disease was diagnosed he uttered the words, "This is the happiest and most peaceful I've ever been in all of my life."

God has a funny way of rewarding people sometimes. Ben finally gets his head on straight and then a month later, *Bam, take that*!

We still haven't told the kids yet. Brady has started to ask questions lately about why Daddy can only play baseball with him for a few minutes before he gets too tired and needs a break.

Isabella thinks Daddy looks funny with his "long face." She remembers him being much thicker a couple years ago. And without a head full of grays.

At two, Lucy is oblivious to the situation right now. I just pray she'll get to spend several more birthdays with Ben.

What's so amazing is after ten years of marriage Ben and I are the closest we've ever been. We barely survived the seven-year itch, and I was within inches of filing for separation.

Now, through his ordeal, he's changed to become such a better man. He was a good man when we got married. I always knew he had a great heart. However, sometimes it wouldn't show up for months at a time.

Now, he radiates love. Every second he's with me and the kids, he gives us one hundred percent of his attention. No more daydreaming. Talking about this makes me choke up.

He has so much to offer and now it might all be gone in less than six months. Just yesterday the doctors shortened his prognosis from six to twelve months to three to six.

Of course, there's always hope for a miracle, which is why I've started to visit St. Patrick's church every morning before Ben heads out to work. He thinks I'm hitting the gym. Which, if I get up early enough, I do both. But I haven't missed a day of prayer in the last five weeks.

I'm trying to take as many pictures and videos as possible right now. We just saved up enough to buy a nice Sony HD camcorder. The first set of pictures and videos came out awesome.

The scary thing is comparing Ben's pictures to a few years back, from our other camera. You can see the weight in his cheeks evaporate as the days go by. He still has that million dollar smile, but it kills me to see him suffer. Especially when I know I haven't always kept up my end of the bargain.

To love and honor, through sickness and health, richer or poorer. And so it goes. If I only knew the nightmares he was dealing with the past few years, I would have been much more patient and loving with him.

But how could I know? I just assumed he was being a typical guy. Selfish, tough to communicate with, and only worried about one thing.

I'm so ashamed of not asking more questions. I'm

supposed to be his best friend. He had no one else to talk to about his problems. Yet, he did it all alone. I only pray we have a second chance to make things right.

6. Reuniting

Ben

I can't believe that kid woke up from the grave.

How random is that. Jimmy and I were inseparable back in high school. I would stay over at his house on average three out of every four weekends per month. Anything to get away from my mom's constant nagging and bitching. The only reason I wasn't there every weekend is because my mom felt compelled to ground me once a month, just so I'd spend some quality time with our family. How ass backwards is that? Talk about empowering someone, not.

My mom did the same thing with church. We didn't really know why we went; we just "had to." Perhaps that's why it took me fifteen years to get back into it once I lived on my own?

Anyhow, when I left for college it never struck me that Jimmy and I wouldn't stay close. He came up to visit the first weekend of my freshman year. Boy, did we get hammered.

But once he left for boot camp at the Corps, we drifted pretty quickly. I can't blame him; hell, I could never make it through the shit he went through. He's only shared bits and pieces of the hazing, but it makes my fraternity stuff look like a kiddie camp.

We wrote letters to each other during the first few months of our new lives, but over time other things started to take priority.

Jimmy left for Kuwait during the first Iraqi conflict within about six months of completing boot camp. Since email wasn't around at the time, we simply drifted apart.

When was the last time I even saw Jimmy? I know, we went snowmobiling. We partied for a few nights with some of the old boys around the lake.

Snowmobiling when you're wasted is not the best

idea. Jimmy nearly got decapitated one night. In complete darkness, we rolled out onto the lake on Christmas Eve. Swerving back and forth, he caught his neck on a wire that was dangling near one of the fishing docks. Two more inches to the left and he may not be here right now. Of course, the tough bastard recovered in a day and we were up drinking again the next night.

I still have two hours before quitting time and definitely don't have the motivation to bug the hell out of a few prospects and convince them to get off the fence.

Most people wouldn't understand why I'm still going through the motions and putting in a full forty-five-hour work week while my body is failing, but for me if I just sat at home, I'd feel so useless.

Geez, I wonder what Jimmy will think when he sees my scrawny ass. He'd never guess that this is actually the happiest I've ever been in my life.

Sure it sucks that I'm dying, but from an emotional standpoint, I'm finally enjoying life to its fullest. The past few years have been hell, but things were finally turning the corner after my thirty-fifth birthday.

Three-ten p.m. If I leave now, I can get to the Dog around four, finish up a little paperwork in the car for twenty-five minutes, and then head in early. If the old Jimmy shows up, he'll be there around four-thirty anyway and try to down two full ones before I slap my butt on the stool.

He likes to scope out the place, find the hotties, and get in good with the bartender before anyone else in the posse shows up. Manchester to Plymouth should take about an hour, not accounting for traffic, that is.

As I close the door to Joe's Heating and AC, a chuckle emerges. So I guess I've made it, I mock myself. On the surface, especially to those from Bristol, it certainly appears so.

I've been with the same company for over ten years and keep getting promoted. Now I'm essentially my own boss in a pretty good sales gig. But I'm not sure if this is what Keene State College had in mind for me—selling payroll solutions to a crabby small business owner as he haggles me down to barely any profit.

A cold beer sounds nice right about now. The doctors would frown upon it, but one won't kill me, will it? I owe it to Jimmy, especially since he actually took the initiative to call me. That's got to be a first.

The rickety old door slams shut. That was loud. I double-check to make sure it's locked; you never know these days. One, two, three. I used to do twenty checks back in the old days, since that's my lucky number. Boy was that tiring.

I get there in fifty-six minutes. Not bad. I haven't been to this place in years. It's nice to see nothing has changed. They haven't even fixed the graffiti on the door. "PSC sucks." No doubt from a rival Division Three school.

"What's up, stranger? Man you look skinny!" Jimmy says as I walk up to the bar.

Seeing my face drop, he realizes he's hit a soft spot and tries to recover. "Oh, sorry, man. Don't worry, the chicks still dig you." Smooth as always.

"You look pretty fat yourself, been eating too many of those greasy fries?" I banter back. Back in high school his soft spot was Bob and Edith's.

I let Jimmy get settled in at the bar while I hit the head. No doubt Jimmy is working on softening up the bartender for a few freebies. In the old days he usually made quite an impression on the girls.

When I get back to my seat, an ice cold Miller Lite greets me. Wow, stepping up. No Milwaukee's Best? Must be a special occasion.

The bartender is a hot blond, so I assume Jimmy's already got her wrapped around his finger.

"What's her name?" I say. "No idea. Didn't ask," Jimmy replies calmly.

Boy, that's a first. In the old days Jimmy would have

already determined the likelihood of taking her home in the first ten minutes.

"So, I assume Sarah told you the news?" I might as well get it out of the way.

"That sucks." Jimmy sums it up nicely. "Should you even be drinking?"

"Well, not much I can do about it right now, so let's talk about something else. And one beer won't make it any worse." Actually, this is the first beer I've drank since being diagnosed, but he doesn't need to know that.

"What's new with you?" I say, changing the subject. "By the way, what made you decide to pick up the phone and call my ass? We haven't talked since what, the snowmobile incident?"

Jimmy nods. "I forgot about that." He grabs his neck, grimacing in pain. "I was one lucky SOB that night. I've only been back in Bristol for a year and let's just say it ain't like riding a bike. This isn't exactly a war zone."

Back in Bristol for just under a year? I'm ready to give Jimmy a hard time, but think better of it. He's probably been at the heart of every major US conflict for the past fifteen years. Bosnia, Kuwait, Iraq, Afghanistan. Lord knows what else.

"I've spent the past week working on that crappy car and trying to make a few bucks here and there," he responds.

I've never understood how our country has treated vets like crap when they come home from battle. Apparently vets have almost double the unemployment rate compared to the general population, which is an outrage. These guys should have a job set up for them within the first month back, or at least some interviews, for Christ's sake.

Turns out Jimmy's been working off and on for our old baseball coach's construction company. But it sounds like they only need him about fifteen hours a week and that won't pay the bills.

He's officially done with his service, but I have a

feeling he'll re-up at some point. Again I think about giving him a hard time for not calling me the day he moved back to Bristol, but hold off.

Physically, Jimmy looks the same, maybe even a little skinnier than when I last saw him. But emotionally something isn't quite right. He barely makes eye contact with me, which is something Jimmy always took to heart growing up. I'm sure it even intensified once he became a Marine.

One thing that doesn't change is his ability to pound beer. Jimmy's on his third already and I'm not even halfway done with my first.

"You hooking up with anyone these days?" I ask.

Jimmy just shrugs it off. "Too busy."

Too busy to hook up? Is there an alien that has taken over my old buddy's body?

"Sarah has always been talking about setting you up with Casey Hollister. Remember that chick who went out with Doug James in high school? She was two years behind us." I try to see if there's any life left in my old buddy.

"Oh yeah, her body is smokin'," Jimmy reacts. "I'll think about it."

"You all right, dude? How are you adjusting to life back home?"

"About as well as the rest of my Corps friends. One day at a time, baby, isn't that the rule we're supposed to live by?" he says sarcastically. "One shitty day at a time."

7. One Last Beer Among Friends

Jimmy

What is your problem? Can you at least enjoy a few last beers and a good laugh with a buddy that's dying, a few hours before you pull the plug?

Maybe I shouldn't have accepted. The cold beers are waiting for me back in the garage fridge.

Why am I so angry? Gee, perhaps it's the hell I lived in for several years of my life?

Stop feeling sorry for yourself. You made the decision to pull the trigger. No one else. Why couldn't I have just held up? A marine is responsible for making right decisions in the blink of an eye. Yet I failed. You didn't fail, hindsight is 20-20. You mean to tell me that any of the other guys wouldn't have pulled the trigger in similar circumstances? Hell, civilians and the enemy are living in the same damn shacks. Just two weeks before, my buddy Adam was shot in the face by a ten-year-old boy who came up to him asking for food. Blame yourself all you want, but war isn't black and white, no matter how much a soldier would like it to be. I could analyze shit every day for the rest of my life and what good would it do? His face is as vivid as the day it happened—must have been no older than twelve, and in a painful irony, looks like me as a child. Just the Iraqi version. God, to know you and only you are responsible for taking away all of that kid's hopes and dreams, it's like hell all over again.

"You want to call it an early night?" Ben asks. It's obvious to him my mind is someplace else.

Meanwhile, on top of all the other crap going on in my head, I now wish I could trade places with him.

This guy has it all, and it's being taken from him. Yet another reason why I really don't believe in God anymore.

If there were a real God, he would inflict me with the disease and let Ben continue to be the model of life. He's the one dying and yet he still keeps an incredible attitude. No wonder he has it all.

8. Moving Day

1987

Ben - 12 years old

I still don't understand why we have to move. This sucks and it's not fair. Mom keeps saying it's what's best for the whole family. What does she think, I'm stupid? How in the world is a divorce good for any family?

Sure, my parents have been fighting a lot, but so what, we can just go in our room and watch TV when we hear them start to raise their voices. That doesn't mean I have to move to the middle of nowhere, does it? Where the hell is Bristol anyway? I've never even heard of it and it's not like New Hampshire is that big.

I was prepared to try out for the Nashua Junior Varsity Baseball Team in three months and now they're ruining it for me. And I was finally starting to get in with the ladies. Suzie Meadows and I just started going out last month. I was planning to go for second base soon, but that's obviously going to have to wait.

Man, was I scared to death the first time we made out. I'm sure chicks talk about that stuff all the time. But my buddies and I have never once talked about it. A few of my thirteen-year-old friends talk about getting laid and how amazing it feels, but first base, never.

So, I had to practice making out with my pillow for a couple weeks and watch *Sixteen Candles* about twenty times. Even with all of that preparation, Suzie still had to take over.

We had three close calls where I was just about ready to pull the trigger, but got nervous. On the fourth try, during recess, she finally dragged me behind the building and let me have it. That was pretty cool, I have to admit. Although I still don't have the tongue thing down yet. And now I probably never will, thanks to my parents.

"Mom, how big is Uncle Tommy's place? Does it have a nice yard?" I ask. At least if I can practice hitting off the tee in the front yard the time will go by faster.

Mom claims we'll only spend the first two months at my uncle's house while we look for an apartment closer to town. But I don't believe her.

My two sisters are just going with the flow. Mary just turned nine a few months ago and only has one real friend that she'll miss. She kind of keeps to herself a lot, but maybe that's just normal for a fifth grade girl. I don't really remember.

Suzy is six and thinks we're going on a permanent vacation. It still hasn't hit her yet that Mom and Dad are splitting up. I guess they've done a decent job at hiding it from the girls. But they can't fool me.

"Why isn't Daddy coming up to Uncle Tommy's, Mommy?" Suzy asked yesterday.

"He has a lot of work travel right now. Don't worry, he'll come up soon."

Yeah, right.

I heard their whole conversation the night after Mary's birthday party. Those there were some pretty harsh words.

"I should have never married you. I always knew you couldn't provide for us," Mom fired at Dad.

He just sat there and took it, tears welling up in his eyes. That was the first time I ever saw my Dad cry. It kind of freaked me out. It was then I realized this time it's serious. No more weak threats; this time my mom was really taking us.

My friend Danny's parents got divorced last year and he's seen his dad about four times since then. He says it really sucks.

Danny was one of the best baseball players on our Little League team, but now he doesn't have anyone to practice with at home. I guess his mom tried to get out there with him once and throw the ball around but she couldn't even throw it ten feet. He gave up after about two minutes. I know that's going to happen to me too. There's no way my mom can catch a baseball. I guess I'll just have to stay after school longer every day and find some kids to practice with during the off-season.

Oh man. Trying to make new friends is going to suck too. I'm not much of a butt kisser and sometimes I'm too competitive, so I can piss kids off if we're playing sports. I just hope there are a few cool kids up there in cow country.

9. The Log Cabin

Ethel

"Mary, don't use up all the warm water. Your brother still needs to take a quick bath." Jeez. Don't these kids realize it takes about twenty minutes to heat up more water on the stove?

Tomorrow's the big day. First day in the kids' new schools. I've convinced myself that living in this old cabin for a few months isn't so bad. The kids complain a lot, but it's kind of growing on me. Plus, it's free, which means I can actually treat myself every once in a while instead of scraping for every penny.

"But Mom, I've only been in here for about five minutes. Ben got to take a long shower last week," Mary says.

"Mommy, the TV's not working!" shouts Suzy.

"You know we only get a couple of channels, Suzy," I yell back.

"Ben, can you twist the antenna for Suzy and try to get it to come in?" I can't handle another meltdown.

Ben fiddles with the coat hanger for a few minutes, but to no avail. You can hear Laverne talking, but a fuzzy black line keeps blocking the picture. "I hate this place," Ben rants. "Why can't we go back to our old place with Dad and a normal house, with real TV and warm water? I'm in eighth grade now and I can't even watch TV."

By now I've heard enough complaining for the night. "Suzy, Ben, get on your pajamas! You're skipping showers tonight and going straight to bed!"

They think life revolves around them? I'm just going to have to teach these spoiled brats a lesson.

"Ben, after you both get on your PJs help your sister with the pee bucket unless she needs to do number two, then take her outside." I can't wait for a little peace and quiet.

It was another eight-hour day on my feet at the restaurant. Tuesdays are dead there. Thirty measly dollars isn't going to cut it. Thank God for Tommy. He always has been good to me, even though we're not blood related.

Mary's water slowly drains out of the makeshift showerhead, which looks to be made of an old watering can. Tommy must have put this together, I think with a laugh. He always has been pretty handy. Well, it does the job. And besides, beggars can't be choosers.

Just then I look up to see something dripping down in between some of the logs from upstairs. It's shooting straight down onto the floor, next to the stove.

What is that? I look down and notice it's yellow. Urine!

"Suzy, are you going in the bucket?"

"Sorry mommy. I missed it."

"Suzy, how many times do I have to tell you to concentrate when you sit over the bucket? If you can't do it, next time you just have to go outside to the real toilet," I reprimand.

"But Mom, it's freezing outside. She can't go out there," Ben butts in.

"I wasn't talking to you, Ben. No more complaining. We're lucky to have a place to live and Uncle Tommy did us a nice favor by letting us stay here for a few months," I remind them.

After Mary takes care of her business neatly in the bucket, I grab it and open the back door for the daily dumping. Splash. The stale smell of day-old urine steams in the cold February New Hampshire air.

After the kids fall asleep, I can finally enjoy a little peace and quiet. I grab my book and nestle on the couch.

Lover's Quarrel. So far it's very entertaining. *A young man loses his wife just days after the honeymoon. Ready to give up on life, he decides to move into a remote part of the Appalachian Mountains. Little did he know a young widow herself would be waiting in the wings.*

I've always wondered how these writers become so creative, especially on the book covers.

As I settle in, one thing is missing, my tea. I hop up, open the cabinet, and to my disappointment, the box is empty.

Oh well, I know Tommy's wife Nancy must have some. I look at the clock ten-fifteen p.m. Well, they're probably still awake.

The phone rings eight times. They must be brushing their teeth. I'll give it a few more rings.

"Hello?" Tommy says in a raspy voice.

"Oh, hi Tommy. It's me, Ethel. I just ran out of tea, can I borrow some?"

There's a long pause. "You woke me up so that you could have some tea? Are you serious?" he grumbles. "Ethel, I have to wake up in about four hours to catch a flight out of Logan. Can't you just wait until tomorrow? I don't want to wake Nancy up."

I concede and hang up.

As I open up to page eleven, where my bookmark sits, I remember that nice older lady Joanne down the street told me if I ever needed anything, don't hesitate to call.

Where did I put her phone number? Oh, it must be in my purse. I wrote it down on a napkin a few weeks ago. Searching through my purse, I'm reminded it's probably time to buy a new one. This one is too small. Especially for all of the things I like to keep in it.

After looking for about ten minutes and tossing out a few ketchup-stained napkins that don't have any numbers written on them, I decide on a much easier route, walking.

Her house is only a few hundred yards to the left, once I walk down the long cabin path. It's likely no more than half a mile total.

I take a flashlight just in case. Ten minutes into the walk I realize Joanne lives further down than I thought. I can see her house now, but it's still a good ways down. Well, it's a nice night, so I'll enjoy the fresh air.

Her house is much smaller than what I remember. But I really only saw it briefly, when Tommy introduced me to her. She asked if I wanted some tea and of course I accepted. It was decaffeinated ginger, one of my favorites. We ended up staying at her place for over an hour, as she made us some sandwiches for lunch as well. Tommy didn't stay for lunch, but I couldn't pass it up.

She's a nice lady. I'm sure she won't mind me swinging by for a little tea right now. Plus, she must know what it's like to have a craving and realize you are out.

There aren't any lights on inside the house, but the outside light is on. I ring the doorbell, but it doesn't seem like it works. Hmm, maybe I should just knock? I close my fist and give three decent size pounds at the glass window.

A minute passes, and I'm about to knock again when I hear something move inside the house. A light flutters on. I can see the little woman through the window. Yes, there's hope; tea please.

She seems a bit surprised to see me, but she just may not recognize me with my hat on. I give her a friendly wave and say, "Hi, Joanne. Remember me? I'm Tommy's sister. Can I ask you for a favor?" She opens up the door and lets me in.

"Is everything OK, dear?" she asks. I notice the dark circles under her eyes. Wow, she must have a hard time getting a good night's sleep.

"Oh yes, things are great. I just ran out of tea and was hoping you had some. Remember the other day when you told me to call you if I needed anything during my stay? Well, I couldn't find your phone number, so I decided to walk down here. You know how it is when you're craving tea, right? Anyhow, can I borrow some?"

The nice lady doesn't say a word. She walks straight over to her cupboard and brings me the entire box of English tea bags and drops it in my hands. There must be thirty tea bags and it looks like a fresh box. "You can have all of them. Is there anything else you need?" she says.

I'm just about to say no thank you when I remember that amazing banana pudding she offered me last time. I'm sure she wouldn't mind.

"Well, it sure would be nice to have something sweet to go with my tea. You don't happen to have any more of that banana pudding, do you?"

I must have made her night because the look on her face is of pure joy. With her mouth wide open she speeds back over to the kitchen, gets a brown bag, and throws the whole thing in there along with some cookies for good measure.

I open up the cookies and try one just as I'm leaving. I might as well show her how much I enjoy them. That way she'll remember me the next time she bakes them.

As the door closes, my mouth is too full to say thank you. Oh well, she likes helping people. I'm sure she won't notice.

Back at the cabin, it is now twelve-thirty a.m. I'm getting tired, but the English tea keeps me going. This time I go with the caffeinated tea.

I finish six steamy chapters, sipping on the hot tea while taking care of the entire batch of banana pudding. Boy, the kids would have liked this. Oh well, maybe we can stop by and ask her to make a little more in the morning.

I wake to the sound of the phone ringing. Looking up, I realize its morning and time to get the kids off to school. Oh, wait; they're busy eating cereal at the table.

"Can one of you get that?" I say.

Ben calls back to me, "its Uncle Tommy."

I crawl off the couch and grab the phone.

"Did you stop by Mrs. Huckabee's house last night asking for tea?" he yells.

"She told me if I needed anything to stop by," I

defended. Why can't he understand that some people like to go out of their way to help others in need?

10. Ben's first signs of OCD

The Next Morning

Ben

It's seven-forty a.m. I have five minutes before the bus comes. If I miss it, I'll have a good two-mile walk to school, which means I'll be late on my first day. That's not what I need right now. It's bad enough we have to piss in a bucket and have an outhouse.

Is that even legal, to have kids living without running water? What the hell was my mom thinking dragging us here to mooch off Uncle Tommy? She hyped this place up pretty good.

Boy did she pull one over on us. A big yard? Yeah, right. If you count the woods, sure, we have plenty of land. Otherwise, all we have is a long dirt driveway leading up to the old filthy cabin.

I throw my sneakers on and am just about ready to head out the door. "Don't forget to brush your teeth," Mom yells out.

I knew I forgot something. *Sixteen, seventeen, eighteen, nineteen, and twenty! Done.* I spit out the remaining toothpaste in the kitchen sink and gently place the toothbrush into its proper spot.

No, that's not right. Get back over there and fix it. I'm just about ready to head out of the bathroom when I realize the toothbrush needs to be adjusted.

One more time. I take the toothbrush out of the holder, wipe it off again, and place it in the third opening.

Don't you remember? It has to be in the third opening. Not the fourth one. I move away, then look up again. *No, it was the fourth spot, you idiot. That was the spot you used when you hit five threes in a game.*

At this point I'm just staring at the mirror, helpless. Almost in a trance. *Which one is it, you moron? Hurry up; the bus has probably already left by now. What is wrong with me? One more time. There, that is perfect.*

I run towards the front door, grab my lunch bag, and head down the stairs. I close the downstairs door, tugging at it to make sure it sticks. *One, two, three, four, five…seventeen, eighteen, nineteen, and twenty! Done!*

I head out and rush towards the street. Just then I see the bus turn down Prospect Street and out of sight. Missed it, you moron! Why can't you just concentrate?

11. Jimmy's First Day of School

One Year Later

Jimmy

This school is so small. I'll bet the sports suck here. Hell, they don't even have football. What a disgrace.

Is it me or do all the kids here look like they haven't showered in weeks? There's even some ninth graders with beards. What is up with that?

Where are we, Alaska? I told Mom I didn't want to move. It's all her fault.

At least my first two classes of the day were pretty easy. I guess they figure a new kid going through a divorce has enough issues without taking on homework on day one.

Now it's time for science class and there's still another hour and a half before lunch. I'm starving. Why do they eat so late at this freakin' school? I'd better wolf down a snack.

Believe it or not my mom actually decided to pack me something today. Not sure what got into her, but I'll take it. Usually she's still sleeping when I leave for school, but for some reason she got motivated. She gave me six Ritz crackers filled with peanut butter. Since they're not the easiest to scarf down before class, I decide to wait it out.

The only seat left is up in the front row. Great, where all the nerds sit. I plop myself down in between two dudes with perms.

No wonder this school doesn't have football! Although these aren't the first guys I've seen here with perms, so maybe perms are in style up here north of the border. I notice they are involved in a debate over whether the Sox will ever win it all with another kid sitting at our table. This one doesn't have a perm, but still looks pretty goofy.

I try to sit without interrupting or drawing attention to myself. But I don't think new kids come around much in this school, so they instantly make me the center of attention.

"You must be the new kid from Mass?" the non-permer says.

"Yeah, I'm Jimmy," I respond quietly, hoping not to draw any additional attention.

"Hi, I'm Ben. Nice to meet you. This is LaFleur and Rankel. Do you play any sports?"

"I play football, but I guess you guys are still trying to get a team together?" I add.

"Cool, man," Rankel says. "What position?"

"Running back," I say confidently.

"Maybe you can pick up baseball with us. Sounds like you have some wheels," Ben says.

"I'd give it a shot. Why not?" I respond, surprised at myself for committing so quickly considering I haven't picked up a bat in two years. Well, I guess my dad used to throw the ball in the yard with me when I was young, but it's been a few years since I put on a glove.

"Sweet man. We need a few more players. Only ten guys even tried out last year and two of them hadn't ever played organized baseball. We have some high hopes this year, man," Ben adds. He clearly matches my passion for football with his love for baseball.

Soon after, Mr. Sutton walks in and the class begins. Unlike my two previous classes during the day, he doesn't take the time to embarrass me in front of everyone with an introduction. He probably realizes the whole school knows about the new kid by now.

I keep peeking up at the clock as my stomach lets out some vicious growls. There's no way I can make it another hour without eating. I walk up to the front of the class and grab the bathroom pass.

Still finding my way around the hallways, it takes me

a few minutes to locate my locker. Nice Mom. The crackers are looking awfully good. Thanks for actually being a parent today. I scarf three down, then put them in my pocket. I'll save the rest for lunch.

Walking back into class I underestimate the need to wash down my snack with some liquid. As such, I walk back in, mouth half open, and try to swallow the mashed peanut butter and crackers without Mr. Sutton noticing. But it was too late.

"Jimmy, what is that you're eating? I hope you brought enough for the rest of the class!" he says sternly. I try to say sorry, but my mouth is still full. Instead, I put my hands up, trying to gesture a symbol of apology. That doesn't go over very well with Mr. Sutton.

"OK. I'll take the rest of those now," Mr. Sutton says sternly. "I know it's your first day of class, but I would hope that your schools down in Massachusetts shared similar rules about eating in class. It's just not acceptable."

My survival instincts kick in and I grab the bag of crackers and hold them out in front of me, away from my science teacher. They look so delicious. As I turn to my left, I notice my new friends looking up at me. Then something comes over me which I can't quite describe. Perhaps it's guilt for losing the one and only snack my mom has given me since I was a toddler.

Anyhow, just as Mr. Sutton is about to snatch my bag of peanut butter crackers, I reach in, grab all three, and stuff them straight into my mouth.

By this time the entire class is watching. Stunned, Mr. Sutton raises his hand and points towards the door.

"For that, Jimmy, you are headed to the principal's office. I want you out of my class now!"

As I walk towards the door, I look back to seek the approval of my three new friends. They each have their hands covering their faces, unsuccessful in their attempt to hold in the laughter. Ben throws me a final thumbs-up as I exit the class.

I take the long way to the principal's office and stop at four different water fountains along the way.

Those crackers really do go better with liquid. I'll have to mention that to mom when I get home. Either way, finding a great friend is well worth a trip to the principal's office.

12. Making A New Friend

Ben

Today is not like every other boring Monday. We actually have a new kid in our school. I know, that sounds like something pretty lame to get excited about. However, when you live in Bristol, New Hampshire, a town of about 3,000 people, getting a new ninth grader in the school isn't a regular occurrence.

Plus, I hear the kid might play sports. Heck, he's from Mass, so he must play something. I heard a few of the kids talking about him in between periods and he sounds like a tough guy. Hopefully he can play baseball. Even if he can't, I'll teach him. We're not going into the new year having to pull up an eighth grader to the varsity squad, that's for sure.

I know exactly what he's going through. Moving up to this tiny little hick town was quite the adjustment for me last year, but it starts to grow on you.

Oh crap, I forgot to do my science homework. I'd better see if I can grab one of the girls. They owe me one after I covered them in math class last month.

I notice Lisa Scheffler mingling outside of Mr. Sutton's class. "Lisa, can I bum your homework from last night?" I ask.

"Geez, Ben, again? You know I won't be there when you go to college, right?" she says sarcastically.

"Maybe we can be a package deal, Lisa. We can both apply to the same schools." I laugh, jotting down the answers quickly.

"Thanks, sweetie, you're the best. I'll strike out ten for you in our first game. Sound good?"

"Eleven. Make it eleven." She laughs.

I stroll into class just before the bell. Mr. Sutton is one of those teachers you just steer clear from most days. He generally won't bother kids unless they test him. If that happens, he takes it personally.

LaFleur and Rankel are already involved in their typical debate. "The Sox are going to suck this year. You know Rice is getting old as hell. I hate to say it, but they had their chance and it's gone now," LaFleur argues.

"Are you talking about the Sox again?" I insert myself. "You know the only chance we have of winning it all rests with the Celtics this year. Don't get your hopes up with the Sox. I love them too, but they'll break our hearts again," I say, realizing I sound just like my dad.

Then I look up. "Hey look, this must be the new kid. Nice, he's coming this way," I say.

"Don't scare the kid before he sits down, Ben," Rankel says.

"I'm surprised you haven't run a background check on the kid to see if he plays baseball." LaFleur laughs.

I introduce myself.

It turns out Jimmy doesn't play baseball, he plays football. But he does seem like a tough kid. I'll bet he can hit. With a little persuading, I can convince him to play with us this year. He's got the build of a catcher.

Halfway through the class Mr. Sutton asks everyone to turn in their homework assignments. I give Lisa a wink and a smile. That's when I notice Jimmy walking up to grab the bathroom pass. Man, this kid isn't bashful, that's for sure. I don't think anyone dared to walk out of Mr. Sutton's class for at least a month into the school year. The kid has balls. Or maybe he just doesn't know any better.

I can't wait for this day to end. I'm supposed to go out with Mom to look for a new baseball glove. My dad gave me the money, or I should say, gave her the money. I really want a black glove this time. They look much cooler than the traditional brown gloves.

I've had my glove, a hand-me-down, since I was eight. Last year during Babe Ruth All Stars the guys couldn't believe how small it was. They made a game out of trying to fit in on their hands. I lied and told them I was superstitious and changing gloves would give me bad luck. I'm sure some of them knew it had to do with money issues, but I certainly wasn't going to be the one that said anything.

Look, the new kid is back. What the hell is he eating? I watch as he shoves the crackers in his mouth like they were his last meal on earth. This kid does have some serious balls!

Hell, even if he can't hit, just having him around for humor is good enough for me. Meet our eleventh member of the varsity baseball team.

13. Male Bonding

Ben

I hope LaFleur and Griswaltz aren't getting jealous of Jimmy. We've pretty much been hanging out every day after school for the last few weeks. What can I say, that kid is funny. And ballsy! I bet he can kick some serious ass. A good friend to have for a guy like me.

I'm five foot four and a hundred ten pounds soaking wet. He's built like a linebacker with the broad shoulders of a grown man. Oh, and did I mention that I have kind of a big mouth and love sarcasm? Yeah, I think Jimmy will be a good guy to have around.

He rides his BMX bike to school and thinks the bus is for sissies. A ton of chicks in the school already dig him. Sure, part of it is because he's the new guy. But if Amy Ashton likes him, that's saying something. She only dates upperclassmen, but it's pretty obvious the way she hangs around Jimmy's locker that she's willing to break that rule.

We have a lot in common. His mom and dad are also getting divorced, so he knows how shitty life can be when that happens. Although when it comes to our moms, his problem is the opposite of mine. She lets him do whatever the heck he wants and could really care less about it. He has no rules. It's like he's thirteen going on twenty. He even has his own beer in the fridge.

Meanwhile, I'm living under a control freak. To give you an idea, I have to call my mom every morning when I get off the bus to let her know I arrived at school. The office assistant has gotten used to it, but it's still weird using the school phone every morning.

Tonight Jimmy and I are headed out to Game Heaven, a really cool arcade and mini-golf place fifteen minutes away in Moultonborough. I'm still in shock that my mom let me out. But since Jimmy's mom agreed to pick us up and his older brother is dropping us off, my mom gave in.

Since its Friday, I'm going to spend the night at his place tonight. I brought enough clothes for the whole weekend and would give anything to get away from that nasty cabin for a few days.

So much for living there a couple months. It's been over a year and Mom is getting pretty attached to living rent free. Unless the outhouse overflows into the cabin, I don't see us leaving anytime soon. Well, I guess Uncle Tommy could lose it one day and toss us on the street too. He can only take my mom in small doses.

Jimmy's brother Al drives like a complete asshole. I can't believe we made it to Game Heaven alive. I think I know where Jimmy gets his balls from now.

Al polishes off two cans of Budweiser on the short ride over. He doesn't even bother hiding the open containers at the stoplights.

"He's going to end up in jail," Jimmy whispers to me. "And I won't come visit his ass."

Boy, if Mom could see us now I'd be grounded for life.

Even though I've only known Jimmy for a few weeks, I can already see what motivates him. He desperately wants to make sure he doesn't end up like his brother. He also takes pride in doing the right thing, which is pretty odd for a teenager. I'm not saying he's a saint, because he can cause trouble with the best of them. It's hard to explain, but it's like he knows he's destined to do great things in life. That leads me to believe he won't stick around Bristol for long after high school.

Al swerves into the parking lot and before the car stops, Jimmy kicks open the door and we both jump out.

"Good luck getting those wieners touched, boys," Al says so politely.

I've been wanting to go to this place ever since I turned fourteen, but every time Griswaltz and LaFleur have invited me, I always had some family commitment my mom would make up.

They say there are tons of hot chicks here. Griswaltz made it to third base with some chick visiting from Vermont last summer. They almost got caught hooking up inside the lighthouse on the seventeenth hole. That must have been awesome.

Jimmy is wearing his football jersey from when he lived down in Mass. So I decided to wear my baseball jersey from last year. I look like a little kid while he could probably buy beer at the local 7-11 and not even get carded. OK, I'd better stop with my man crush on Jimmy. I don't want anyone getting the wrong idea.

"You want to start at the football toss?" Jimmy says predictably.

"Sure, man. You lead the way," I respond. Ever since we decided to come here, Jimmy's been pumped about breaking his high score of seven-fifty.

As we make our way down the stairs to the sports games I'm in awe of how huge this place is. There must be hundreds of arcade games here; it's packed! We head over to the football game and of course, there's a line. A handful of guys wearing Laconia High School football jerseys are throwing five-dollar bills down, challenging each other for the high score. The machine says it's six-fifty.

"Hey, Jimmy, didn't you say your high score was seven-fifty?" Right after the words come out of my mouth, I want to take them back.

"Oh, we got some tough guys over here, fellas!" the biggest guy says. Donning number fifty-six, this kid is built like Jimmy, but at least three inches taller.

"So you got seven-fifty, huh, kid? You want to put your money where your mouth is?"

Jimmy looks at me with a deep glare, then back at fifty-six.

"Thanks, guys. We're just here to have some fun. Not

looking for any trouble," he says calmly.

"What are you, a pussy? Ten bucks says I whip your ass in this game," fifty-six snarls.

"You're on, Snaggletooth!" I blurt out, holding all the money my mom gave me before we left my house. "Come on, Jimmy, show this guy what real football is like. None of this weak Minor League New Hampshire shit. He played down in Mass, where the big boys play."

Even though Jimmy accepts the challenge, I could tell he doesn't feel very good about the situation. The way I see it, if we lose, so what, at least I show Jimmy that I backed him. If we win, we double our money.

What I fail to take into account is what Jimmy knows all along, losing is not an option for these jackasses.

They flip a coin to see who goes first. "Nice nickname, kid," Jimmy whispers to me as we back off to give our enemy some room. I laugh. It was pretty quick on my feet. That kid definitely has pointy front teeth and they cling to his bottom lip when he smiles.

Snaggle starts off really weak, but then gets into his groove with twenty seconds left. He nails five in a row when the throws count for seventy points instead of fifty. The final tally is six hundred eighty.

"New record, baby!" Snaggle cheers for himself. Then his buddies give high fives and conclude the celebration with a group chest bump.

"Your turn, Masshole," the scrawniest dude in the group says. He still outweighs me by about twenty pounds.

As Jimmy steps up to take his spot, he looks around and realizes we've drawn a crowd of at least twenty kids now watching. There must be ten hot chicks who made their way over.

As he rolls up his sleeves, Jimmy gives me one last glare. I'm sure he'll give me some hell for putting this kind of pressure on him later. That's what I get for opening my big mouth.

Jimmy starts off super cold, throwing bricks that make the floor shake as they clank off the metal football players and bounce back at him like boomerangs.

Just as the loudmouths start to give Jimmy crap his luck changes.

Three hundred. Three fifty. Four hundred. Five hundred. He looks like Joe Montana up there. Still twenty seconds left and he only needs about four more. Five fifty. Six twenty-five. Ten seconds left. He's gonna do it.

I watch as another spiral makes its way towards the large open cylinder. Clank! What the hell is that? A basketball comes flying in from the side and ricochets off the football just before it makes its way through the hole. Then another. Then another. Those bastards are sabotaging his game. I turn in disgust as the buzzer sounds. Jimmy falls short by fifty-five points, or one ball.

"That is bullshit! You cheating bastards!" I yell.

Two of their guys get in my face. Another three get in Jimmy's.

"Pay up, fellas. You lost," Snaggle says.

"In your dreams, man. You cheated. You owe us," I fire back, completely oblivious to their size and numbers.

Jimmy grabs me and pulls me aside. "Let this one go, Ben. I'll handle it. All right guys, how about double or nothing? You win again, we pay you twenty," Jimmy says.

"What are you, nuts? I don't have another ten bucks. I'm out of cash and you know these guys are going to pull another fast one on us."

He gives me a wink and focuses his attention on the game. "Well boys, can you handle one more game?" Jimmy asks confidently.

"You're on," Snaggle accepts.

"Fellas, can we have a quick pregame pep talk?" Jimmy asks. They nod, and he pulls me over in a mini-huddle. "When I start to run, you take off. Meet me at the front entrance. Got it?" Jimmy says with a twinkle in his eyes.

"You go first again, hot shot, seemed to suit you well last time," Jimmy offers.

Snaggle takes him up. This time the guy is red hot. He hits his first ten tosses in a row. Just as number eleven is thrown, Jimmy sneaks behind him, grabs a hold of his shorts, and pulls them straight down. Bare ass and all is showing to the unsuspecting crowd. The last thing I remember seeing is a hug red zit on his left butt cheek before I took off.

Meanwhile, Jimmy grabs both tens that were left sitting on the front of the game and runs for his life. We weave in and out of people, darting past the video games and towards the entrance. Snaggle must have taken a while to pull up his shorts because they are at least fifty yards behind us. We haul it up a bunch of stairs towards the final destination.

"They're gaining on us!" I say to Jimmy. Now it hits me. If these guys catch up there will be no mercy.

Jimmy looks to his left. Sitting in the corner are two large metal arcade game movers. They are a cross between a shopping cart and forklift. Without hesitating, he grabs them both and shoves them down the stairs. They smash down each stair, one by one, and eventually steamroll into Snaggle and his friends.

We don't stick around to see the extent of the damage, but it's safe to say there are a few bruises. We sprint outside into the parking lot and deep into the woods surrounding Game Heaven. We finally catch our breath and sit on a tree stump a good half mile into the woods.

"You crazy bastard!" I laugh and give Jimmy a high five.

"I had to do something after you ran your mouth there big shot." He chuckles.

Before we have time to reminisce, we hear sirens. "They called the cops!" I yell.

As we peer through the opening in the trees we notice

flashlights coming towards us.

"Run!" we both say in sync.

Jimmy and I make it back to his house right as the sun comes up. We must have walked fifteen miles. But to us, it was a total bonding experience. I guess that's natural after two friends almost get their asses kicked.

I learned a whole lot about Jimmy Keller that night. How all he ever wanted in life was to have a normal family. He's the only kid I've ever told about the log cabin. I still never took him there. There's no way I could live with the embarrassment of having my best friend see the piss bucket or outhouse.

Some might wonder how we could be best friends and he never sees where I live. It's simple. He could sense my shame when I talked to him about our situation and that was it. He never once pushed the issue. It was always just assumed that we would hang out at his place.

He didn't even flinch when I told him my sisters and I qualify for the free lunch program at school. As a matter of fact, Jimmy started packing an extra lunch every day to share with me. We now use the free lunch ticket to stock up on snacks. I'm sure other kids have it much tougher than us somewhere. But right now, as two early teens trying to make their way through life, that doesn't make it any easier.

14. The next day

Jimmy

Man. What a night. That's one for the record books. I still can't believe how far we walked home. Even crazier is how Mom didn't say a word when we saw her this morning. Did she not even notice we didn't sleep last night? Did she try to pick us up at Game Heaven?

So this kid Ben is pretty cool. Cocky, yes. Enough testosterone for both of us, without question. But I give him credit. He's got some firepower. He's the only kid I've ever talked to about my family. What can I say; my guard came down after mile thirteen. I started spouting off and rambling about how shitty my life is. I hope I can trust him not to say anything to anyone at school. I mean, I've really only known Ben for three weeks.

My gut tells me I can trust him. And heck, it's not like he didn't spill his guts to me too. Those living conditions sound horrible. I swear I remember reading something about a family that got separated by social workers because they were living in similar conditions. Not that I'd ever rat him out, but that is pretty sick.

A piss bucket? And crapping outside in a wooden outhouse in below zero temperatures? That will give you some thick skin pretty fast.

We'll never admit it to anyone, but we both shed some tears talking last night. He started to break down when he talked about how much he misses his father. That was the first time I've ever hugged another guy. Not even my dad has earned that honor.

You know what's crazy? When that big kid, Snaggle, as Ben called him, got in my face, I felt so alive. I could have easily cracked him in the face. But I've learned from Al to stay away from uneven rumbles. Five against two isn't very good odds, especially when I've never seen Ben rumble. Not that he couldn't hold his own, he probably is scrappy.

Still, I made the right call walking away. Or should I say, running away. Hah!

And how about those freakin' metal shopping carts? I wish we could have snapped a picture of those guys when those things came storming down the stairs at them. Classic!

I have a feeling there's going to be more where that came from now that Ben and I are tight.

15. Football Game

Jimmy

"Hurry up, Ma! We're gonna be late for my first game," I say. Whenever I talk to my mom, I can't help but to overplay the Boston accent. Her accent is so thick, even my friends who were born and raised here in Mass can't understand her.

Why does this always happen? Can't we just be on time for once?

"Why didn't you ask one of your brothers to take you?" she responds.

"I tried. They're in Al's room with the door locked."

"All right. All right. Throw me my keys."

I run out of the house with my uniform pants halfway down to my knees, belt hanging off and my shoulder pads caught up in my jersey.

Ma's 1970 El Dorado is blowing a ton of smoke out of the rear and barely putting along. But at least we're on our way. I pray we'll make it on time. My coach told me at our last practice that I'm starting at running back today. I'm pumped.

"Will Dad be there?" I ask, knowing full well the answer to my question.

"You know he has to work, honey. But he told me to ask you to score a touchdown for him. Can you do that for him?"

"Yes, Ma," I reply, disappointed he won't be able to watch my first game. I don't know why it hits me so hard every time. He's never around.

I guess I always hold out hope that one of these days he'll just cut out of work a little early. What's the point of owning your own business if you can't make your own hours? But Dad does work hard to pay the bills. I know that.

My mom's cigarette smoke is overwhelming. I brush it away with my hands as she tells me it's rude to do so.

"Didn't the doctor say you need to quit smoking, Ma?" I lecture her.

"Mind your own business, Jimmy. I put up with a lot of shit around here. You think I need my eleven-year-old son giving me lip?"

"I'm almost twelve," I remind her. Mom hasn't been working for as long as I can remember. My brothers tell me she carried a full-time job for years in one of the plants up in Lawrence back when I was little. She was doing something with chemicals.

Anyways, over the years they took their toll on her. Now there's some lawsuit pending where about a hundred former plant employees are saying they're sick because of working there. We still haven't seen a dime of the money yet, but Ma says its coming.

Her cough is getting worse by the day and she gets tired walking up the four stairs going into our house. Now she mainly sits on the coach and watches soap operas while smoking about two packs of Camels per day.

I look at the clock; it's ten-fifty a.m. Great. The game starts in ten minutes. Coach told everyone to be there at least thirty minutes early for stretches, but I couldn't get my lazy brothers out of their rooms.

I turn on the radio in order to calm my nerves. Steve Miller Band, "The Joker." Nice! One of my all-time favorites.

Some people call me the space cowboy, yeah
Some call me the gangster of love
Some people call me Maurice
Cause I speak of the pompitus of love……
I get my loving on the run… wooo… wooo

Love that tune! Now I'm jazzed up and ready to hit some people. "Ma, can you pick it up please?" It's eleven o' three and we still have a mile to go. They probably already kicked off. Coach Johnson is going to ream me a new one.

We finally pull up to the field at eleven o' seven. I run out of the car in a full sprint, cleats untied with shoelaces slapping onto the pavement.

"You're late, Jimmy. We're already down seven, mainly because our second stringer fumbled on the second play of the game," coach squabbles at me.

"Sorry coach, I won't let it happen again."

"Grab a seat at the end of the bench; you'll be sittin' for a while," he says without taking his eyes off the field.

Yup, he's pissed. I'll be getting the silent treatment for a while. In Massachusetts youth football is a big deal. It's even worse because our local NFL team, the Patriots, is brutally awful.

It's pure agony watching my offense head back onto the field without being in the huddle. I see our starting QB, Butler, staring me down.

"Sorry, dude," I say under my breath.

Halftime rolls around and we're down 17-0. We huddle up as a team, sucking on some fresh oranges, while coach lays down our game plan.

"All right, boys, we played decent on defense, just couldn't put up any points. We're going no huddle in the second half. Jimmy, I expect big things from you."

"Thanks, coach." I take a deep breath; appreciative he opted not to sit my butt on the bench the rest of the game to teach me a lesson.

We have a decent kick return down to the 45 yard line and start in our no huddle. Butler calls the play, "53, PA – LEFT OUT." That's me, dog.

I step out of the huddle with the adrenaline pumping. Butler fakes the handoff to me, then I brush off the linebacker and head left a few yards. I turn just as the ball is in front of me and pluck it before it hits the ground. I have just one man to beat. I fake right then cut left, as the DB dives for my feet and misses. Daylight, baby! I take it fifty-five yards into the end zone!

Butler is the first one there to congratulate me. "We could have used that in the first half, Dawg! Nice run!" I look up in the crowd. Where's my mom?

Then I see her yapping it up with a few of the other moms in the upper deck, totally oblivious to my TD. Dad, of course, is nowhere to be found either.

For the next twenty-four minutes we steamroll over the Lowell Green Giants, scoring twenty-eight more unanswered points and end up winning 35-17. There's no better feeling than having your teammates and coaches look at you with pure appreciation, knowing you made the difference in the game.

"Nice work, Jimmy. You came through big time, buddy. Sorry to see your old man wasn't here to watch," Coach Johnson says.

"Maybe next time," I mumble. Yeah, right.

16. Halloween

October 1988

Ben

Too old for candy? Yeah, right. I'll dress up until I'm twenty if it means getting a big sack full of candy bars.

Wow, squeezing into mom's old dress is tougher than I thought. Good thing she never wears this ugly rag, I've stretched it out a few sizes at least. Now, a little more bright red lipstick to go with this eyeliner and I'm ready to rock. There. Perfect!

"Jimmy, what do you think?" I yell upstairs.

He comes barreling down in his typical football uniform, which I swear he has worn every year on Halloween since I've known him.

"You're a hottie. If I had a few beers in me, I'd take you home," he adds.

We probably aren't the only fifteen-year-olds running the streets tonight, but I doubt many are focused on candy. I know for a fact that some of the guys will be egging houses in full force tonight. Maybe we can meet up with them after we get our sugar fix.

As we trek through the neighborhood, both of our pillow cases look pretty full. My eye shadow is smudging from the humidity, but by now I could care less.

My goal is to keep going until I have to use a wheelbarrow to carry it. Last year the candy only lasted two weeks since the whole family decided to purge it when theirs ran out. This year I want it to last through Christmas.

As we turn the corner we're now right in front of Billy Thomas's house. Billy T, as they call him, is one of the most popular seniors in high school and makes it a point to give me crap whenever he can. I don't need to deal with his comments in this outfit.

Before I can get a knock in, the door opens wildly. "Well, looky here. If it ain't the football star and his prom date," Billy T jokes.

"Funny, funny. Just give us some candy," I fire back.

"Looks like the queen over here needs some help catching up to you again, Jimmy," he says sarcastically, and then throws in one piece of Starburst in each bag.

Before that scumbag said anything I didn't even notice who had more candy. Now it's irking the hell out of me.

"Let me look at your bag, Jimmy? Do you really have more than me?" As he opens up the bag, sure enough he somehow has more than me.

"How in the hell is that possible?" I grumble. "We've both been going to the same houses all night."

Just then we hear some giggling coming up the hill. I can tell from the distance it's my neighbor, Cindy Starks, along with a few of her girlfriends. They're dressed up as rocker girls. I look better.

"Come over here, I have an idea. Hide with me," I say to Jimmy.

We nestle ourselves in a wall of bushes down the end of Billy T's driveway.

"How the hell do they have so much candy?" I complain to Jimmy. Why can't I just let it go?

"This is going to be funny, watch me." As the girls make their way down the driveway, I jump out and lunge towards Cindy's giant bag of candy. She starts screaming and before you know it, all five of the girls are yelling at the top of their lungs.

"LEEAAAAVVE US ALOOOOOOONE!" they yell in harmony. I'm dragging Cindy like a ragdoll along the pavement as she hangs on to her candy for dear life. Soon after the other girls grab onto her pillow sack as well. What a sight.

To someone watching, it probably appeared to be a total chick fight. Little did they know I'm a dude in disguise. Now I'm pulling five girls down this driveway; what a workout.

My father would kill me if he witnessed this debacle. Too bad I haven't seen him in four months. Am I bitter? Maybe just a little.

I make one final pull, like in a tug of war, and yank the bag from the girls as they all tumble to the pavement crying.

"Let's go," I yell to Jimmy. He's nowhere to be found, so I haul it.

Sprinting for about ten minutes straight without stopping, I come into the back woods of Jimmy's house. Now I can enjoy the catch. She must have doubled my candy intake. What a score! Just then I see Jimmy walking into the yard.

My chest sticks out, proud of my accomplishment. Now who has more candy?

He sits down next to me without saying a word or even looking up at me.

"Why didn't you help me pull while those chicks were hanging on?" I ask.

He just looks up at me and shakes his head. "You got issues."

"No, I got my fill of candy through Christmas," I say proudly.

Later that night, while lying in bed, a towering sense of remorse overcomes me like a giant tsunami. Why am I such a prick? I'll never forget the look of sadness on those girls' faces. This is not the man I want to become. My broken family is taking its toll on me. I know one thing. Jimmy would never have taken that candy.

17. Jimmy's First Stand

Winter 1986

Jimmy

I'm pretty pumped about going to the Football Awards Banquet tonight. Sure, I'm only thirteen, but football is the most important thing in my life right now. Our team made it to the championship this year, but we couldn't close the deal, falling short 20-7. Too many turnovers. As Coach Johnson always says, "In this league, if you turn the ball over you lose. It's that simple."

Personally I had my best year ever, scoring twelve touchdowns in only ten games and also throwing for two. We don't keep good stats of yardage, but I'll bet I had close to a thousand. Anyway, last year Teddy Newcome beat me out for our team's MVP award. Coach said it was close, but since it was Teddy's last year in the eleven-to-thirteen-year-old division, he got the edge.

I'm pretty confident it's my turn tonight. I hope he sticks with the same trophy size. Man, I remember seeing Teddy holding that bad boy above his head. It was probably four feet tall and sparkling silver. The trophy place must have shined it right before the banquet because the lights were reflecting off that thing like it was the North Star.

After that night, I set a personal goal for myself to take it home the following year. I fell short on our team goal of winning it all, but one of two ain't too bad. My mom is supposed to take me there early so I can get a good seat. Last year we missed the first ten minutes and coach gave me a dirty look.

She says dad is coming this year, but I'm not holding my breath. I'm sure at the last minute some work thing will come up. He'll leave a message on the home machine saying how sorry he is and that he'll make it up, that way he won't have to talk to me in person. I guess it's easier to disappoint your son that way.

Mom peels into the driveway, cigarette in hand, at five-fifty p.m. The banquet starts at six p.m. I'm pissed.

"Sorry, honey, I had to stop by the post office before it closed. The line was out the door," she says.

"Let's go, please. You know how important this is to me!" I fire back.

"At least I'm going Jimmy. Where's your father? Probably drinking with the guys, right?" Boy, she really knows how to make me feel better.

At least she knows to pick up the pace and this time we hit all the green lights, all two in the town circle, and pull up at six on the dot. I sprint in and breathe a sigh of relief when I realize things haven't started yet. Thank God.

Still, all the good seats are taken, so I'm stuck in the back row with Adam Stinchler. Or Stinky, as members of our team affectionately call him. Stinchler doesn't have an athletic bone in his body. The running joke is that his dad keeps signing him up for sports to prove he's not gay. The jury is still out in my book. When I look at him, I see more of a golfer rather than a gridiron player.

The oldest kid on the team, he missed the cut off by a few days. He's portly, about 5'1" and 150 pounds. The old-school glasses don't help either. During football games he wears broken "rec specs". Either his family doesn't have the money or he's too afraid to ask for new ones, probably because he hardly sees any action. This year the most he played in a game was about ten snaps. That was in the game against the Falcons, and we were up 43-0. Even Stinchler couldn't give up that lead.

He's actually a half decent kid if you take the time to speak to him for a couple of minutes. Stinchler is no doubt the smartest kid on our team. Yet his looks, combined with his quirks, make him easy pickings. At the end of every practice the guys usually rotate giving him full-throttle wedgies, just for the hell of it. Stinchler takes it like a man and hasn't complained once. He might even like the attention.

The only real interaction I've had with him is at McDonald's, after one of our games. He showed me how to eat for free with salad croutons and mustard sauce.

"They never ask to see your receipt. A few packets and you got yourself a meal," he said to me.

Weird, I thought, but never made much of it. Anyhow, now I get to spend the evening sitting next to him. Great.

"What's up, man?" I say to him.

"Hey, Jimmy. Awesome season," he says.

"Yes. Awesome running Jimmy. Way to take that pigskin and run with it!"

I look to my left and see an older dude who looks just like Stinchler.

"Oh, that's my dad Jimmy. He's a big fan of yours."

"Thanks to both of you. Um, great year too." I'm embarrassed for hesitating, but the words just don't come out right away.

Coach Johnson saves me by standing in front of the group and starting his pep talk. "We were just a couple big plays away from winning it all this year, men. Not bad after going 3-7 the year before, huh?" Coach says with enthusiasm.

He goes on to say he's changing around the format of the awards presentation this year. "I'm giving out the big ones first!" Wow. That means I won't have to suffer in anticipation for two hours. To coach's left there is a long brown table stacked with trophies. One of them is huge. That must be the MVP. It looks even bigger than last year. They go down in size from there. Usually he gives out a Defensive Player of the Year and a Coach's Award too. Then I see a bunch of smaller trophies, probably six inches tall. Nice; he must have gotten the whole team trophies to celebrate the championship appearance. That's a first.

Coach grabs the MVP trophy and puts it directly in front of him. "This year it's a pretty easy choice for me, guys. Our Team MVP is someone that I've had the honor to watch mature into a young man over these past few years. He's not the biggest guy on the team or the fastest, but without question he's got the biggest heart," he says.

This is it. He always tells me how much heart I have. Yes, the trophy is finally mine. I look back and remember my dad still isn't here. Wait, where the hell is my mom? I look out the window. She's puffing on a cigarette.

"Our MVP scored more than one touchdown per game, ran for over a thousand yards, and demonstrated tremendous leadership ability. Jimmy Keller, come on up here and collect this bad boy!"

Blushing, I walk up, grab the beautiful piece of metal, and shake coach's giant hand. Everyone in the crowd is cheering. This is probably the proudest moment of my life. Who gives a crap if I can't share it with any of my family. I'd be much better off if I start assuming the worst. That way I won't be disappointed.

Coach moves down the line with the other two awards, giving the Defensive Player of the Year to Freddie Ryan, a tough SOB who plays safety for our team. Then he gives the Coach's Award to Sam Cunningham. Sammy, as we call him, always plays tough defense. He's probably the biggest kid in the league, standing 5'10" and weighing well over 225 pounds. While he isn't the most agile kid, he makes about twenty tackles a game playing inside linebacker. He also has an awesome attitude, leading the team in our pregame workouts, and we know he always has our back if someone messes with us.

Finally, coach calls up each player to collect our team trophies. "I got every one of you a trophy this year to celebrate our tremendous season. Next year, when we win it all, they'll be even bigger!"

The whole team is pumped, even Stinchler. His dad gives him a high five. That's probably the first time I've seen that kid smile. As each player goes up to accept, parents and teammates send out a loud cheer.

Stinchler is the last one up. As the coach announces his name, no one cheers. Then, one of the parents, Mr. Weaver, lets out a soft "boo". Stinchler walks up and shakes coach's hand, full of smiles. Someone from the crowd yells, "That kid didn't even play. He doesn't deserve a trophy. Look at him. He can't even throw a football." It's Mrs. Weaver. Their kid, Jesse Weaver, is the star wide receiver on the team. He caught eight TDs this year and was probably my toughest competition for the MVP trophy. Yet, as you can tell from his parents, he's got a real attitude problem. Come to think of it, he's usually at the front of the line for the wedgies after practice.

Then the front of the crowd starts chanting, "Stinky sucks! Stinky sucks! Stinky sucks!" Of course, Jesse is leading the chant, but I'm shocked that a few of my other teammates follow suit. Next thing you know half the room is chanting and "booing", ruining Stinchler's one and only good memory about sports. The visibly shaken thirteen-year-old looks up, drops his head in embarrassment, and then scurries back to his seat.

I look up and see his dad. He's got tears streaming down his eyes. Yet he remains strong and hugs his son, trying to somehow reverse the evil actions that were just on display. But the damage was already done.

"Why is everyone chanting those mean things, dad? Did I do something wrong?" Adam asks.

I'm enraged at this point. Without thinking, I stand up, walk to the front of the room, and grab the microphone. The chants keep on.

"Stop it! Stop it right now!" I yell at the top of my lungs. Where did this confidence come from? I never like to talk in front of a crowd. I'm even nervous using my mom's karaoke machine when no one is watching.

"This is no way to treat your teammate! I'm embarrassed to be in the same room with you people." I look up and see Stinchler and his dad turn their heads towards me in shock.

"This team won because we all came together. How many of you even know Adam Stinchler? How many of you have even taken five minutes of your time during this long season to speak with him?"

I realize at that moment I'm just as guilty, unless you count our short McDonald's conversation.

"He may not be the best football player in the league, but he has guts to stick it out with this team. For that, he's my MVP." I walk towards Adam and hand him my trophy. "All you buddy. Don't listen to what these guys have to say. They're a bunch of jerks."

As we leave the parking lot, I see Adam and his dad laughing as they struggle to fit the huge trophy inside their little Fiat. That image kept me going for several months whenever I felt down about my miserable home life.

"How did it go in there, Jimmy? Did you win any awards?" Mom asks.

Looking down at my tiny team trophy, I respond, "More than I ever knew possible."

That was my first experience of true sacrifice. Yes, it was only a football trophy. But at the time it was everything I ever wanted.

This moment would set the stage for many more great sacrifices. No matter how often I give back, the feeling of euphoria never grows old. Years later I ran into Stinchler's dad at a high school football game.

He went on to share that Adam is now happily married with three kids living down in Georgia. He's a history teacher and best of all he coaches' junior high football. Mr. Stinchler hugged me like his own son and again the tears were flowing down his cheeks.

"I'm so proud of you, Jimmy," he said, like it happened yesterday. That was the only time in my entire life I heard that phrase. It felt incredible.

18. PTSD Emerges

Summer 2010

Stephanie

I've only been dating Jimmy for a month, yet I find myself completely falling for him. Maybe it's the cute nervous twitch he gets in his lips when things get serious, or perhaps knowing I'm one of the few who has seen the soft heart underneath that tough-guy exterior. I always knew going to the supermarket on a Friday night was a good idea. I just never thought I'd drum up the courage to start up a conversation with a guy, especially one as hot as Jimmy.

Maybe this is a new approach for me. The aggressive type who asks for a phone number and date within the first five minutes of talking. Heck, it worked that time. Either way, I keep reminding myself to just let things happen one day at a time. The last thing I want is for my mom to be proven right again.

"You fall for guys faster than birds flying south during a blizzard," she always says. Whatever that means? Aren't all the birds gone by the time it snows?

Anyhow, this week should be a great time to just relax and get to know him even better. He's been looking pretty stressed out the past week or two, so this will do him some good. Plus, the fact that my friends will be there too makes things a little less daunting. If he turns into some crazy man, I'll have backup. But I can't imagine my sweet Jimmy doing anything to hurt a fly.

It's nine fifteen a.m., barely enough time to get a manicure and pedicure before picking Jimmy up at eleven for the long drive down south. This is the third straight year for our Virginia Beach Girls' Getaway. I know, it morphed into a couples' getaway after year one. We realized one night of girl talk is enough and then we want some male company.

This year my three best friends are finally able to all make it at once. Jenna, who just recently finalized her divorce, is bringing her new beau, Austin, a Texan she met on a recent business trip. If he's half as good looking as his Facebook pix, then he's a true hottie. Ashlie is coming with her husband, Max. They're leaving their two kids at home, which should be a nice break.

Finally there's Sharon, the wild one of the bunch. She's been divorced three times already and swears she'll never wear another ring. As of last night she was still deciding between inviting Lance or Dominic. Boy, can she manipulate people when she sets her mind to it. I told Jimmy that I would give him the lowdown on everyone during our ten plus hour drive.

It's now twelve forty-six p.m. I just left the salon and should be right on time to pick up Jimmy. Oh, this must be Sharon calling me. "What's up, girl? So which man did you decide on?" I ask her.

"The Latin sensation, Dominic," she says, giggling.

"I thought he was Italian?" I say.

"Well, maybe he is, either way, he satisfies me. So, are you sure you know this guy well enough to spend a full week with him?" Sharon asks me.

"I've spent almost every night with him for the past three weeks, honey. I'm counting quality time spent with him, not the total amount of time I've known him. And based on the math, I know him better than half of my exes," I add for good measure.

"All right, girl, but you know some of these military brats have pretty bad tempers. Just don't let your guard down fully quite yet."

I start to get defensive, but realize she has a point. I have only known Jimmy for a month. Still, I know they'll fall in love with him after this week. I just know it.

Before I can ring the doorbell Jimmy props open the

front door and picks me up off my feet. A long, wet kiss follows. It sends chills up and down my spine. As he puts me down, I feel lightheaded. Wow! Still the same reaction as our first kiss three weeks ago. Maybe there is such a thing as a permanent spark!

"So, how many days are we going to be gone again?" Jimmy asks.

"Huh?" I respond, still fantasizing about that last kiss. "Oh, we're coming back a week from today."

"OK, so seven pairs of boxers sound good to you?" he asks.

"Boxers? You're going to be naked the whole time," I respond. His face turns beat red.

"Never thought I could make a marine blush." I laugh.

"That's not blushing, just excitement," Jimmy says.

It's six hours into the drive and I've already spilled my guts out. By now I've managed to tell Jimmy about my last five relationships, how we broke up, how long each one lasted, and some other key embarrassing moments of my childhood. I even told him about the senior prom, which might go down as the worst moment of my life.

"OK, now it's your turn to tell me some embarrassing things about you," I say.

"I never get embarrassed," he says.

"Aw, come on, nothing in high school? OK. Then what about the military?" I ask.

"Embarrassing probably isn't the right description for my years in the service. And I doubt you'd want to hear about any of it," he says abruptly.

"Sure I would, Jimmy. I want to know everything about you."

"All right, honey, how about I tell you some stories right after I nap for an hour or so? Sound good?"

I say yes, but don't lose sight of the fact that he never wants to open up about anything when it comes to his life experiences.

Three hours later, as we approach the campground, I can tell Jimmy's getting excited. His ears move when he gets curious. I know; it's weird that I know this about him after only a month. But trust me, it's true.

Hard to believe he's traveled halfway across the world on his tours, but has only been further south than New York twice, and each time it was to Camp Lejeune in North Carolina. Those don't strike me as enjoyable road trips.

"How far are we from the beach again?" he asks.

"Walking distance. Like a quarter mile," I say.

A smile lights up on his face. OK, looks like it should be on the left about a mile up. Let's keep an eye out for First Standing State Park.

"There it is, at the next light," Jimmy yells excitedly. "Sweet, it looks like we have a lot of trees around us."

I remember that from the way Sharon described this place; it has the best of both worlds. A private beach nearby and plush trees around the campsite for maximum cover and shade; all for only thirty-two bucks per night per campsite. Hard to beat that.

After getting our parking pass, we pull up to campsite G21. I already see the group hanging out around the fire with cold beers in hand. Before we can even open the car doors a big, clean-shaven guy with a cowboy hat hands Jimmy a cold can of Budweiser.

"I'm Austin. You must be Jimmy. Thanks for your service. Have a cold one!"

Jimmy downs it in about ten seconds and smashes the can with his fist.

"Woohoo, Semper Fi!" Looks like Jimmy will fit in here just fine.

Sharon comes over to greet me and pulls me aside.

"You didn't tell me he looks like Brad Pitt," she says.

"Back off." I smile. "He's all mine."

We spend the next hour trying to catch up to the rest

of the crew, who has been drinking since around seven. They left pretty early this morning to get a nice head start.

The girls have managed to separate away from the campfire into our own section, while the guys are standing up practically on top of the fire. Jimmy, Austin, Max, and Dominic seem to be getting along just fine. I'm sure on a Monday morning they couldn't be more different people, but out here in the woods on a beautiful seventy-degree night, with cold beers in hand they are like old high school buddies.

I try not to eavesdrop, but can't help hearing Dominic's distinct and loud Massachusetts accent. "So Jimmy, did you kill anyone over there?" he asks. I watch Jimmy as he tries to ignore the question.

"Nah, man, it's just a giant party over there, right?" he says, trying to laugh it off.

"Oh, come on, man, I got a buddy of mine who served in the army and he's told me some pretty sick stories. He told me about some sand nigger who they caught trying to steal some weapons. They tortured his ass with a blowtorch." Dominic pushes. I look over and try to get Jimmy's attention to distract him, but he's already committed to taking this head on.

"Sounds like your buddy is a pretty stand-up dude. Must be quite the tough guy," Jimmy says sarcastically. "I guess your buddy never had the chance to talk about all of the innocent kids that are being killed in the crossfire, did he? Or about the roadside bombs that are ripping apart the intestines of twenty-one-year-old kids? Has your buddy ever had to hold on to the hand of a dying friend and promise to lie to the kid's parents and say he died with a gunshot wound to the head, rather than shit himself while all of his guts are spewed on the road? Guys, did you ever hear about Uday and Qusay's rape camps? Now that is a good one. You see, they set up torture chambers in one of their mansions. The basement had five different rooms with handcuffs, blowtorches, long poles, stun guns, and a whole arsenal of goodies to torture the hell out of young virgins. It even came with a cache of HIV test kits. I guess they figured safe sex is better than consensual sex. Oh, if that isn't funny, how about the dozens of mass graves we found just outside of Tikrit. Now that is a good one. Did he mention the smell that was so hideous, you would puke within five seconds of getting out of your car? You see, they only buried the bodies about two feet deep, which means it didn't take long for the flesh to resurface. Yeah, I bet your buddy didn't tell you about that one. So, did I kill someone? Which day are you referring to?" Jimmy finishes.

Then he walks off into the woods to smoke a cigarette. I sneak away from the girls to follow. Hopefully, they only caught small snippets of Jimmy's rant. "I didn't know you smoked," I say.

"Only when I camp in Virginia," he says.

"You OK?" I ask, trying to read his eyes.

"Nothing a couple of Buds can't ease," he replies.

"I'm walking over to take a quick shower, in case you happen to see a man in a ski mask," I tell him.

I make the hundred-yard walk over to the campground bathrooms and shower stalls. At least there's plenty of light. Other than the spider webs in every corner, I can live with this. Then I look down and notice a large pool of standing water leading into each shower stall, no doubt leftovers from the campers earlier tonight. I open shower door one, yuck! About an inch of stagnant water is blocking the drain. On to door number two. This one doesn't have any water in it, but the three piles of matted up hair make me dry heave. Let's see if door number three is a charm. Not too horrible.

I lock the door, check it again, and start to run the shower. There are two small hooks to hang up my dry clothes and towel. I have to put my old clothes on the bench, which has a mixture of sand, dirt, and water covering half of it. Thank God I brought my flip-flops. Athlete's foot is the least of my worries in this place.

I hop into the hot shower. Ah, that feels good. I close my eyes and try to forget about the surroundings. Instead of looking up at the large daddy longlegs about five feet from my face, I try to picture a nice waterfall in Hawaii. That works for a minute. I quickly apply the soap, shampoo, and conditioner. No shaving tonight. I'll do it tomorrow night, if by then I can adjust to this nastiness.

Funny, Sharon didn't tell me about this part.

As I walk out of the shower, it becomes quite the challenge to put on my clean clothes while standing in a small pool of water. Hopping on one foot, I'm able to put on my underwear without getting it wet. Just then I hear a soft tapping on the door.

"Hello? Jimmy, is that you?" I say. No response, but now another knock. "OK, funny joke." I cover up with the towel and open up.

But instead of looking up to see Jimmy, I'm horrified to see a half-naked man pleasuring himself in front of my shower door. I scream at the top of my lungs "Ahhhhh! Help me!"

Then I slam the door and lock it. I can hear him take off into the woods. OK, calm down, he's just some pervert, probably not a rapist.

I try to remember what he looks like so I can give a description. Tall, skinny white guy; probably in his late twenties. Red baseball cap. I don't remember what it said on the front. His shorts were down to his ankles, but I do remember he was wearing Sambas, the black and white striped indoor soccer shoes. Then I hear Jimmy's voice.

"Steph! Steph! Are you OK?" he yells. "I'm fine, Jimmy. In here." I open the door, still wrapped in a towel.

"What happened?" he asks.

"Some pervert knocked on the door and when I opened it, he was taking care of himself," I say.

"What did he look like?" he asks.

"He's a white guy, probably mid-twenties, wearing a red baseball cap and those indoor soccer shoes," I say. "Sambas."

But before I can get the final word out of my mouth, Jimmy takes off. "Wait, wait, I think we should just let the police handle it," I yell. But he's already gone.

I hurry and put on the rest of my clothes, then jog back to the camp. Everyone is still sitting around the campfire. After I quickly explain what happened, the group offers to help me find Jimmy. Dominic takes the lead and starts running at a pretty fast pace. The girls are dragging behind ten to twenty yards.

As we run down the narrow side road along the campground, it gets eerily quiet and dark. By now it's probably past one a.m. and the only lights we see are lanterns sporadically shining throughout various campsites. Hard to believe a place like this doesn't have street lights, but I guess that's the fun of camping. At least until some guy jerks off in front of you.

After running for what seemed like at least a mile, we can see lights in the distance. It's the main entrance to the campground. As we get closer, I hear yelling.

"Show your face, you scumbag! I know you're in there!" That's Jimmy's voice. He's standing outside of a green storage shed, adjacent to the main bathrooms.

As he looks over at us approaching, without hesitation, he continues to bang on the door with his fists. "I'm going to count to three, pervert. If you don't open the door at three, you will wish you did. One. Two. Thr—" Before Jimmy gets out the last vowel, the door slowly pops open. The squirrely man with the red hat and Sambas puts his hands up in the air surrendering.

Jimmy grabs the pervert by the front of the neck and lifts him squarely off the ground. His feet are dangling six inches off the ground as Jimmy's giant hand appears to be squeezing the life out of the man. He slams him against the shed, the back of his head putting a small head-sized dent in it.

"You like scaring women and acting like a pig, you pervert?" His tone sounding like a Marine sergeant. "How about I make sure you never do that again?" At that point Jimmy drives the man into the concrete with a body slam and starts kicking him right in the family jewels. Then he jumps on top of him and starts laying haymaker punches squarely on his nose and the rest of his face. Blood is spewing everywhere and the man is screaming in pain.

"Jimmy, please stop. You've taught him a lesson. Now let's get the police involved," I plead.

I pull on his shoulders to pull him off, but in the violent rage he throws me to the ground with one arm. My head hits the pavement and I can feel the knot forming instantly. I'm shocked. This is not the same man I started to fall in love with. He was so gentle. This man is a psycho.

A few more punches to the face and the man is barely conscious. Blood is all over the man's clothes and Jimmy's hands. He doubles over in pain as Jimmy stands up. "This is your lucky day, punk. We're going to avoid calling the police this time and say that you just received your punishment, the old-fashioned way."

All of my friends are in shock, even the guys. Dominic and Austin pick me up to my feet and start escorting me back to the campsite. I take one more look at the pervert. You can't even recognize his face under the bloody mess. There is no question he needs stitches and he may have broken bones in his face. Then I look back towards Jimmy.

His face is still locked in a rage, and he is breathing heavy as he mumbles to himself. He looks down at all of the blood on his hands and I can start to make out what he's mumbling. "God, please help me. I'm a killer."

19. The Long Ride Home

Jimmy

Boy, do I really know how to screw things up. Here is a girl who is totally into me and I scare her half to death by nearly killing a guy with my bare hands. She hasn't said it yet, but I know we're done. I'm surprised she didn't just pack up and leave the campsite after it all went down. I guess she figures if we act like nothing happened, maybe her friends would forget about it. Based on the way they've looked at me, that's highly doubtful.

I spent the last two days exchanging small talk with Austin. He seems to be the only one who isn't scared to death of me. Max won't even throw a football with me on the beach and Dominic avoids eye contact. Obviously the entire group camping dynamic got thrown out of whack after my incident. No more group campfires, every couple seems to do their own thing. That is, except for Stephanie and I. She hasn't even talked to me since everything happened. I've tried to make small talk by asking if she wants anything on my Starbucks run, and she replies with a soft "No, thank you." I'm a pretty good mind reader. My gut tells me she is not really upset, just sad and disappointed. Like she thought I was someone she could trust and be with for a while, but now that's all vanished.

I can't really blame her. However, at the same time, that pervert deserved what he got. Hopefully, I spared some other woman down the road. I just wish I had pulled him in the woods and given him the beating of his life alone, rather than in front of a big crowd. In Iraq that guy would be castrated before getting shot in the head. So I consider him lucky.

I've been driving for nearly three hours since we left the campground and Stephanie has been just zoning; looking out the window with a blank stare. I try to put my hand on her leg as a sign of affection, but she slowly pushes it off and squirms into a different seating position.

I really do mess up everything. Now I see why so many guys re-enlist and go back for two or three more tours. We're trained killers. Guys like me, who try and convert back to a kid glove society, are a walking time bomb. It's like asking a wild lion, who has been hunting for food his entire life and fighting off anything that gets close, to one day live in New York City. Something bad is bound to happen.

I end up driving the entire eleven hours, with the exception of a five-minute gas and bathroom break. Midway through the trip Stephanie decides to lay in the backseat and sleep. Probably a good idea; at least I don't have to see her sitting comatose out of the corner of my eyes.

During the last hour she begins to sniffle a lot. Sounds like she is crying. I realize this may be the last time I ever see her. It's times like these where I miss my buddies, especially Tyler. Life can be so unfair. Why couldn't I stop it? We were always together. Like twins. Yet, just like most things in my life, Murphy's Law takes over. The one time you don't need something to happen, it does. Pulling down her street, we pass a vandalized stop sign lying on its side. I chuckle. Those were the good old days. Boy, could I use a laugh like that right now.

20. The Stop Sign

Summer 1990

Ben

Working around Newfound Lake during the summer was a prime gig for high school kids looking to get their parents off their backs, while making a few bucks on the side. Supposedly ranked as "One of the Cleanest Lakes" in the U.S., Newfound Lake is about four miles outside of downtown Bristol and attracts a ton of what we like to call "Massholes." The term affectionately refers to our lovely neighbors south of the border in Massachusetts that infest New Hampshire during the summer months.

Jimmy came from Mass, but since he is a regular here now, the term doesn't apply to him. In Bristol, the population triples to a whopping 9,000 people during the summer, mostly because of our middle to upper income friends. The lake is really quite a hidden spectacle. You'd never know there could be such a serene place after taking a stroll through dilapidated downtown Bristol just a few miles up the road. With two stop signs and no red lights, there are a few antique shops, a barber shop, a local mini-mart, and not much else.

The buildings look circa 1930s, with their lead-based paint peeling inside out. It's always an adventure figuring out how to spend your Friday and Saturday nights in Bristol. There are the occasional parties, but those are few and far between. Mostly it's left up to our creative imaginations to fill the time.

Tonight the plan is to meet at Greg Rankel's house around nine p.m., then brainstorm about how to cause the most trouble without getting caught. Rankel, a senior, ran into Jimmy at a party last weekend and set the stage for the night's activities. I haven't hung out with him much, but he seems like a decent guy. Word travels fast in this tiny town, so there's a fine line between being known as a group of kids that pulls off harmless pranks and being labeled troublemakers. I probably fall somewhere in the middle at this point.

A couple of other buddies also wanted in on the action, LaFleur and Grizwaltz. As the gang arrives, we meet up in Rankel's garage for some serious brainstorming. The typical ideas are being tossed around; egging and toilet paper rolling keep coming up. But tonight seems like a night that's destined for something more exciting. Not the same old same old.

Jimmy has that look in his eyes. The look right before we do something crazy. "How much white paint do you have over there?" He's referring to the supply sitting underneath Rankel's dad's tool supplies.

We pop off the lids and see that each of the two buckets is at least half full.

"Where are you going with this, Jimmy?" Rankel asks. He seems a little hesitant to take one for the team. At least until he hears more about the idea.

"It's a surprise," Jimmy says. "Just trust me on this one."

We pile into my '85 Ford LTD station wagon; a chick magnet, of course. This is one of the few times my mom actually lets me use my driver's license. Normally she forces me to mooch rides from everyone. I accidentally sit on top of the shovel Jimmy threw in the way back. Wow, that feels good.

We start to drive around aimlessly on some back roads until the LTD stops sharply at the stop sign on the corner of Prosperity and Hunter Road.

"Hop out, boys," Jimmy says enthusiastically.

We then proceed to dig about two feet into the ground and yank out the eight-foot stop sign, pole and all. Oh boy, this is getting good.

Of course, none of us take the time to measure the length of the interior space in the LTD, which by my estimate was pretty darn close.

After twenty minutes of maneuvering the sign and post, along with getting dirt in just about every nook and cranny of the Wagon, we finally accept the fact that it won't fit with the windows closed.

So, we're off to the next phase of our journey; the six of us and a large stop sign with about six inches of metal pole sticking out the front passenger window. Oh, but the green blanket covering the pole outside of the Wagon made it look much less conspicuous. That's male high school logic for you. Good thing the Bristol PD has about three active duty officers.

"Next stop, The Ledges," Jimmy emphatically pronounces.

At this point we all start to put things together. The group approves with an almost synchronized man chant. "Nice!"

"The Ledges" is a five or so mile narrow stretch of road adjacent to Newfound Lake. The road can't be more than twelve feet wide covering both lanes, raised about fifteen feet above the water with only inches to spare before the drop-off. The other side of the road is occupied by steep cliffs of granite which range anywhere from ten to fifty feet, depending upon the section of "the Ledges".

Every so often you'll see a summer home on top of the granite ledges. Driving these roads is treacherous in broad daylight and like playing Russian roulette at night. The speed limit is around 20 mph, but most people drive about 10 mph, since they're just visiting and on vacation time.

We hit the windy road going about 30 mph with the stop sign pole hanging out the window, reminiscent of a dog taking in the fresh summer air. Weaving back and forth I pray a stray vacationer won't decide to hit the streets. Odds are 50/50 as to whether or not the road could even handle two cars driving at the same time. Jimmy pops the high beams on as we hit a patch of road that gives about twenty feet of visibility in front of us, the most thus far.

"This is it," Jimmy barks. "Ben, Greg, you get the sign. I'll take the brushes. LaFleur, Grizwaltz, I need one on each end of the road, about forty feet up, playing lookout." I'm not surprised that Jimmy took the reins on this project like he's done a hundred times before.

Lookout sounds good initially, until I realize we have nowhere to run, even if I'm able to give the group a proper warning.

We stumble with the awkward sign and drop it in front of Jimmy. He's already put the first touch of fresh paint on the unsuspecting road. He quickly finishes the job with two coats of paint, making an almost perfect stop line stretching about six feet long and one foot wide. Then he stands up, proud of his work, and orders, "OK, start digging. Right here." His foot stands over the dirt to the left of the stop sign, with about two feet between the road and the ledge.

I grab the shovel and start digging. After about two minutes and roughly a foot of depth, Jimmy stops me.

"OK, that's good enough; it doesn't have to be perfect. We need to get movin'!" Rankel grabs the sign and slams it into the newly formed hole while Jimmy follows by throwing some dirt over it to secure our work. "Perfect!" We all approve.

"LaFleur! Grizwaltz! We're done, come on back!" Jimmy yells.

We all take a minute to appreciate our work. What a sight. There along the windy and dangerous road lies a random stop sign with paint to match. We all start howling.

"OK guys, let's enjoy this now," Jimmy says.

We hop back in the LTD and drive a few hundred feet past our masterpiece. There we find a long driveway to park.

We all run back towards the stop sign and hide along the embankment, hoping we'll soon be able to witness a seriously confused motorist.

Ten minutes goes by, nothing. Then we see some lights.

"Here we go, fellas," Jimmy yells.

It's a small sedan, looks like a Toyota Corolla and going pretty fast considering the road. Suddenly it slams on the brakes in front of the stop sign. We all start to cackle. The driver leans forward and looks completely befuddled. Just then, I'm sure out of pure instinct, she looks both ways to check for oncoming traffic. Looking ridiculous, she peruses the water on one side and cliffs on the other. Ten seconds go by and she finally starts to inch past the sign, pumping her brakes every few feet as if she's driving on snow.

What a riot! If I could capture her face on camera, it would go down as a classic! She slowly rolls past us as the group sprints onto the road giving high fives.

"That was AAAWWWWSOME!"

Before we can celebrate too long, we notice another car coming in from the opposite direction. We dive back into the shallow brush and hope for similar results.

Then I see a big pickup approaching on the other side of the road. Our second victim, I say to myself.

Almost perfectly, both drivers cross paths. The pickup stops sharply right when the driver sees the sign. The other car, a Volvo, reacts by stopping as well, even though he doesn't have a stop sign on his end. They both look at each other and give a "what the hell?" look. Each holds up their hands in dismay. Rather than just proceed, neither knows who should go first so they each move forward a few feet, and then slam on the brakes again. Then the pickup truck owner waves out the window for the Volvo to go. Watching this, we are all rolling on the ground in tears.

"Are you kidding me? LaFleur says.

At that point we all realize this one is an instant

classic.

A few days later while sifting through the local paper, I come across the following headline. "Mysterious stop sign causes major confusion for Newfound Lake travelers." I get out my scissors and clip that one out for a rainy day.

Little did I know my creativity would come back to haunt me later in life.

21. Ben's Big Game

Spring 1991

Ben

This afternoon's game is the most important of the season. Actually, it's probably the most important of my career so far. We're 8-6, with only two games left in the regular season. The standings just came out in the *Manchester Union Leader* and we're currently in a tie for sixteenth place with Mascoma High School and Inter-Lakes High School. I know we're better than both of those teams, but the only thing that matters is what's in the final box score. Potential means nothing.

If we win our next two games we're a lock to make it into the tournament. We can worry about the fact that we'll be ranked number sixteen playing the number one seed in the state later. This is disappointing considering last year our team made it to the state semifinals and lost a heartbreaker to the eventual champs, Belmont, 3-1.

I'm on the hill tonight, as we face the eight and six Mascoma Royals for the second time. They're a cocky bunch and my blood boils every time I think of those wiseass faces. We lost the first time we played them in week one, 10-5, on our home field. However, we're a better team now, so I'm confident we can come out on top. Now we have to travel to Canaan, New Hampshire, to their home field.

Marking a recent tradition, everyone on the team is wearing our baseball jerseys in school today. I figure it will get everyone thinking about the game and pumped up, especially when some of our classmates wish us luck. The cool thing about playing road games is that we get to leave school a couple hours early. The game officially starts at five o'clock, which means the team bus leaves around two-fifteen p.m. Works for me.

It's now eleven-thirty a.m., but the day is dragging. Hopefully, once we get through lunch, time will go a little faster. Jimmy and I are meeting up in the cafeteria in five minutes. Today is chickwich day, a great pregame meal. Usually I'm able to bum a second one from Jeanie, the cafeteria lady, assuming her boss isn't paying attention.

My coach told me after last game that it's likely there will be a few scouts at the game tonight. Mascoma has a stud player on their team, Gabe Watkins, a 6'1" 210 pound lefty first baseman that is leading the state in batting average and home runs. Obviously, the scouts aren't there for me, but like coach says, they're still watching the whole game. If I play well, I can force some of these colleges to notice. It's not very often scouts venture up to Bristol, so I'm not bashful piggy-backing off of Gabe to get a chance to play college ball.

As of now my expectation has been to try out for a Division III team such as Plymouth State or Keene State. However, D III doesn't offer scholarships. I hear UMass and BU scouts might be there today.

"Yo, Clemens, you up for a big day today?" Jimmy says, strolling in with his Number 53 jersey. While Jimmy's number one sport is clearly football, his tough-guy approach has been a nice fit for our team. He plays right field and back-up catcher, but his hitting has really started to come around this year. Last game he hit a bomb over the right field fence and he's now moved into the number five slot in our batting order.

"You better believe I'm ready. Time to shut down those Mascoma loudmouths! You want me to try and pull you an extra chickwich?" I say.

Jimmy gives me the thumps-up. Jeanie discreetly serves me up four and we head over to the table. I wolf down mine in about three bites when I look up and notice Jason Wockerman come into the cafeteria.

Wocker, as we like to call him, is a freshman that sits the bench for our team. He's a real quiet kid who, if he adds a little weight and about six inches, could be decent someday. Right now he's about 5'3", 120 pounds, and has played no more than five innings all year. If we had a junior varsity team, he'd be much better off playing on it. However, we have eleven total players on the varsity squad, including Wocker. We're probably the only high school team that he would make.

I've tried to keep an eye out for him this year, for a few reasons. First, the kid has zero confidence. Most of the time he's looking straight down and hardly ever makes eye contact. The second reason, one that hits home with me, is his family's financial situation.

Wocker lives a few houses down from the log cabin, which we stayed in my freshman year. We rode the bus together and I saw his living conditions.

My guess is he doesn't have running water at the shack where his four siblings and mother reside. I say this because his wardrobe consists of about four outfits. Well, technically eight. Four in the winter, and four that cover the other six months of the year up here in sunny New Hampshire. All of his outfits have some type of rip or stain on them and they're stiff like sandpaper. I would imagine this is because they hang dry clothes outside. I can't tell you how many times kids on the bus made fun of Wocker after seeing his tighty-whities outside of their bus window, just dangling on the clothesline.

He sits in the corner of the cafeteria by himself, shoveling food down as fast as possible, so that kids won't have time to pick on him. He's always very careful to only walk through the lunch line when no one is around, so kids won't notice he gets free lunch. I can totally relate. I went through that for about a year and as petty as it sounds, for a teenage kid, there isn't much more you can do to embarrass the hell out of him.

I walk over to him in an attempt to invite him over with us to finish his lunch. However, just as I approach, he engulfs the last few bites of his chickwich.

"Wocker, you want to join us?" I say.

He shakes his head no, without making a sound.

"Hey, why aren't you wearing your baseball jersey? Today's a big game. We may need your speed out there on the bases." Saying this, I know it's highly unlikely he will get on the field today.

"Oh, I forgot. It's in my bag, so I'll make sure to have it for the game."

****

We arrive at the ballpark with plenty of time to stretch and take some batting practice and grounders in the infield. I warm up in the bullpen with Jimmy, and my curveball is breaking sharply.

"That is nasty. You break those off like that today and we're winning big," Jimmy says.

His prediction proves to be accurate. Through five innings, we're up 3-1, with their only run being unearned due to a misplay in the outfield. I've only given up two bloop hits, and managed to strike out their all-star Gabe Watkins twice so far.

In between innings I've noticed two guys in baseball caps, who must be the scouts. Each time I walk off the field, I make sure to look their way. One of them, with the BU cap, takes notes after my eighth strikeout. Hopefully he's writing "bad ass pitcher."

Gabe is on deck, and there are two outs. I need to concentrate on getting this guy, so that I don't have to face their all-star with a man on base. After falling behind 2-0, I manage to battle back and even the count at 2-2. Our catcher, Charlie, calls for the curveball. I snap it hard and the hitter makes contact, a shallow pop-up heading into shallow left field. Our left fielder, Joe Wilson, has some serious speed and a great glove. He tracks down the ball, but doesn't see our shortstop, Marty Bailey, running backwards to make the play. At the last second Joe calls off Marty, but it's too late. They collide. Somehow, Joe manages to hang onto the ball and make the catch. Out number three. Yes!

Marty gets up with a limp, but Joe is still down. The coach runs out to him. After about five minutes, Joe is helped off the field. He can't walk on his own. Looks like a severely sprained ankle. When he gets back in the dugout, Coach walks down to the end of the bench and sits next to Wocker.

"OK, buddy, we need you. You're playing right field next inning. Jimmy, go to left."

Wocker stands up and that's when I notice his uniform. It has what appear to be ketchup stains down both legs. He must not have washed it after our game last week. It's wrinkled so badly you can barely make out his number, twenty-nine.

We go down one-two-three in the top of the sixth. It's now me against Gabe for the third time. Each of his at bats so far I've stuck with breaking balls, since the book on him is that he crushes fastballs. However, sooner or later he is going to sit on one of my breaking balls. Charlie calls for another curveball, but I shake him off. He gives me a hard stare then throws down one finger, signaling for the fastball. He also motions his hand towards his left knee, which means keep the ball outside. I fire a perfect strike right into the outside target. It catches Gabe completely off guard, as he watches the ball slam into the mitt.

Now I want the breaking ball. I snap off a nasty one; this time it hits the inside target at the knees. Again Gabe leaves his bat on his shoulders. My confidence is building and I can't help but to smile at the two scouts while heading back to the mound. High heat baby! Who is the college player, huh? I think to myself.

Charlie is thinking on the same page as me. He signals for the fastball, but uses both hands to remind me to keep the ball up. That's all I need is to serve one up for Gabe while up 0-2. I rear back and let it rip. Right away I can tell the pitch is not high enough. It makes contact with Gabe's bat right below his right armpit and it's hammered. No need to even look back. A solo homerun that must have cleared the fence by thirty feet.

Now its 3-2. Charlie hops out to the mound and reminds me to stay calm. "We're in good shape, Ben. Just hit your spots and get out of this inning," he says firmly. I manage to get the next three batters out on hard ground balls.

We go into the final inning, top of the seventh, still with the lead. Jimmy is up first. Mascoma's pitcher, Billy Wheatley, has pitched almost as good of a game as I have although he hasn't posted nearly as many strikeouts. He's more of a groundball pitcher.

Jimmy walks up to the plate and pounds the first pitch over the deepest part of the ballpark. As he rounds first base, he continues to sprint, not in the least bit concerned about a home run trot. The whole team congratulates him when he crosses home.

"Not bad for a football player, eh," Jimmy says, smiling. "Now go close it out for us, Clemens."

Our next three batters hit weak fly balls to the infield. We're three outs away from practically locking up a spot in the state tournament. I start to do the math walking out to the hill. If we win, we'll be 9-6. That would leave Mascoma at 8-7. Our next game is against 3-11 Winnesquam. So it's very likely that if we win this game, we're in.

Concentrate. Just three outs. In the on-deck circle I see their number eight hitter. *Whatever you do, don't walk him. Wait a minute; your math is off there. Mascoma could still tie us if they win their next game, right?* Oh crap, not now. I don't need this now. *Will you concentrate for Christ's sake!*

Charlie calls for the fastball. Just as I'm about to throw, I see the BU scout in the corner of my eyes. *Is he writing about me? How many strikeouts do I have again? Eight, no nine.* Ball one. Way up high. *I told you, don't walk this kid. He's the number nine hitter. Wait, do I have nine or ten strikeouts? Let me think here. Two in the first, one in the second, two in the third.*

Ball two, low. *You're blowing the game. Why does this always happen? Just don't think about anything except throwing strikes. That's it, I forgot about Inter-Lakes. If they win the next two games, we still might not make it into the playoffs. Wait, do they have eight wins or seven?*

Ball three. Just inside. *You are going to blow this game, you asshole.* I notice the BU scout get up and walk behind the backstop. *Is he worried about my pitching motion? Maybe he sees something he doesn't like.* Ball four. Way outside.

Charlie heads out to the mound. "Ben, are you in this game? You didn't even acknowledge my signs. Where is your head? Come on now, buddy, the tying run is coming up to the plate."

Now it's the number nine hitter. This guy probably won't even swing the bat. *Did I bring home my math book? Oh man, I have a test tomorrow and I forgot it. Wait, what time is the class? Oh, first thing. How can I study? Maybe one of the other guys brought their books home and I can borrow it.*

Ball one, high. *Wait, maybe I did bring it. It might be in the front pocket of my backpack.* Ball two, low. *Are you going to blow this game, you loser?* OK. Step back and concentrate. *Wait, who does Inter-Lakes play their last game? Are you sure they have seven wins? I thought they have eight?*

Ball three. That is seven balls in a row. I step off the mound, take my hat off, and wipe the sweat pouring off my head. Then I remember the lucky ritual. How the hell could I have forgotten it? *Touch your nose twice before throwing the pitch. Then wipe off the mound twice with your glove after you throw the pitch.* I perform the ritual two times in a row and wouldn't you know it, I fire two strikes right down the middle. The batter didn't even move his bat, proof that if I can just fire one more strike, he will K. *Touch your nose twice.* I fire the ball. It's just off the outside corner. Ball four, the ump calls.

Crap! Two men on and no one out. Are you kidding me? Now I face the top of the lineup. The winning is run coming up to the plate. *Wipe off the mound two times with your glove. Do I swipe left to right or right to left? It's got to be left to right, since I'm a righty. Last pitch I must have went right to left. No wonder I missed with that pitch.*

Charlie looks up at me, wondering where my head is. Can't you just act normal and get your head in the game? *Think positive thoughts. Actually, on second thought, don't think about anything. Just look at the glove and throw the ball.* My ritual works for the leadoff hitter as I gun him down on four pitches.

One out, two men on and we're still up 4-2. I start off the next hitter with two balls. *Am I missing one of my good luck rituals? Oh yes, I forgot to tap my left cleat before throwing. I tap it one time, after I wipe off the mound and before I touch my nose.* Now I fire a strike and he fouls the pitch off. Then another strike; this time he looks at it. I'm back in the saddle at 2-2.

Charlie calls for a curve ball and I pull the string. The batter barely makes contact, with a squibbler that could be trouble. At first I think it hits off his leg, but the ump doesn't signify a foul ball. It must have bounced off the front of home plate, which means it's fair unless the ball rolls into foul territory. I stumble towards the ball, which is up the third base line halfway between home and the mound. The only play I have is at third. With my lower half on the ground, I try to shot-put the ball towards Marty at third, but we're too late. Now the bases are loaded.

I look up and for the first time notice how many fans

are in the crowd. There are at least fifty, which for one of our games is like a capacity crowd. I then notice the UMass scout standing up next to the Mascoma dugout.

For some reason I now feel really nervous. I walk back to the mound slowly, so I can recite my prayer. *Father, Son, Holy Spirit, amen. Lord, please help me to throw strikes and do my best.* Amen. The rituals are working again because I entice the next hitter to swing at a bad pitch. He lunges towards the high, inside fastball and pops it straight up behind the plate. Charlie makes the play and now we're one out away from locking up the win.

Lord, thank you. Please. One more, Lord. Father, Son, Holy Spirit, amen. I'm not typically a very religious guy, but at times like this I definitely feel calmer when I pray. *Swipe the mound, kick my cleat, and wipe my nose.* Charlie calls for the fastball on the outside corner as we face their cleanup hitter. He hits a high popup to right field. This should do it. Yes!

I watch as the ball starts to drift deeper at an angle towards the foul line. Then I remember that Jimmy is no longer in right, but rather it's Wocker. Come on, man. Stay under it. Two hands. The ball takes forever to come down. Wocker gets under the ball, but then at the last second dives backwards. The ball drifts a bit with the wind and pops in and out of his glove onto the ground.

Is it fair? I look up to see the ump making the signal for a fair ball. I think Wocker was technically in fair play when the ball fell out of his glove. He takes forever to get to his feet then overthrows the cut-off man. I run to back up home. The winning run is heading to the plate. By the time our first baseman, Ray, picks up the ball in the infield, Mascoma is already celebrating the winning run.

We all walk off the field, devastated. No one says a word. I find Wocker and pat him on the back. "That was a tough play. Don't be too hard on yourself. Besides, we would have never been in that situation if I would have thrown strikes," I say. However, he's in his own world.

Wocker finds a seat at the end of the dugout and buries his face in his glove. Thirty minutes later, the coach has to pry him off the bench so he won't miss the team bus back home. That kid's confidence must be devastated. And really, it's all my fault.

22. Big Mac Trick

Ben

I sit in my favorite bus seat on the way back home, number twenty, which is about five rows from the back. I've been watching Wocker off and on for the last ten minutes of the bus ride, to see if he snaps out of his misery. A few of the guys behind me start to whisper and I can tell something is up. Then Pete, our outspoken second baseman, sneaks up on him and takes his glove.

"Guys, look, now I know why he missed the ball. There's a huge hole in his glove," Pete says sarcastically. He squeezes a few of his fingers through the webbing to portray the image. Wocker sits and takes it without even moving.

Pete can be a real dick sometimes. He doesn't mess with me, of course, because he knows I would throttle him. But he definitely isn't afraid to mess with some of the weaker guys.

"Leave him alone, Pete. It was a tough play," I say, jumping in.

"Tough play? Why are you sticking up for this siv, Ben? He cost us the game and probably a trip to the playoffs. Look at him. Stand up, Wocker."

Then Pete grabs Wocker by the shirt and yanks him up so that he is standing in the aisle. He points down to his uniform. "This kid can't even wash his uniform. Look at the ketchup stains all over it. I don't remember eating before the game, do you? If he doesn't take pride in looking like a ball player, he'll never be one."

Then Pete pulls out a bleach stick pen from his bag and throws it to Wocker. "Put this on your filthy uniform, Wocker, you need it more than I do."

At that point I look over and can see Wocker starting to tear up. I lose it.

"You mean bastard!" I grab Pete by the throat and

start to choke him. I've never, ever gotten in a confrontation with anyone at school, especially on a ballclub. Pete and I usually are cool, but I can't stand bullies. Jimmy reaches over to pull me off of him, but I resist at first.

"You need to apologize to Wocker right now or I'm not letting go," I say. Pete's face is bright red but he has the wherewithal to nod yes.

"Sorry, man," the coward says. Then I stand up in front of the team.

"Guys, today was a tough game. We had plenty of chances to win it and one play didn't decide anything. If you want to blame someone, put the blame on me. I walked two guys in the last inning. If we win our next game, we still have a really good shot at making the playoffs. I don't want to hear anyone else giving Wocker or another player crap for this loss. Understood?" The whole team nods and coach gives me a thumps-up.

I go up to sit behind Wocker and he whispers, "Thank you."

"Anytime. I'm hungry. How about you?" I say, looking forward to our Mickey D's stop. The one thing that can quickly make you forget about a loss is some hot, salty fries and a Big Mac.

A few minutes after the fiasco, the team bus pulls up to McDonald's. We all march out. As I'm walking past the bus I notice one silhouette still sitting in his seat. It's Wocker. I climb back onto the bus.

"Come on slugger, let's grab some food."

"I'm not hungry. Thanks anyway, man," he says.

It hits me that Wocker likely has zero money.

"My treat. Let's go."

I pick him up and lead him outside. A sadness hits me as we walk through the front doors. I suddenly realize he's done this for every road game. While we were all hanging out laughing and eating some comfort food, Wocker was sitting on the bus alone. I guess I just used to assume he wasn't hungry. The reality is no one really cared enough to pay attention.

I reach in my pocket; three bucks. Just enough to get Wocker a Big Mac meal. "What are you going to eat?" Wocker asks.

"I have a little trick up my sleeve, Wocker. Eat and enjoy." I laugh.

As everyone is eating, I remind Jimmy to leave me the last two bites of his Big Mac. "Of course, bro, you think I would forget your master deception?" He laughs.

Wocker joins in the fun. "The suspense is killing me. What do you do, rob the place?" It's great to see the kid engaged with the group. Hopefully this is a first start to coming out of his shell.

"OK, OK. Here we go. Jimmy, mostly eaten Big Mac please," I say. Jimmy hands it over, with no more than two bites left, or one big one, depending on how you slice it.

"Next step, hair color please," I add. Charlie is positioned by the front counter and then after looking in the back at some of the workers, he heads back.

"Looks like three of the workers putting the burgers together have black hair, one with red," he says.

"Our lucky day." I laugh. "OK, we're skipping the red and going with the sure thing. Wocker, would you like to do the honors?" I say to him. He nods yes.

"Just hank out two long strands of your hair," I say, trying to keep a straight face. Wocker pulls out two gems, each strand about three inches long.

"That might be the best pull yet," Jimmy says.

Then I open up the tiny remainder of bun left and carefully place the strands of hair across the top of the burgers. The hair strands are so long they actually stick out of the side.

"This one will take some balls," Pete adds.

He's right. Usually I have the hair under the bun to make it less conspicuous. "Wocker, you want to join me up there for some fun?" I offer.

"OK. Do I have to do anything?" he asks hesitantly.

"Nope, just look upset, like you just ate someone's pubes."

We walk up to the front counter. Wocker puts on his best angry face.

"Hi, ma'am', sorry to bother you," I say. "My friend here was eating his Big Mac and realized there is a hair in it. He almost threw up when he noticed. Can you please get us another one? Oh, and make sure to ask the workers in the back to be more careful," I finish.

The worker, no more than seventeen, looks at me in disbelief. She appears ready to challenge me, but then retracts. That's the beauty of this trick. It's not worth the risk for a worker to question me. If by a slim chance the hair really was in there from the beginning, they would look like total assholes arguing with me.

As she heads back to talk to the kitchen workers, Wocker looks back at the rest of the team. They're a few seconds away from erupting into laughter. "Here you go, sir, we're terribly sorry about the inconvenience," she says, handing me a freshly cooked Big Mac.

"We understand, ma'am, nobody's perfect." I hold in my laughter.

Wocker and I walk back to a greeting of high fives. I'm now nine for nine with the Big Mac trick. Luckily, I've yet to try the trick more than once at the same location. Jimmy always jokes that he'll soon see my face on a "wanted sign" plastered across every McDonald's in the state.

I split my Big Mac with Wocker, who accepts without an apology this time around. We take our time enjoying the fruits of our labor. Or, better put, our conniving.

Funny, I definitely have a hard time softening up with people. But it comes much easier when I come across a guy like Wocker, who has really been dealt a shitty hand in life.

I guess that's why Jimmy and I have always been

such good friends. No one's been dealt a shittier hand than him.

23. Jimmy's Best Friend

1988

"Run, boy, run! Two more miles. Let's finish strong."

Cognac doesn't need any motivation from me; he enjoys this trail even more than I do. Running these back roads near my house is one of the only times I feel free. No cars, no one bothering me. This is an experience I couldn't get in Mass. I guess New Hampshire is starting to grow on me.

I quickly jump over a large divot in the ground, narrowly averting a sprained ankle. A few years ago I didn't think dirt roads like this existed. The hustle and bustle of city life toughens the skin and makes you take things for granted. As the dirt kicks small dust clouds behind me, I think back to the first time I took Cognac home.

The Wilmington Dog and Rescue down on Elm Street was my first visit to a pound. It was two months ago and I had just turned thirteen. There he was, with those big brown droopy eyes that made my heart sink.

"What kind of dog is this one?" I asked the young girl working the front desk.

"Oh, we just got him in the other day. We think he's a mix of English Setter and Black Lab, but don't know for sure. He was found out on Highway 495 North, just outside of the guardrails. Lucky for him a police officer spotted him and took him in. No tags."

Has anyone come by looking for him?" I asked. Mostly because I cared, but also 'cause I didn't want to get attached only to find out he had to go back to the rightful owner.

"Nope, and I'm not holding my breath. Matter of fact, if they do, they're going to have to go through me before ever being able to take this one home again!" she said.

"What do you mean?" I asked curiously.

"Well, as we were giving him a bath, we noticed he kept wincing every time we touched him. When we flipped him over to his belly we found a bunch of small burns which fit the bill of cigarettes. Then we got to his ears and the burns were everywhere. Made me want to throw up!"

"How in the hell could anyone do this to another creature, never mind a beautiful dog like this? If you find that guy, I want first crack at him!" I said, hoping to impress.

"You want to play with him?" she knew what my answer would be.

As the cage opened, the dog winced and slithered back into the back corner.

"OK, boy, I know, you've been treated real bad. Don't worry, I'm not like that."

I sat on the ground with my hand out, inviting him to take a sniff. Little by little he crept forward and we eventually met eye to eye. His thick black fur covered his face like a Maine Black Bear. He proceeded to sniff my hand. After approving, he suddenly licked my face with his bright pink tongue, catching me totally off guard.

"His tongue is huge," I laughed. "How big do you think this one will get?"

"Tough to tell since we don't have any history, but based on his mix, could be up to a hundred pounds."

Mom said nothing too big, since our house is already cramped. She expected me to come back with some type of poodle, but that's not my style. Don't get sucked in, I thought to myself. This was my first visit and I shouldn't make any rash decisions.

As I stood up to distance myself a bit, he rolled over onto his back in a completely submissive posture. That's when I noticed the scars. At least twenty small burns which pierced the skin. After pulling myself together and ignoring the anger, I rubbed his belly gently. He accepted by wagging his tail uncontrollably.

"I think he likes you," the girl said.

"I like him too, but need some time to make sure I'm making the right decision for both of us," I explained. "It's probably time for me to go. You got a restroom?" I figured it would provide a quick getaway. No need to make a decision based on pure emotions.

"Down the hall and to the left."

Two minutes later, as I went to open the door, I felt it stick. I pushed a little harder and noticed a black nose sneaking its way through.

"Sorry," the girl explained, "he didn't want to go back in his cage and went looking for you."

I caved. "All right, get the paperwork."

I wrote my check for $165, covering the vaccination, rabies shots, and certificate. Then I took home my new best friend.

In the distance I hear the running water. "Almost there, boy! You ready to swim?"

We sprint the last hundred yards to our favorite spot. Profile Falls is the best-kept secret in town. Two gushing waterfalls dropping about forty feet into a serene water hole, surrounded by nature. We plop ourselves on the giant flat rock positioned perfectly above the falls.

Cognac doesn't wait long to cool off. He weaves his way down the rock slope and belly-flops into the water. No fear. I tell myself it is too early in the morning to get cold, but I can't leave him hanging.

"Watch out below!" I cannonball right next to the big bear. "Owwwwwww!" I chant, freezing my ass off. I quickly jump out and climb back to my lounging spot, soaking in the early morning rays. Cognac continues to explore.

The jog back always seems so much longer. My hair is the only part of my body still wet. But it's enough to give me the chills each time a brisk spring New Hampshire wind makes its way through the trees. I start to pick up the pace and turn to check on Cognac. He starts to wander off a side road. Then it hits me - that's Old Man McGillicutty's land. I run back and yell his name, but he doesn't listen.

As I pass the first of many No Trespassing signs, my nerves start to run wild. "Cognac, come here boy!" But he keeps moving forward; clearly he smells something worth exploring. Must be the chickens.

As I turn the corner, his trailer is in clear view. The poster child for white trash, the brown and white hunk of metal is surrounded by about a dozen old rundown cars. Most are half put together and propped up on cinder blocks. A couple are in the woods with large weeds now pushing through the frames.

Mom warned me not to run with Cognac off his leash, I keep reminding myself. Just then the chickens let their presence be known with a loud cackle. This isn't good. I sprint to the back of the trailer and up to the barb-wire chicken coup. Cognac is on his hind legs trying to jump the fence.

"No, boy, get down now!" I grab his collar and yank him back with me. Still no sign of the old man. I peek around the corner; coast is clear.

Just as I start to run back onto the dirt driveway, the sound is deafening. Two gunshots echo through the woods. I turn and see the black shotgun pointed our way.

"Get over here, boy!" the old man cackles with his sinister laughter.

Running enters my mind, but God knows he's a good shot. I hear him out here almost every day taking target practice and decide this is no time for egos. I hold my hands up high, ready to pay the price.

"Sorry, Mr. McGillicutty, Cognac got excited and wanted to see the chickens."

"Boy, can you read? How many times do I have to tell you to keep that grangy mutt off my property?"

As I start to apologize, he cuts me off. "You ain't in the city anymore. You know what the law says about shooting people or mutts that roam onto your property in the great state of New Hampshire?"

I shake my head no.

"It says if I feel threatened, I can shoot. No questions asked," he remarks snidely. "That big mutt must weigh about ninety pounds, perty scary, don't ya think? And my chickens just about had a heart attack. Sounds like just cause to me. What do you think, boy?"

He reloads and my heart drops. I realize, looking at the old, worn-down man, that he wouldn't even lose a minute's sleep if he killed us both. He would bury us somewhere out in the woods and we'd never be found.

"I promise, sir, we'll never let it happen again."

He reaches his dirty fingers into his mouth and pulls out the large chunk of chew, then hucks it on my sneakers.

"You damn right it won't happen again. Next time I won't be so forgivin'. You got thirty seconds to get that mutt out of here before I change my mind."

Before I take a step, Cognac is already sprinting ten yards in front of me. He must have sensed the old man's temperament could change again at any moment.

We make it back to the house in record time, counting our lucky stars. Yet in the pit of my stomach I know this wouldn't be the last run-in I'd have with McGillicutty.

24. The Poop Game

LaFleur

"See you Sunday afternoon, Mom," I say quickly, trying to scoot out without much attention.

"Where are you going again?" she asks quizzically.

"That new kid Jimmy is having a few people over, kind of a welcoming party to the neighborhood."

Funny how we still all refer to Jimmy as "that new kid," even though he's been here like over a year now.

"As long as his mom is fine with watching you boys, it's OK with me. You behave now."

"Don't worry, Mom, you know I always do, right?"

Little does Mom know the last people to show up for the weekend would be Jimmy's parents. His dad stayed down in Mass when his parents got divorced. I'm not really sure where his mom goes; I think she might be dating some guy down in Hampton Beach, but who knows.

As I pull into Jimmy's dirt road, I notice only one other car there. It's Grizwaltz's ratty old green Renault. Heck, who am I to talk. My bright yellow Dodge isn't exactly a chick magnet.

As I knock on the front door, I hear a loud commotion. I push and it opens up. Darting in front of me comes Jimmy, wearing a bright red motorcycle helmet. He's carrying something in his hand, which I can't quite make out. Upstairs I hear another voice. "You're sick, kid." It was Ben. Then Grizwaltz comes around the corner.

"What the hell is going on?" I ask. Grizwaltz is in tears he's laughing so hard.

"Just take a seat, kid, and watch."

Just then Ben knocks Jimmy down with a broom and rushes past him down the stairs. Wearing a blue helmet and dish gloves, he scurries down the basement stairs before seeing me.

"All right, now it's your turn, scumbag," he yells. He flings something across the room at Jimmy. It hits the window and rolls across the floor in front of us.

"Is that dog shit?" I ask Grizwaltz.

"Oh yeah, and there's a whole lot more where that came from. Come with me."

We walk down into the basement and the stench starts to kick in. Smells like a kennel. I look down and see dried-up dog feces everywhere. There must be a few hundred pieces all over the cold basement floor.

"Are you kidding me?" I say to Grizwaltz.

"Yeah, apparently Jimmy's mom left her poodle down here for about two weeks. He refuses to clean it since it isn't his, so instead they're having a shit fight."

Jimmy treats his own dog Cognac like a family member and is probably closer to him than just about any creature on the planet. He would literally die for him. But his mother's poodle, Thelma, doesn't get the same treatment. I'm sure the resentment he has for his mom avoiding her responsibility has a lot to do with it.

Just then Jimmy runs by me and tackles Ben into the cement wall. Their helmets save them as they fall to the floor, laughing hysterically, each now with dish gloves on, trying to smear old poodle shit on each other. These guys are nuts, I think to myself. But it's pretty funny.

The fun is just about to get good when we hear some laughter through the basement windows. We look up to see Jimmy's brother Al and a couple other stoners smoking some joints.

Jimmy tells us to hide, but it's too late. Al knocks on the window and motions for us to come outside.

Al is a big, intimidating dude. He's at least 5'11", 220 pounds, and strong like an ox. His two buddies aren't lacking in the size department either. I've heard a lot about Al from Jimmy, but hadn't run into him myself, until now, that is.

"Hey look, if it isn't the young jocks from Newfound

High School." Al laughs.

"Shouldn't you guys be out somewhere practicing?" his red-headed friend says sarcastically.

"Ben, you want a hit?" Al mocks him. He knows that although Ben is little bit of a troublemaker, in the grand scheme of things, he lives on the straight and narrow. Heck, he just tried his first beer last summer and I don't think he even knows what a joint looks like.

"Get out of his face!" Jimmy yells. He stands chest to chest with Al. "Why don't you leave us alone and get back to your drugs."

With that, before Jimmy can react, Al head butts him across the bridge of his nose. Blood starts gushing down Jimmy's face. But, in typical fashion, he shrugs it off, spits the blood in the air, and charges Al. They tumble to the ground and exchange blows.

Ben and I move towards them, but Al's two cronies get us each in full nelsons, rendering us useless. They outweigh us by about forty pounds each and have at least four years on us. Heck, they might even be twenty-five. Who knows with these guys? They probably flunked out of high school back in the early eighties.

I turn around and hear Jimmy yelling out in pain. "All right, uncle, uncle. Let go of me, you jerk!" Al has Jimmy's right arm in a chicken wing behind his back, pulling up with his full body weight. Finally he drops Jimmy to the ground, releasing him from his grasp. We walk over to help Jimmy up, but he wants none of it. I'm sure he's both embarrassed and pissed off.

We stick around, even though Jimmy stays in his room for a while. Grizwaltz and I watch a *Rocky-a-thon* on the tube. Hours later Jimmy emerges from his room, heavily favoring his right shoulder.

"Are you OK?" I ask, accidentally grazing his elbow.

"Ahhhh!" Jimmy winces in pain.

For the entire weekend he heavily favors his right

arm, but he refuses to see a doctor. You can see a lump near his shoulder blade protruding through his shirt. At the very least it has to be a severe sprain. Yet Jimmy never mentions it again.

25. Worst Hookup Ever

1990

Jimmy

I lost my virginity as a freshman in high school. I guess it's a little young for a guy, but not creepy young. I had been dating my ex, Amanda Wright, for over six months. She was also in the ninth grade, and had experimented before me. I think I was her second or third. I never could really get a straight answer from her. Anyway, after six months, we both felt we'd waited long enough. To me, it was a great feeling, but I don't really know what all the hype is about. Then again, it only lasted about two minutes, and that's with a condom on. I'm sure it would have been about two seconds without one.

It's the first Friday night after my junior year has ended and maybe I'll meet lucky number two tonight.

After Amanda and I broke up our sophomore year, I fooled around with a few different girls, but haven't hit the home run. As Ben would say, "I'm perpetually stranded at third base."

We're heading over to a party at the lake. I'm not even sure whose house it is, but I heard it might be one of the summer houses. It's the whole crew tonight. Ben, LaFleur, Griswaltz, and yours truly. This time it's LaFleur's turn to drive, so that means I'm getting hammered.

He pulls up into my driveway, nailing the huge pothole which has sat in the middle for years, and almost loses his muffler. I'm the last guy picked up, since I live the closest to the party. Everyone else already has a Milwaukee's Best, "The Beast," cracked open. Ben hands me one.

"You're already two behind," he says, pushing me to catch up. During the five-minute drive I manage to knock back a full one and get a second halfway down. I chug the rest of it before we walk into the party. The house is a typical Newfound Lake summer cottage, furnished with a bunch of stuff from the disco era.

It's only nine-thirty p.m. and the place is already packed. We take our standard full circle walk through the joint to see what kind of material we have to work with. There are a lot of older people here. At least half the party appears to be over twenty-five, some even thirty. Here we are, barely sixteen, strolling in with our $8.99 case of "The Beast."

Finally, we notice a couple of local seniors, which gives us enough reason to stay. Our crew decides to set up shop on the screened-in porch. It's a perfect setup for quarters. After grabbing a small coffee table from inside and a large pitcher from one of the cabinets, "anchor man" is set.

This happens to be my favorite drinking game, mainly because it combines quarters, which I'm really good at, along with team play. The rules are also really easy to pick up, so anyone can play. The first team that gets three quarters into the pitcher wins. You take turns back and forth and the winning team gets to pick the losing team's order of drinking the pitcher. The reason that's critical is because each player can only drink the pitcher one time, so that means the last player, the "anchor man," needs to pick up the slack for his teammates. I've seen "anchor men" who end up drinking nothing because his teammates want to hook him up. Then I've seen times where the anchor has to drink over twenty ounces, since his teammates were a bunch of sallies.

The four of us sit down to play. Then Griswaltz walks inside to find two more players. It's much better to play with three per side. "Look who I found," Griswaltz says, coming back in with two big women in his arms.

"Hello boys," Ms. Zaborski says.

Holy crap. What the hell is she doing here?

Ms. Zaborski is the high school art teacher. She must

be in her early thirties and most of us think she's lesbian, although that has never been confirmed. I couldn't care less if she's gay. Actually, most of us think it's kind of cool. She wears glasses, stands about 5'2", and weighs about 220 pounds. Very nice lady, just not the looker we were targeting when we walked into the party tonight. She is joined by a substitute teacher I've seen here and there at the high school, Ms. Kaldy.

Ms. Kaldy, who also has been rumored to be a lesbian, is also short and overweight. She stands at around 5'1" and probably weighs 200 plus as well. Either way, they're a lot of fun, and from what I hear, they love to booze.

We split up the teams. It's me, Ms. Zaborski, and LaFleur on one team and Ms. Kaldy, Ben, and Griswaltz on the other. Griswaltz assures us that he'll only play one game, since he's driving. We quickly get ahead two to zip, after Ms. Zaborski and I sink the quarter on our first attempt.

"Stop calling me that, call me Zab," she says.

"OK, that's a cool name, I like Zab," I respond.

"Thanks, you were making me feel so old." She laughs.

I look up at Griswaltz and we both chuckle. Who would have thought we'd be partying with teachers tonight? And having fun doing it.

LaFleur makes it a perfect three in a row for our team, as he sinks one that barely makes it over the front rim of the plastic pitcher, which looks like they stole from Pizza Hut. Our team erupts in a loud cheer.

"Oh, let me pick the order," Zab says.

She decides to make her friend, Ms. Kaldy, the anchor woman. Then she proceeds to have Ben go first and Griswaltz second. Ben downs about a third of the pitcher, leaving just enough so that his teammates don't remain thirsty. Then Griswaltz takes the pitcher and without taking a breath for thirty seconds, finishes all of it. He then lets out a loud belch. Ms. Kaldy, or "Kal," as she now asks us to call her, is impressed.

"Thanks, Grizzy, you saved me," she says. We all laugh.

"Yeah, Grizzy, thanks, honey!" I cackle. Griswaltz knows that will haunt him for the rest of the night, or maybe the rest of his life.

Five games later, we're out of beer. Luckily one of the older guys brought some extra Natty Lite, and we're able to buy a case from him. "OK. Best of seven," Griswaltz slurs. "We're gonna catch up to you assholes."

At this point, we all realize he isn't driving us home, so it's every man for himself later, when we all scavenge for pull-out sofas.

Of course, they win the next game, which makes it even at three games apiece. The final game is down to the wire, with both teams having sunk the quarter twice. Next up is Kal, who has yet to even come close to sinking one. Then it's my turn. I've probably finished close to a twelve-pack myself, but that hasn't hurt my playing ability thus far. I bet I've sunk half our team's points.

Kal shoots the quarter high up in the air, probably three feet higher than the pitcher. Somehow it then takes a weird fall and lands smack dab in the middle of the pitcher. After their team calms down from the victory dance, they choose me to be anchor man. By now, Zab is smashed, with both of her arms hanging on my neck, and LaFleur is lying on his side, "taking a break," as he put it. So I decide to impress everyone and chug the entire thirty-ounce container. That's the last thing I remember.

I wake up to the bright sunlight beaming through the bedroom window. You know that feeling of waking up and wondering where the hell you are and how the hell you got there? Well, I have it. I'm buck naked, in a bed I've never seen in my life. Just when I think things can't get any weirder, I look to my left and see a large woman sleeping under the covers next to me.

"Is she naked?" I say out loud. I pull back part of the covers and see her large and pale white body, uncovered. She does have big boobs, but they're very saggy, hanging down almost to her belly button. Down below, well, let's just say she doesn't wax frequently.

Oh God, please tell me nothing happened. I get up and walk to the bathroom. Midway through pissing I notice two used condoms on the floor; one clearly has some excrement in there. Then I hear, "You're awake, you animal." It's Zab. "I went back to sleep after you wouldn't move this morning. But man, last night you certainly moved. That was the best I've ever had. And what you do with that tongue, oh heavens."

My first instinct is to sprint out of the house, but I manage to keep my calm and give her a half smile. You never know if she will be my teacher next year. That's all I need is to fail art.

I quickly pull on my shorts and T-shirt, then start heading towards the stairs.

"Don't forget your friend," Zab yells to me. I walk back towards the other bedroom upstairs and notice Griswaltz, naked, lying next to Kal. For a brief second, I forget about the nightmare of last night and burst out laughing.

"Wake up, Grizzy Bear," I say to him. "He pops up, like he just saw a ghost, and grabs his clothes, now beginning to process what happened.

"You were fantastic, Grizzy. Hopefully I'll see you again soon. Maybe I'll sub more," Kal says, dashing Grizzy's hopes.

On the car ride back home we make LaFleur and Ben swear on their mother's lives that they will never tell a soul about what happened. I'm completely horrified with my lack of control last night. I can only pray that this doesn't get around the school. I would never live it down.

Griswaltz and I never mention it to one another again.

The only saving grace is that I have a counterpart who made the same mistake. Misery truly does love company. At the time this registered as one of my worst all-time memories. Boy, would that change.

26. Jimmy's Worst Childhood Memory

Summer 1991

Jimmy

As I pull into the driveway after a long day of hanging drywall, things seem too quiet. I realize Cognac is not on his rope, like he was when I left early this morning. The water dish is turned over and food is spread everywhere. Ma must have brought him inside because it's hot out.

"Maaaa," I yell. "I hope you gave Cognac some water, it's empty outside." No response.

I walk over to my mother's room and hear the shower running. I try to pop open the door but it's locked. She must have Cognac in there with her. He's always loved the sound of a steaming shower.

I head over to the fridge, pop open a Coors Light, and turn on the tube. Nice, Sports Center is just about to start. Ten minutes later my mom opens up her door.

"Were you sayin' something to me, Jimmy?"

"Yes, I was asking you about Cognac's water. He ran out. Do you have some in there with him?" I ask.

"I haven't seen Cognac all day," she responds. "I thought you might have taken him with you to work today."

My heart sinks. Oh God, please tell me he's OK. I run back to his cage and inspect the leash. Weird, the hook which attaches to his collar looks cut. Just then I notice the leash is tangled around the lawnmower. He must have panicked when he got stuck and forced his way out of the leash. Oh no, the chickens!

I sprint down towards Old Man McGillicutty's house. My heart races with fear. That old man is just waiting for the chance to hurt something. My mind races as memories of

Cognac as a little puppy appear.

Two more minutes, I mumble to myself, now in a full sprint. I pass the No Trespassing sign and turn down the old man's long dirt driveway. Everything seems eerily quiet. Even the chickens aren't making any noise.

Then, in the distance, I notice something lying on the driveway.

"No! No!" I shout in a panic. I slow down to a nervous walk as the image gets clearer. It's a black animal lying on its side. My heart drops as I get closer. It's Cognac. Flies are buzzing all around him and there is a pool of blood underneath his precious head.

That bastard shot him! I cradle Cognac's warm body as it lies in the hot sun; his eyes still open, now locked in a daze. I'm ready to cry. But I hold it in, realizing I owe it to Cognac to get revenge. Did he threaten the chickens? Even so, that bastard knows he can't get to them in that cage. Right then my detective instincts take over and I notice his body is facing towards the end of the driveway. The bullet wound is in the back of his head. I'm no forensic scientist, but it seems clear that he was running back to our house, away from this asshole.

I walk towards the woods and grab the first thing I can find to carry him. It's an old tarp he probably uses for his cars. I pick up Cognac's lifeless body and gently place it on the tarp. Then I pull it down the road, just past his mailbox and into the common area and out of the hot sun. Now it's payback time, bitch. I sprint back home in record time and head straight for the garage. Dad said to only use the rifle for emergencies. Well, this qualifies in my book.

I fiddle with the combination lock. "Shit. Come on, open! Twenty-three, fifteen, twenty-nine. That's gotta be it." We each picked our favorite number for the lock. I slam it down against the concrete floor hoping to pry it open. I notice the last number is slightly off center, so I flip around one more time and land directly on twenty-nine. Bingo!

Perfect, a few shotgun shells are left in the box. I load it up and slam the door shut.

As I run back down the hill I notice Al's truck in the driveway. He must have pulled up without even noticing me. My heart is racing a mile a minute. I've never been this scared in my entire life, but something needs to happen. I need to teach this bastard a lesson. Tears are streaming down my face, but I'm determined to show no fear. I make it past his mailbox and start to plan my route of attack. I want to see him scream for mercy. I'm going in balls to the wall. No stealth mission here.

I walk like Arnold in *The Terminator* with my rifle in hand charging towards his front door. Without hesitation, I kick open the rusty door and there he is, sitting his sorry ass on the couch with a beer in hand.

"Get your weak ass up, you sick dog killer!" I demand.

"I warned you, son, don't say I didn't. That dog had it comin'," McGillicutty says.

"Don't say another word, you asshole, and follow me." I lead the worthless human out the front door, down the driveway, and directly in front of Cognac's lifeless body. "Is this how you treat animals?" I yell. "I want your last image to be of him as I blow your brains out."

He looks up at me with those rotten teeth, the stench almost too much to handle. I cock the barrel to make sure it's fully loaded and watch him squirm. "Get ready to join the rest of your family in hell," I state.

"Bang!" At first I look down, thinking the gun went off early. Once I see the maggot still smiling, I look behind me to see Al with a pistol pointing at me.

"Don't ruin your life on this scum, Jimmy. Let him go," he says.

"He killed Cognac! No, he deserves to die," I plead.

My brother walks up to the old man and smacks him across the face with the butt of his pistol. Knocks him out cold. "He'll get his Judgment Day." Then he gently hugs me and walks me back towards the house.

As we walk home I know two things about today. It's the worst day of my young life, and I guess my brother isn't always a selfish prick.

27. Trash Bag

One month before boot camp

Jimmy

Every summer for as long as I can remember, I've made the trip down to Hampton Beach with some of my old buddies from my elementary days. This year is much needed, given the extra hours I've been putting in hanging drywall.

I only have a month before boot camp begins down at Camp Lejeune, so this probably will be my last long weekend partying. The extra money will definitely help pay off some final bills before this new chapter of my life begins.

This year I decide to head down with my brother Al, since he has some old buddies that will be hanging at the beach as well. Ever since I started working at his construction company last month, our relationship has improved a bit. Don't get me wrong, we still could blow up at each other at any given time, but at least we're cordial at this point. Plus, I think Al appreciates the fact that I'm actually driving this time.

I just got my pickup truck fixed as a graduation present to myself (catalytic converter) and I no longer have to bum rides off of him. I even filled up the tank without asking for his help. My 1981 Ford F150 isn't the greatest on gas, but it does real well on the back roads of New Hampshire.

Ah, the smell of salt water. Each year as I make the drive towards the "strip," I'm always filled with mixed emotions. Initially I'm always disappointed at the sight of so many dilapidated buildings and the lack of attention received during the off-season. Hampton Beach looks like it hasn't had a makeover since the sixties. Some of that is nostalgic, like the old fried dough joints positioned throughout the boardwalk. However, the old restaurants with paint peeling off the sides and the constant litter in the streets quickly remind me why I only make this trip once a year.

The old motel sits about six blocks from the beach, just enough to get the cost down to less than $75 per night per room. Which means $25 a night since we're triple shacking. It's Al, myself, and his buddy Jake. Most of the crew is already situated when we get there. There are well over fifty kids here, most between seventeen and twenty-one.

I make my way into our motel room and it's definitely adequate. There are two bedrooms and a pull-out sofa in the living room. Granted, the beds look to be either full size or twin beds, but after a nice buzz, they should work fine. Al's buddy isn't here yet, so I lay claim to the smaller bedroom and throw my black trash bag filled with clothes on the bed. Mom keeps saying she'll get me a suitcase before I head down to boot camp, but I'm not holding my breath.

As I unload my toiletry bag, I realize I forgot to pack the most important thing, condoms. I keep hearing from just about everyone whom I tell that I've enrolled in the Marines, "Better get your ass now, because you'll have quite the drought during boot camp."

If years past are any indicator, Hampton Beach has plenty of decent-looking and willing talent. I try to bum a condom off of Al, but he tells me that Jake is bringing a twelve-pack.

"Just ask him when he gets here," Al says. "But don't go wasting it when you strike out, just to make us think you got some." He really knows how to build confidence, I tell you.

We spend the day pounding beers and playing volleyball on the beach. I've already noticed three or four hotties, one of whom is playing on my volleyball team. Sheila is her name. I'd probably give her an 8.5, and that's when I'm sober. Which means later tonight she'll be a ten. Sheila just graduated from Billerica High School. She has a tight body, probably weighing no more than 110 pounds, with a nice, dark tan. Oh yeah, she also has curly blond hair. Probably dyed blond, but I couldn't care less.

We chat a bit here and there during our game and she tells me that field hockey is her sport. I can tell. Those legs are tone. Instantly I think of her wrapping them around me.

As nighttime approaches, Sheila and I start to get closer. I make the first move and hold her hand as we walk back towards the motel. She doesn't resist, so I'm happy.

When we get back, Al has already started the grill in the parking lot and it smells delicious. He smiles. "Pork ribs baby, in Al's special sauce." He hands me a small slice and it tastes heavenly. Then he grabs me and pulls me close to him, "Look in your top dresser drawer, I hooked you up."

Sweet, Al actually remembered. Now if I can just close the deal with Sheila, this would be a perfect going-away present.

The next few hours are spent singing Steve Miller, The Beatles, James Taylor, Cat Stevens, and other classics which are on an incredible mix tape that someone put together. "I need to get a copy of this mix," Sheila says to me.

As we talk more, I reveal to her that I'm heading down to boot camp in a few weeks. She tells me she's going to travel across the United States with her best friend for six months, before trying to enroll in a community college next year.

We actually have a lot in common. She loves sports, is still unsure of what she wants from life, and loves to party. Neither of us has ever dated anyone longer than a year.

I've tried to pace myself tonight, especially when I realized I actually had a shot with Sheila. This is probably only my ninth beer, which stretched out over eight hours isn't that much. She's starting to get a little tipsy, so I start drinking a little of her beer to slow her down. The last thing I want is for her to pass out tonight before the deed is done.

Just then the mix tape ends. I hop up and ask Al if he

knows who is in charge of the music. He points to one of the older girls sitting in a circle, near the other side of the motel. "It's Julie. She'll hook you up," he says.

So I head over with the tape and ask if she has any more. She has a whole case of mix tapes under her chair. "Take the whole thing," she says. I start to walk away and then remember how much Sheila likes the first tape.

"Any chance you can make me a copy of this mix tape and send it to me?" I ask.

She smiles. "I have two more at home. Go ahead and take it." Nice. Sheila's going to love this. I pop another tape into the player and walk over to her.

"I have a surprise for you," I say. Sheila loves the tape and starts making out with me.

"Let's go back to your room," she suggests.

We go at it pretty steamy once we enter my room. Sheila's body is even hotter up close. As we start to rip each other's clothes off, I remember the condom. I drop my boxers on the floor and then pop open the top drawer of the dresser. Yes, there it is, just like Al promised.

We stick with foreplay for ten minutes before she tells me to put on the condom. I'm drenched with sweat. The back window of my room is open. I'll bet this place doesn't even have AC. The next five minutes are the most intense I've ever experienced in my short life. I almost lose it twice, but try to think gross thoughts to hold out. Random teachers come to mind. Then I notice things feel different. I pull out and the condom is hanging off. It's ripped at the top, no longer any good. "Shit," I mumble to myself.

Sheila knows what's wrong. "Don't you have another one?" she asks.

Feeling like a total fool, I tell her to hold tight. I wrap a towel around my waist and go out into the living room in search of Jake's toiletry bag. I find nothing but a pair of boxers and an old T-shirt in his gym bag. Then I head to the main bathroom. All he has there are a few bottles of pills. No condoms.

Blue balls start to settle in. OK. My choices are to go in without a skin, or avoid the home run and stick with a long triple. Wait - a thought pops to my head. Maybe a plan C? I slowly creep back into the room. There it is. I grab the black Hefty trash bag that I used to carry my clothes. These things don't break even in the worst conditions. I've seen their commercials.

I wrap the full bag around my crotch, giving me a triple layer of protection. "Great, you found one?" Sheila asks.

"Kind of." I lie on top of her and try to maneuver my makeshift condom back into her warm body. Just as I penetrate she stands up.

"What the hell is that? A trash bag? Are you kidding me? Do I look like a whore to you?" She picks up her clothes and storms out of the room. I quickly throw on my shorts and go shirtless outside trying to chase her down.

I hear a door close a few rooms down and start to yell out her name.

"Sheila, I'm sorry. That was stupid. I was just kidding around." But we both knew that was no joke. In one of the stupidest moves of my life, I did in fact try to use a Hefty bag as a contraceptive.

Sheila never did answer the door that night. I went back to the room and jerked off for twenty minutes before giving up. Blue balls were probably the weakest punishment I should have received for my actions. I made up some bullshit story to Al and Jake that the Marines called and I had to finish up some paperwork to send to them ASAP, so I left early the next morning.

Jake was able to give Al a ride back. That was my last trip ever to Hampton Beach. I still don't know if that story ever made it around to the group. If it had, I'm sure Al would have given me a hard time. Then again, he could be waiting for the perfect moment, like during my wedding reception.

To this day, every time I look at a black trash bag, I let out a nervous laugh. Part of me thinks it's hilarious, but the other half worries what that night might have done to Sheila's confidence. She had to feel so used. Maybe she can take comfort in knowing I'd get my payback tenfold in the deserts of hell.

28. The Head

Fall 1991

Ben

These first few weeks of college have been amazing. Finally free from my mother's grasp, I've been able to do whatever the heck I want. This includes walking home from parties at four in the morning, taking a nap for three hours during a perfectly sunny day, and eating fast food whenever I want. Not only fast food, but the dining hall food is all you can eat. Man, I've eaten more this month than I probably had all summer at home. I know we didn't have much money, but one hot dog with a little corn just didn't cut it.

I must admit, so far I haven't paid much attention in classes. I've been more focused on the social scene. It's been much easier to make friends here than in high school. I'm sure a lot of it has to do with the fact that I've been drunk longer than sober during this period.

I've been attached at the hip to my new partner in crime, Eddie, ever since we both blacked out during one of the first nights here and caused all kinds of havoc on the dorm room floor. He impressed me after pissing all over the RA's doorknob at around five in the morning one night after we pounded two bottles of Mad Dog and a twelve-pack of Natty Light. As a matter of fact, Eddie and I decided to room together after we both got complaints from our roommates about the excessive noise and partying.

It took Eddie about fifteen minutes to move his clothes and futon across the hall into my dorm room. He grew up in Revere, Massachusetts, and let me tell you, fit the stereotype perfectly; tall, lanky, slicked-back dark hair, gold chain, and the Italian suave to boot. We also both love sarcasm, women, partying, and a good laugh. I've noticed he even has a warped sense of humor that rivals mine, which I've always thought impossible.

Tonight we're heading out to another big party off campus. There's a pack of about twelve guys walking through the small downtown area on our way to Franklin Drive. Passing the local market, Eddie and I notice a very short man in a wheelchair, who just left the store with a twelve-pack of Budweiser.

After a double-take, we soon recognize this is no ordinary man. Standing barely over a foot tall, the disfigured man's body is comprised of almost all head. He has tiny arms and legs, probably no more than six inches each, which dangle off a miniature torso that has to be less than four inches long. Then, the other ten inches was all head. He has glasses and a full beard.

At first we're both taken aback by this man. Then we can't help but to crack a small laugh after seeing the beer in his chair. One of the guys in our group nearly bumps into him when the man yells, "Watch where you're going, asshole." The rest of the walk is uneventful and after a few hours of drinking games, we're all feeling pretty buzzed. That's when Eddie says, "Man, did you guys see that man in the wheelchair with the beer? That was pretty messed up."

One of the sophomores in our group pipes in, "Yeah, I used to feel bad for that guy until I realized what everyone else on campus already knew, he's a major dickhead." After this comment, Eddie feels like he has the green light to start cracking a few jokes.

"Wouldn't you be a dick if all you were born with is a giant head?" Several of us started howling with laughter.

Then I jump in. "We should call him *The Head*. Next time I see him I'm going to say, hey, where you headed?"

As the crowd of guys gets louder with laughter, it seems the whole party has formed a circle around us. Eddie and I are on a roll. We spend the next hour trying to one up one another with "head jokes."

"Hey Billy, when that asshole bumped into you, I would have fired off, 'use your head, hell, it's all you got!'" I say.

"How many beers do you think that guy can drink before he gets smashed? There is no way he can drink a twelve-pack. It goes straight to his head," Eddie responds.

At the time, Eddie and I were really making a name for ourselves, especially amongst some of the upperclassmen. I haven't laughed that hard in months.

Never once during this tirade did either of us even remotely consider how insensitive our comments were. For the next four years on campus, I would venture to guess we made fun of that man hundreds of times. Granted, we realized he was a pretty mean guy. But making fun of a man that was dealt such a horrible fate is so tasteless.

I learned a few years after we graduated that "The Head" passed away. Heart failure was the word on the streets. As I look back upon our mean-spiritedness, I'm so ashamed. Ashamed that such hate came out of my mouth. Ashamed that we made a mockery out of this man's suffering. Disappointed in myself that I lacked even an ounce of compassion and never once during my four years in school gave any thought to how rough his life must have been. Little did I know I'd get a little dose of karma later on in life.

29. The Urinal

Ben

It's time for a shower. Prior to hopping in the nasty stalls, I decide to take a leak. These urinals suck. They're the kind with no divider in between, which means someone can look at your package if they want to. God, I hope no one plops their nasty ass next to me. As I finish playing asteroids by peeing on the wad of gum in the urinal, I can sense someone standing next to me.

Don't turn your head. I focus intently on keeping my eyes directly in front of me, but my peripheral vision catches something to my right. *Look in front of you, idiot.* But it's too late. I can't tell if I caught skin or just shoes. Either way, I know it isn't good. Ten minutes from now I'll be regretting this experience.

Did you look at that guy's package? No, of course not. Well, at least not intentionally. Are you gay?

Oh God, here it comes. *If you aren't gay, why did you look at his package? I didn't look at his package, those were his shoes. Was it though, I think there was some skin. Even if it was, that doesn't mean I'm gay, does it? Well, let's think about this for a minute. One guy looks at another guy while pissing. That sounds gay to me. Did my thing move? I didn't notice it. Well, then, I'm not gay. How in the hell do I think I'm gay? I love women, really love women, especially naked women. Well, could someone be gay that never has been attracted to a dude? How do I know I'm not attracted to that dude? What if the next time I start hooking up with a chick I start thinking about that dude's package? Would I be gay then?* Snap out of it, this is tiring. *Actually, that would mean I'm gay, right? Let me think. If I fantasize about other dudes, of course I would be gay. Right? Well, what if I didn't mean to think about it, but stuff just popped into my head? Oh, in that case I wouldn't be gay. Right? Wait, no dude thinks about other dudes unless he's queer. What the hell is wrong with me?* Stop worrying about this stupid shit; you're not gay, dude! You hook up with a different chick every weekend. Why in the hell would you think you're gay?

This ridiculous back and forth not only follows me into the shower, but I actually spend the next two weeks convincing myself that I might be gay. Even though I have never hooked up with a guy in my life and I'm extremely attracted to women. And only women!

Almost every waking moment is spent arguing with myself. There's usually a point during each day where I will temporarily relieve the pain by coming up with the perfect rebuttal for my obsessive thoughts. Yet, they quickly return when I wake up the following morning and stay until something more pressing occupies my mind. This can't be normal. Can it?

30. The Brown Crawlies

It's two months into our freshman year and Eddie and I are really making a name for ourselves with the ladies. Mostly it's because neither of us could give a flying crap what they think of us. So, while we may offend many, there are others who get a kick out of our immaturity.

And when it comes to hooking up, let's just say there's plenty of fish in the sea. We've developed a secret code to let each other know if one is getting lucky in the room. On our dry erase board, which hangs on the dorm room door, we simply write a big "L" for Lucky. So far none of the chicks have picked up on this highly sophisticated coding.

Last night the ace of spades was in my pocket as I took home a hot blond chick from Connecticut. We were both pretty wasted and ended up having passionate sex. In the middle of it, the condom broke, but I kept going. I've been praying nonstop that I won't catch any STDs, especially AIDS. The prayer goes something like this: Hands folded together, *"Lord, please protect me against all illnesses, especially STDs and most importantly AIDS. I'm sorry for being promiscuous. Please help me live a long, happy, and healthy life. Father, Son, Holy Spirit, amen." Knock on wood three times and sign of the cross five times.* Done. I started doing this prayer after my first risky hookup about four weeks ago. Since then, it's not an understatement to say that I recite this exact prayer every thirty minutes, all day long. Basically any time a bad thought pops into my head about getting an STD, I say the prayer.

As I walk towards the shower stalls with a towel wrapped around my waist, I can't help laughing as I pass by some of the remnants left over from last night's adventure. I'm not quite sure why, but Eddie gets a thrill from ripping down anything and everything that hangs on the dorm's hallway walls.

If I were the dorm monitor, by now I'd just give up. However, he's a persistent bastard. Within a day or two there's always new posters hanging.

I've found that midday is the best time to shower, since the stalls are pretty empty. Yes, my choice of stalls. I'll take the handicap shower. It's the most sought after stall because it has nearly twice the walking space. Since no one is handicapped on our floor, guys gladly use it whenever possible.

Just as the warm water hits me I notice a nasty wad of matted-up hair stuck in the drain. Good thing I always wear my flip-flops. That is nasty. I wonder if that guy has an STD? Then the prayer comes again. Hands folded together. *"Lord, please protect me against all illnesses, especially STDs and most importantly AIDS. I'm sorry for being promiscuous. Please help me live a long, happy, and healthy life. Father, son, Holy Spirit, amen." Knock on wood three times. Sign of the cross five times.* Done.

As I wash my body with soap, I notice something moving down in my pubic hair. What the hell is that? Oh shit, it's small, white, and appears to be moving. Hands folded together, *"Lord, please protect me against all illnesses, especially STDs and most importantly AIDS. I'm sorry for being promiscuous. Please help me live a long, happy, and healthy life. Father, Son, Holy Spirit, amen." Knock on wood three times. Sign of the cross five times.* Done.

I scrub for several minutes and it appears whatever is down there may be gone. After throwing some shampoo on my hair, I start drying off with Eddie's towel. Mine is still wet from last night's shower, so I grab his. I'm sure he won't mind. He uses my stuff all the time.

As I go to put on my underwear, I look down into my pubes one more time just to make sure all is clear. Oh no, there they are again. At least three or four white things. I put one in my hand and it moves slightly to the left. It must be crabs. Oh shit. I knew I shouldn't have kept going last night without a rubber. "You stupid asshole!" I swear at myself walking back to the dorm room.

Immediately after getting dressed I head down to the local pharmacy and pick up A2000. *"Fight those little critters with Advanced A2000 protection. Gets rid of body lice, crabs and other scary pests."* The label certainly gets to the point. I run home and open up the package. A small white comb comes with the A2000 liquid formula.

For the next week I'm supposed to apply this crap on my pubes three times per day and then comb out the dead crabs after I dry off. Man, if anyone in the dorm finds out about this, my sex life is forever gone.

Two days go by and so far no one has suspected anything. Not even Eddie. Of course, I've had to wake up an hour earlier than normal to ensure I'm alone in the morning, but other than that, things are easier than I expected. The funny thing about all of this is that I'm barely itchy. Maybe once or twice a day I itch for a few seconds down there, but that's normal for a guy. I guess my crabs aren't biting as much as other ones typically do.

Then on the third day, I make a mistake. Instead of putting away my toiletry bag and hiding it in my dresser drawer, this time I casually leave it open on the desk. That's when Eddie notices it. "What the hell is that?" Eddie says inquisitively.

I finish throwing on a t-shirt and run at my bag. "Nothing, dude, give that back to me," I say. But Eddie eludes me and jumps on the top bunk with the medicine.

"A2000. Fight those little critters?" he says and then starts dying laughing. "You have crabs? You dirty bastard!"

My face is bright red as I humbly nod yes. Eddie spends the next ten minutes staring at the medicine and comb. In the middle of his laughter, I remember something. I used his towel the other day.

"Hey, Eddie, does it say on there that crabs are

contagious?"

"Extremely contagious. Do not make sexual contact with others or use others' clothing," he reads.

"Oh, OK. Well, just thought I'd let you know that yesterday my towel was still wet, so I used yours," I say, trying to contain my laughter.

"You asshole! If you gave me crabs I'm going to piss on your toothbrush every morning for the next four years!"

Later that night Eddie starts to feel some itchiness down below. Now we're both using the A2000. Trying to keep the medicine hidden is hard enough for one person taking a shower. With two, it's nearly impossible. Eddie figures out that it can fit inside his soap container, so that's how we conceal it.

At the dining hall a few nights later we overhear one of our buddies talking about crabs. "I had those creepy crawlies once in high school. Man, those pesky little brown critters can run, boy. I'll tell you what; I must have had ten of them on the palm of my hand, after I dug into my pubes. They were like tiny versions of the crabs you see at the beach. That was the worst week of my life," he says.

I jump in. "Did you say they were brown?"

"Yeah, man, like the color of a Hershey's bar," he adds.

On the way home I stop by the library and head to the section on Health. There I find several books on STDs. As I flip through the pages, I can't help but look at the section on genital warts. The pictures are horrible. Man, if I read this book a few months ago, I wouldn't go near a chick without a note from her doctor. Then I get to the page on crabs. *"These tiny brown pests…"* Are you kidding me? Mine are definitely white.

I run to the library bathroom, lock the stall door, and pull down my new Hanes tighty-whities. There they are, three of them again, and all white. I pull each one out of my pubes and put them onto my hand. Feeling a little bolder after reading up on the critters, I put my hand within a few inches of my face to study them closer. They aren't moving anymore. I grab one and dangle it in front of my face. Then I pull on it. It stretches?

The other doesn't move either. Finally, I walk out of the stall and put all three on the sink and take a few steps back. It hits me. These are pieces of lint, you idiot! My new underwear, which I bought exactly two weeks ago, is shedding white lint pieces. Probably because I didn't wash them before wearing.

Rushing home with a big smile on my face, I couldn't wait to laugh with Eddie. Then I thought twice and decided it couldn't hurt to let him use the whole bottle of A2000 before saying anything.

Three nights later, at a party, I break the news to Eddie. After he tackles me, we enjoy a nice long bonding laugh. Funny how the little things in life can really make you chuckle. I wish all of my life experiences ended on such a positive note.

Little did I know years later I would trade for crabs any day if it meant I wouldn't have to deal with the mental demons that came my way.

31. Boot camp

August 1991

Jimmy

I take pride in the fact that my new beginning has proven to be the best decision of my life so far. While many of the guys bitch and moan about boot camp, to me it's eerily helped me develop a stronger inner resolve. I'm not saying it's easy. It sucks real bad. Just ask the fifteen guys that have already quit during the first six weeks. My point is that we all have a purpose here.

Our platoon, who started with fifty-one and now has thirty-six, will someday be fighting for the good of the United States of America, the best place on earth. It's funny how close grown men can bond when going through bullshit together.

Normally I'm not the easiest guy to get to know. That's why I've never had very long relationships. My family is dysfunctional and even my good friends in high school would probably classify me as "a great drinking buddy." Yet, I've found myself getting pretty tight with Trey Thomas. Actually, to be accurate, it's Trey Thomas the Third. He comes from a long line of Marines and is your stereotypical big southern brute.

Born and raised in rural Mississippi, he can bench press three hundred pounds, even though he's worked out about five times in his life. "Naturally strong," as some would say.

A former high school football quarterback, he stands at 6'4", 210 pounds, and still growing. His blond hair and blue eyes give him the perfect All-American look. And he's got a thick southern drawl to top it all off. So thick, in fact, that he has to repeat himself frequently when trying to

143

communicate to his fellow plebes.

Yet, despite his family track record and huge physical presence, Trey hasn't made it easy on himself during these first six weeks. He's constantly messing up and is the number one man on Drill Instructor Sgt. Harris's shit list.

I can't say I blame Instructor Harris; between trying to get an extra five minutes of shuteye or being the first one to give up during "fitness activities," Trey has a long way to go.

I'm sure the high expectations of the Corps don't make it any easier on him. Rumor has it that Instructor Harris went through boot camp with Trey's brother, Scott. Though we haven't heard full details, it sounds like they had quite the competition and never really got over their quarrels. So Trey knew going in it wouldn't be easy.

Yesterday I overhead some of the guys placing bets on which plebe will go next. Trey had the most votes. I jumped in to defend him. "Don't you think he puts enough pressure on himself? You gotta kick a man while he's down?" My voice was raised. They shut up quickly.

I kind of like the leadership role that I've stepped into. Funny though, I never thought my Yankee ass would be sticking up for a 6'4" southerner.

This afternoon, before dinner, we face our biggest test yet. We run several miles, with full gear on, as we break up into three teams. Now with thirty-six guys, each team will have twelve men. As Sgt. Harris breaks us into teams, Trey and I are thrown together. Just before the drill starts, the sergeant walks over to me, looks me dead in the eyes, and says, "I'm watching you, Jimmy. Don't you go picking up the slack for your boyfriend over here. Someday he'll be on his own against the enemy, and you won't there to help his ass. Understand?"

I look up at Trey, then back and Sgt. Harris, and nod. I pray he can step it up.

We're three hours into the drill and it's grueling. My

guess is we've already gone about five miles, but that's not the hard part. Each of us is carrying 85 pounds of gear, trudging through swamps and transporting different pieces of weaponry and other equipment at various stages of the mission. A couple of guys have fallen on the ground, almost trampled by the crew, before being dragged back up by one of their buddies.

So far Trey is holding his own. Now it's his turn to lead the group, which means he's responsible for using the compass and guiding us towards the next destination. He panics a bit and leads us in a circle, losing a lot of ground. Sgt. Harris comes out of the woods and immediately gets in Trey's face. "You're showing me nothing, Thomas. Nothing!"

Eventually we finish the task. We end up finishing last of the three groups. It takes us thirty minutes longer than the other two. Some of the guys blame Trey. Personally, I think we have a weak group, but his mistake didn't help.

After dinner I notice Trey coming out of Sgt. Harris's office. "He gave me a final warning," he said. "If I screw up again, I'm history."

Three weeks go by and Trey is just starting to turn the corner. He's now in the final stretch, with about three and half weeks left until the end of boot camp. By this point he's definitely become one of the closest friends I've ever had. I've even told him about my dysfunctional family life.

He's revealed to me that despite how it looks on the outside, his family has some pretty major issues as well. I guess they have a fourth brother, the black sheep of the family, who is a homeless coke addict. The family hasn't heard from him in nearly three years. For all Trey knows, he could be dead in some alleyway.

One night, while winding down for the night, Trey asks me to step into the bathroom stall with him for a minute. "What, you are hitting on me?" I laugh. Then he pulls out the newest issue of Playboy.

I haven't seen a naked woman in months, not since the debacle with that chick from Hampton Beach. Hell, I wouldn't even call that seeing her naked, since it was dark in the room.

My first reaction is to tell Trey he's an idiot for bringing that out. "Where the hell did you find that?" I say to him.

"Don't worry about where it came from, just enjoy it," he responds. We spend the next fifteen minutes flipping through as many pages as possible.

Although I thoroughly enjoy looking at the naked women, I can't help but realize I was doing fine without them. Now these last few weeks will be even harder, being reminded of what I don't have. As I hear someone enter the bathroom, I quickly scurry out of the stall and start washing my face.

Trey spends another ten minutes in there before packing it in for the night. During breakfast the next morning, we're suddenly interrupted by Sgt. Harris. He's holding Trey's Playboy magazine.

"OK Thomas, you dipshit. Are you going to own up to this smut?" he says.

Before Trey can say anything, I stand up from my seat. "Sir, my apologies, that is mine."

Sgt. Harris looks at me, shocked. "You wouldn't be sticking up for your loser boyfriend here, would you, Keller?"

"No sir. I snuck it into the barracks yesterday and forgot to put it away. I accept whatever punishment you deem appropriate."

Meanwhile, I'm wondering how Trey can be so stupid. He must have tucked the Playboy under his mattress, thinking we wouldn't have a random search in the final few weeks.

Sgt. Harris gives me one more chance to change my mind. When I stand firm, he responds. "All right then, you'll

146

be joining my grumpy ass at four a.m. every morning for the next two weeks. And when I'm grumpy, that makes two of us."

Each morning during that fourteen-day stretch, as I finished sprint after sprint, I tried to remind myself of my good deed.

Trey made it through camp. He didn't have go back to Mississippi and disappoint his family. Yet, perhaps it was really selfishness on my part. How bored would I have been without Trey? Without my buddy. Little did I know that my good deed actually sent Trey to his deathbed years later.

32. Making friends in Iraq

Jimmy

It's our morning rounds and we're heading a mile or so down towards town to check out some of the damage from last night's firefight. When I first got here, this was one of the moments I dreaded most. Usually we'd find some mass carnage around the target area, especially if missiles were involved. Of course, as American soldiers we went well above the Geneva Convention rules and actually buried enemy casualties whenever possible. Many times this even included hosting a funeral service, which sometimes had enemy fighters in attendance. Crazy, I know, but somehow both sides had enough human decency to call an unwritten truce during these burials.

I never thought I'd get used to seeing body parts strewn all over the place or no longer gag when I picked up heads that were half missing. But as each day passes, the horror of it all starts to blend into everyday life. I guess our minds cope by blocking it out and adjusting as best we can.

"Jimmy, check it out. A soccer game. You want to show these boys how to play?" Trey laughs. Having been serving together for almost ten years now, Trey and I can almost read each other's minds at this point. His southern charm probably goes a lot further back home than in these mean streets.

"I didn't know you southern boys even played soccer. Isn't it the stepchild to football?" I poke back.

To my amazement, literally in between smoldering buildings and in some cases, dead bodies, there is a group of young boys, probably ranging from nine to twelve, playing soccer. Or, as they call it, fútbol.

As we walk closer I notice the ball isn't your typical black and white leather soccer ball. It rattles pretty loud as each of them makes contact. That's when I realize the ball is made up of a bunch of old crushed beer cans taped together with duct tape. They put down cinder blocks at each end of the field to serve as goal posts.

Trey and I grab a seat in the makeshift bleachers, some plywood pieces nailed together on top of more cinder blocks. These kids are having a blast.

We watch for several minutes and catch some serious action. Each team has scored at least two goals and the energy level is high. If I saw this group of kids playing on TV, without the hellish background, it could easily pass for inner city kids in the U.S. Well, if you didn't get a good look at the makeshift ball. Even the poorest kids in the U.S. use the real thing. Heck, most have $75 shoes, who am I kidding?

Just as we're about to get up, a final cheer erupts and the game appears to be over. A few of the kids come by to check out our gear. One in particular, who scored all the goals for one team, points to my gun. "Me hold?" he asks.

"Sorry, kid, stick with soccer." I say. Trying not to be too much of a jerk, I motion Trey to start heading in the other direction. There's a fine line between befriending the local kids and getting distracted while they jump all over your equipment.

"OK, OK, no gun. Hemet! Hemet!" the kid answers.

"Hemet?" What the hell is hemet?" I ask.

"I think he wants your helmet, Jimmy," Trey translates.

"All right, all right. I'll let you guys hold it for a minute. But if you run off, I'm taking you down." Of course, I'm mostly joking, but I also don't want to be the brunt of jokes back at camp because some eleven-year-old outruns me and steals my helmet. There have been plenty of laughs around camp with guys missing anything from helmets to boots, even a water bottle, because they let some kids mess around and they take off.

He puts the helmet on backwards, and all of his

buddies start laughing.

"Here, let me help with that," I say. "What's your name?"

"Amir," he answers. "I eleven years old."

As I clip the chin strap, he lets out a huge smile. Then I realize he has an uncanny similarity to someone I remember from childhood pictures. Who is it?

Just then one of his buddies makes a fake pistol with his hands and pretends to shoot at him. Amir takes the bullet in the chest and with his best American film imitation, staggers to the ground in agony. He flails to the ground and kicks the bucket. All the kids laugh.

"Pretty good kid. I hope that happens to the bad guys, not us," I add.

He then takes off the helmet and places it in my hand. With a final smile, I notice he has big buck teeth, just like I did when I was his age. Wait a minute. Holy crap! That kid looks like an Iraqi version of me. I take out my old cell phone, which I only use as a camera these days, and snap a shot of him. Then the kids all get together for a second shot, this time with the makeshift ball in hand.

At that point I notice a huge scar covering Amir's left leg. He acknowledges I've seen it, then puts his two hands together and lifts up them up quickly, while making a loud noise, signifying a bomb. Wow, that roadside bomb could have done a lot more damage than that, I think to myself. Still, it sucks these kids have to deal with this nightmare. It strikes me how resilient these kids must be to keep their sanity in the midst of this living hell.

For the rest of the day, even as I dig through the carnage, I can't get Amir's smile out of my head. In a place like this, that image can go a long way.

33. Wedding Weekend

Ben

I still don't fully understand what Sarah sees in me. Maybe it's my constant sarcasm? Or perhaps the overly optimistic outlook on life I wake up with every day?

Yeah, right. Regardless, she only has one day to change her mind. So like my buddies tell me, don't give her a reason to change it. That's yet another reason why my mom's decision to crash at our place the night before the wedding is driving me crazy.

At least Sarah won't have to deal with her much this go round. If my mom gets here a little before dinner, it's likely Sarah won't even cross paths with her before making the getaway to the hotel with her bridal party.

It's ten-fifty a.m. and today has been pretty relaxing thus far. Since Sarah has taken on just about every wedding task, my one responsibility has been to pick out what the groomsmen will be drinking in the limo to and from the church and wedding reception.

Initially I was thinking hard alcohol, perhaps vodka shots. Then my better judgment kicked in at the thought of my rancid breath on Father Mac.

I know some Catholic priests have been known to throw a few down, but he may take exception to the hard stuff invading the chapel. So, I've decided on Bloody Marys prior to the ceremony and champagne on the way to the reception. This means I only have one stop today, Total Beverage.

I make my way through the aisles. Bloody Mary Mix. Spicy or regular? Spicy. Why not? Some GREY GOOSE vodka, nothing but the best for my buddies. Finally, some champagne I've never heard of and I'm off. Wait, I almost forget the celery sticks. Wouldn't you know it, this place even sells them. At the checkout line, my phone rings. Hmm, it's Sarah. I thought she'd be in her own world this morning. I hope nothing's wrong.

"Hi honey," I say, answering the phone.

"Guess who is sitting on our front porch waiting for us to get home? I mean waiting for YOU to get home!" she says with her voice slightly raised.

Now normally I'm not a very good guesser. As a matter of fact, Sarah and I already have an unwritten rule of our new household that states I am not allowed to gamble, especially on sporting events. Why? Because it's almost a given that whichever team I predict to win will fail miserably. I think the last time I checked, the average fan has a 45 percent chance of guessing which NFL team will win any given Sunday, without the spread. I would be at around 15 percent.

Well, despite my horrible mental crystal ball, just by the tone of Sarah's voice I know exactly who she is speaking of.

"She's here already?" I say. "What the heck?"

Then I remember Sarah has enough stress without worrying about my over-the-top mom.

"Don't worry, honey, I can be home in twenty minutes and will handle everything. You won't even notice her there," I add, with a small chuckle.

"Now that would be a first," Sarah exclaims, as we end the call.

Great. So much for relaxing on my last official day of bachelorhood. Well, come on, how bad can it be? Mom knows we have a ton going on here; she probably will just hang out, maybe go for a long walk, and stay out of the way. I pull up into the driveway and there she is suitcases in hand. I can also hear Brutus, our miniature dachshund, barking at the top of her seven-pound lungs. Stay positive, I mumble to myself.

"Ben, it's your big weekend! I can't believe my little boy is getting married," my mom utters.

"I know, hard to believe, right, Mom?" I say, thinking maybe this won't be so bad after all. As I make three different trips inside with her suitcases, I can already hear her fiddling around in the kitchen.

"Ben, do you have any tea?"

"Give me a minute, Mom, and I'll check. Sarah usually keeps some around."

I spend the next fifteen minutes combing through every cabinet and drawer in the kitchen, including using a ladder to look deep into the pantry. Nothing.

"Sorry, Mom, looks like we must have run out. Can you go without it for a day or two?"

"Oh, well, sure, if I have to," Ethel says with a disappointed tone.

"All right, Mom, I'm going to start packing for the hotel and honeymoon, then will probably mow the lawn. Do you need anything else before I go upstairs?"

Mom thinks for what seems like an eternity and finally responds, "Well, I think I'm all right for now. I had a late breakfast before I came over here, so I'm pretty full."

Just in case, I let her know about the leftover Chinese food in the fridge from the night before. My favorite, General Tso's. "Just make sure to save me some, Mom, that's my lunch," I add. *China Delight* packs in the food, so unless mom is bringing over a few friends, no need to worry about having enough for lunch. Isn't it amazing how much food they can squeeze into those tiny containers? Don't get me wrong, I'm not complaining. Although I do find it kind of ironic that Chinese restaurants have no problem shoving four portions into one order, yet when you ask for a napkin, they shoot you a death look. And when you ask for more, you'd think you just called their ancestors every four-letter word in the book.

Packing takes longer than expected. I'm the type of guy that always worries the one item I forget to bring will be needed on a trip, so I pack two of everything. This makes

Sarah cringe. I keep reminding myself that we're stopping by the house before we head to the airport for our honeymoon. Sarah hasn't even started packing, so I'm ahead of the game for once.

As I head down the stairs I can hear my mom putting some dishes in the sink. I guess she took me up on the Chinese food.

"Boy, I was hungrier than I thought," she says. "Don't worry, Ben, I saved you some."

It's now twelve fifty-five p.m. I throw on my lawn mowing apparel stained shorts, a wife beater, and my torn-up sneakers. Then I head outside. I should be done just in time to shower and eat before two p.m. That's the nice thing about having a small yard. I could mow it with one hand tied behind my back and still finish in less than thirty minutes.

Just as I'm finishing up, I can see Mom knocking on the window trying to get my attention. I hold up my hand letting her know I'll be done in five minutes.

After I put the lawn mower away, she greets me at the door with my cell phone. "Can I make a call, honey?"

"Do you mind waiting until I take a shower? Who do you need to call?" I inquire.

"Well, I was thinking, didn't you say Sarah is out doing errands? Do you think she would mind picking up some English tea?" Mom says.

I try not to let it bother me, but as Sarah is quick to point out, I'm not very good at hiding my emotions. As a matter of fact, I'm probably one of the most transparent people on the face of the earth. Grimacing, I respond, "After my shower, Mom." Then I stomp upstairs. When she gets something in her mind, forget it.

As I grab my towel from the closet, I catch a glance of Mom's open suitcase on the guest bed. When I look closer I notice that her toiletry bag is left wide open. I walk in the room and see her pill case, full of God knows what, is wide open. One of the pills, an oval-shaped white pill, is actually sitting right on the bed. Luckily we don't have kids to worry about here. However, I don't think Brutus's small frame would handle these very well.

I walk downstairs and give Mom a small reprimand. "Can you please put these in a secure spot, up high, so that Brutus doesn't get a hold of them and accidentally OD?" She agrees to take care of it. Then, just for good measure, I put up the gate and plop Brutus down in the kitchen.

After a nice, hot shower, I take my time shaving and taking care of business on the throne. Wow, I guess that Chinese last night is starting to take effect. I can't wait to go for round two, I laugh to myself. The three S's are one of the simple things a man needs in his life.

Just as I start getting comfortable, there is a knock on the bathroom door. "Ben, I think something happened with Brutus. Can you come here when you're done?"

So much for a nice clean wipe. Can't a man take a dump in peace?

I open the door and see Mom trying to quickly pack up her pills. There are now several of them sitting on the bed, in a variety of shapes and colors. When I look closer, I notice the white oval-shaped pill that I saw earlier is missing.

"Did you put away the white one that I told you about?" I say sternly.

"Actually, I think that is the one Brutus has in his mouth," she replies.

"Where is he?" I yell. She points downstairs.

As I run down the stairs, I see Brutus hovering over the pill, half chewed. I dive to the ground to get it, but he's too fast. Thinking we're playing a game, he runs with it down into the basement. On the way he passes through the kitchen and that is when I notice the gate is propped on its side. Mom must have gone in there for something.

It takes me another ten minutes, but I'm able to pry the remainder of the pill from Brutus's small mouth. Now I need to figure out what the hell he just ate. After grilling

Mom for ten minutes, she finally is able to conclude he ate one of her Lactaid pills. Mom has always had issues with her stomach, particularly with dairy products. However, this doesn't stop her from eating pizza, ice cream, you name it.

While I'm still nervous for Brutus, I thank God it wasn't one of her more powerful "happy pills." Mom hasn't come out and told us directly, but it's safe to say she takes a bunch of different anxiety pills. We know this because there was a period of time two years ago when she couldn't even sit down for five minutes. She would literally pace around looking for whichever lost item was on her mind. Constantly misplacing keys, food, pills, you name it. This, combined with her obsessive habits like reminding me every five minutes about taking her to the airport at a certain time, triggered some insensitive words. "I think you need to talk to your therapist about some new medication, Mom. The stuff you're taking now doesn't seem to be working." At the time I wasn't sure exactly what she was taking, but she had already told us about the once a week therapy visits for "stress."

I never have understood how people can resort to medication for emotional problems. To me it's a sign of weakness. If you're depressed, get up and do something about it. Go for a jog, take up a hobby. Don't rely on pills. Today everything has got a clinical explanation. *Chronic fatigue syndrome, Chronic dry eyes, AHDD, Obsessive-compulsive disorder.* What about just sucking it up? Everyone has issues. Deal with them. Once you start to cave and use medication or blame your problems on everyone else, the crutch will never go away.

It seems like no one wants to take responsibility for their situation today. It's always the parents' fault for how they didn't give the kid enough compliments growing up. Or that the father worked too much. That must be what led to a kid dying their hair purple and tattooing every part of their body.

Where is the vet's phone number? I am not going to

call Sarah for it. I'd rather look up the number in the yellow pages. There it is, *Friendly Paws Animal Clinic*. Hopefully they're still open, given it's a Saturday.

"Hi, Dr. Roberts? It's Ben, Brutus's dad."

Funny how that just slips out now. As I go on to tell her about the Lactaid pill, she advises me to keep an eye on him for the next twenty-four hours and to make sure he drinks plenty of water.

"Hopefully he will excrete the remnants of the pill," she says.

Normally it wouldn't be as much of an issue, but because Brutus is so small, any foreign substance like that has a more significant effect. Before she hangs up she recommends giving him some human food, preferably something that will make him shit a lot.

I have just the right formula. "We both can crap together," I say to Brutus, opening the fridge. My stomach has been growling for the past thirty minutes, but I was able to ignore it. I pull out the Chinese food container and plan to dig in. But when I open it, I see literally two small pieces of chicken and about a spoonful of rice. Is this what she meant by saving me plenty? The woman weighs a buck ten soaking wet, yet she can eat like a horse.

I decide to give Brutus all of it, while I polish off ramen noodles. Once my dish hits the sink, Mom pokes her head in the kitchen.

"Oh, is he OK?"

"He got lucky, Mom. He should be fine."

Then she hands me my phone and asks again if I can call Sarah. Sighing, I punch in the number. No answer. Smart on her part. I leave a detailed message asking her to pick up the English tea.

The next two hours go by much faster since I throw in a movie for Mom. I found the longest one in my collection, *Dances with Wolves*. That will give me the next three-plus hours of peace and quiet. I spend that time working out, showering again, and reading the last few pages of my book, *How to Win Friends and Influence People* by Dale Carnegie. An absolute classic, especially for anyone in sales.

Time check. Three thirty-five p.m. Sarah should be home soon. Should I even tell her about my day with Mom? Nope. That will be a good honeymoon story.

Just then Mom yells upstairs. "Ben, did Sarah call you back?"

"No, Mom, she's probably tied up with all of the last-minute wedding arrangements. I can call her again if you really think it's important."

"Yes, that would be great. Thanks, Ben," she says, with no hint of regret. This time I catch her on the second ring. After the initial shock of me asking for the tea, Sarah collects herself and agrees to buy it. Then I can hear Mom's voice again in the background.

"What did you say, Mom?" I ask.

She responds with more demands. Should I even tell Sarah? You know what; I don't want to deal with it later.

"OK, my mom is asking if you don't mind buying some popcorn and white wine while you're at the store."

Just then I hear the click of the phone hanging up. Hopefully she heard me. As I put down my completed book, I head downstairs. Maybe a cold beer will do me some good. I make my way past the TV, which has the credits running from the movie, when a putrid smell catches my nose. I look down to see streaks of diarrhea in a pattern leading all the way to the kitchen.

"Brutus!" I yell. But the streaks are smeared as well. With someone's footprints on them. "You have got to be shitting me," I mumble. She stepped on it.

I turn the corner into the kitchen to see Brutus guiltily licking his shit-stained paws and Mom, completely oblivious to what she's done, opening the fridge looking for more food.

I spend the next thirty minutes wiping up the fecal matter, forgetting about the cold beer. What a crappy way to spend my last day as a bachelor.

34. Wedding Weekend

Ethel

I know Ben and Sarah aren't expecting me until later this afternoon, so it will be a nice surprise when I show up for lunch. Just a forty-five-minute drive from my house in Concord.

Let's see, I'd better double-check my suitcase again to make sure I haven't forgotten anything. I'm only supposed to stay for two nights, but who knows, maybe they won't care if turn this into a mini-vacation. They'll be on their honeymoon anyway.

OK, I have four outfits packed, my pills, two books, and toiletry bag. Do I need shampoo or toothpaste? No, I'm sure they have plenty. Wait. How about cash? There isn't an ATM anywhere near Ben's house.

I just got my SSI check, which means I have a little extra spending money this time. I'll bring fifty dollars. This should cover my gas, a few snacks, and a bottle of wine. As for meals, I'm sure they have plenty of food to cover me before the wedding. Then it's all inclusive from there. The girls will probably bring some food too or at least snacks.

I'm still having trouble deciding on the right dress for the wedding. I can't wear white, so I'll leave this one in the closet. But I have three that would look really nice. The royal blue classic dress, multi-colored more hip dress, or the yellow summer dress. Maybe I'll bring all of them just in case.

The girls can give me their honest opinion. What about this green one? No, three is enough. OK. I grab all of the shoes that go with these dresses and I'm on my way. I look down and notice the gas tank is on empty. First stop, Citgo. As I go in to pay the cashier (cash of course, which saves me five cents per gallon), I think again about that lovely green dress. When was the last time I wore that dress?

Oh, wait, I remember. It was Ben's college graduation. I got so many compliments on that one. Maybe I should just wear it again. Why not go with something that has already worked? Yes, I'm getting it. Luckily I've only driven about seven miles up north, so the drive back to the house isn't too bad. I run upstairs, grab the dress and two additional pairs of shoes which match. Then I'm back on Route 93 North.

As I pass the Concord Mall, I remember they have so many cute shops. I especially love the new trendy hat shop. As a matter of fact, I need to buy another nice hat soon. The last time I bought one was prior to Ben's graduation. Wait a minute. The green hat! I totally forgot it. Should I go back and get it? Yes, yes. I have to. Ben and Sarah aren't expecting me for a while anyway. I head back to the house again. Now I'm finally on the road for good.

The whole ride I can't stop worrying about what else I might have forgotten. *What about shoes? How many did I bring again? Seven pairs. That should be fine. Oh, my lipstick. I forgot it. I knew it. Maybe I can borrow some from Sarah. Panty hose. I forgot that too. Wait, am I sure seven pairs of shoes are fine? What about the silver pair? Should I turn around and go back again? No, I'm sure the girls or Sarah can help. Why do I feel like I'm forgetting something else? Something really important.*

I look in my right side mirror and notice my gas cap is missing. Oh my gosh. I must have left it on top of the car when I was pumping my gas. I've been driving for about fifteen minutes. I had better turn around and find it. Gas caps can be expensive. Lucky me. Turns out the gas cap is sitting right on the trash can next to where I pumped my gas. I wonder if I left it there or if some nice person picked it up for me? Either way, that saves me at least ten dollars.

I pull back onto the busy two-lane road and hear a loud thump. Was that a pothole? Must have been, but I don't remember a big pothole pulling into the gas station. It sounded like I ran something over. *Oh my gosh, I hope not.*

Father, Son, Holy Spirit, amen. Lord, please make sure I didn't hit anyone. If I did, please make sure they are safe. Oh God, did I hit someone with the car? What if I did and they are lying in the road right now, dying? No. It would have sounded louder if I hit a person, right?

But it could have been an animal. Oh, that would be awful if I hit an animal. But I didn't notice an animal running in front of my car. Oh, Holy Spirit, Lord Almighty, please give a sign that I didn't hit anyone. A church, look. That must be my sign. Everything is fine now. Right? OK, I will drive back just to make sure no one needs help. Could I really have hit someone there? I doubt it. Wouldn't the thump have been a little louder? It was just one single thump, not a really loud thud, right? Wouldn't I be dragging him/her still if I hit them? Wouldn't there be blood somewhere?

Just stop to check it out, will you! So what if I get to Ben's house a little later than I wanted, they will still be surprised. Besides, if I did hurt someone, I have to tell the police. I drive back and forth in front of the Citgo entrance and the only thing I see on the ground is an old muffler. That is it! I ran over an old muffler. *Oh no! What if a week from now I get a call from the police saying they have a witness that saw my car hit a man trying to cross the street? Or worse, what if the guy is lying there now and I have to miss the wedding because I'm in jail?*

OK, now, Ethel. Remember what Dr. Karl says, this must just be your anxiety taking over. You didn't hit anyone. Now get back on the road and enjoy your weekend.

I pull into their driveway with plenty of time to spare. See, that's what happens when you leave early. I start to unload my suitcases and carry them onto the porch. They are going to be so surprised to see me. I can't wait to see their reaction! As I walk back to get the final piece of luggage, I notice something on my front bumper. When I walk up closer, there is a small dent, maybe the size of a quarter. That isn't what concerns me. It's the red stain on top of it. Is that blood? *Oh my gosh. Maybe I did hit someone? Our Father, who art in heaven, hallowed be thy name. Thy kingdom come, thy will be done, on earth as it is in heaven. And give us this day our daily bread, and forgive us our trespasses as we forgive those who trespass against us. From thy bounty, through Christ our Lord. Amen. Lord, please let that not be blood. Please, Lord. Please.* I get on my knees and hesitantly put my index finger on the red mark. It's dry and doesn't come off.

I look a little closer and realize it's a bumper mark, probably from someone in a parking lot. Must be paint. *Thank you, heaven almighty Father. Father, Son, Holy Spirit, amen.* Wow. That was close. OK. Time for some English tea. Thank God Sarah always keeps some in the house.

35. Jimmy's Big Mistake

2005 Iraq

Jimmy

"I see the scumbag. Three o'clock and on the move. He just went inside the two-story building with the blue door. I'm on him," I relay through the walkie-talkie.

I hope this is the break we need to take down the sniper who's been stalking our men. Two dead and one critically wounded just in the past week.

This guy has a great shot. I'll bet he was trained by us at one point in his life. Ain't it crazy how the line between enemies and friends gets so cloudy? It really depends on the decade. As I always say, "the lesser of two evils."

A lot of people bitch about the U.S. helping Bin Laden back in the eighties and now it's come back to haunt us. To those, I say it's a lot more complicated than that. At the time the Soviets were by far our biggest threat. They were the only other country at the time with nuclear weapons and the motive to strike made it even scarier. Initiating a direct conflict with them was not a favorable option, so supporting Afghanistan was the next best thing.

Did we provoke Bin Laden by leaving them out to dry down the road? Maybe, but the man's a fanatic and has vowed to kill non-believers for several decades. If anything, our one-time alliance may have dropped our guard a bit, which enabled al-Qaeda to get stronger. My belief is that history will show we will have many more cases of former allies turning on us and vice versa, instances where we actually support a dictator whom we once opposed, such as the case with supporting Saddam against the Iranians. Pick your poison.

I'm on post watch nine until dusk, which means I'm

flying solo chasing this bastard. Typically, this is a pretty slow rotation, as most of the trouble happens at night. However, something tells me this afternoon will be different.

As I approach the dilapidated house with the blue door, I focus on the two second-story windows where the sniper is likely to set up shop. Just then, a shot whistles past my left ear. Missed me by an inch or two. OK. Left window. Wow, am I lucky. This guy doesn't miss very often.

I make a run for the side of the house and dive into the dirt. No more shots, luckily. One slow step at a time, I scrape my back against the base of building. Reaching the front corner, I take a deep breath and spin quickly. Now I'm facing the front door with my pistol in the ready position. I kick it open. Nothing but dead silence. That bastard is a sitting duck now. I got him, unless he wants to break his legs and jump out the window. No time to call for backup.

The stairs have holes in them and look like they could come tumbling down at any second. I quietly slither up the stairs and see the two bedroom doors. Unless that bastard moved, he's to my left. I remain silent and listen for any semblance of noise. Nothing. I throw the hardest kick of my life and kick open the door while yelling. "Freeze you bastard!" He's nowhere to be found.

A second later, I hear footsteps behind me. I turn and fire two rounds. Direct hit. The body slumps to the ground and a pool of dark red blood instantly surrounds it. I step closer to get a better look at the bastard. I want to look into his lifeless eyes and stare down the scumbag who took the lives of my friends.

As I get closer something isn't right. Holy shit! No! No! It's a kid. God, please no! Next to him on the ground is a makeshift soccer ball. I shot a defenseless kid. Oh God, why? What were you doing in here? I slouch down onto the wooden floor with my hands covering my face. Out of the corner of my eye I notice his left leg. That scar. Amir. Oh Lord no! No!

I run back into the bedroom and through the window I can see the sniper sprinting away. Amir must have been in here playing while that asshole was trying to kill me. I can't just leave him here. I call for backup. That's the last thing I remember about that day.

My mind must have shut down. Trey tells me I sat there until about midnight. He helped communicate with one of our local neighborhood contacts, who knew of Amir's family. Trey then went over to the house with the man, who translated the horrible news to his mother. She broke down in hysterics. Turns out they lost their only other child, Amir's older brother, a year ago to an IED explosion.

I was able to attend Amir's funeral two days later. When the first shovelful of dirt was thrown onto his plywood casket, his mother lay on the ground and started wailing while pulling the dirt off.

The look of incredible sadness on her face pierced a hole in my heart. Then two things hit me. That hole would likely never heal. And I would have to live with knowing my poor judgment took away this woman's last child forever.

36. A Night Out in Fallujah

2007

Jimmy

"Sweet Caroline, bum, bum, bum....Love ain't never felt so good," we all sing, beers in hand. Thank God for American music. Whoever brought this CD player deserves a medal. Not to mention the couple hundred CDs we continually rotate through.

Tonight is our monthly booze fest. On the first Friday of every month, assuming we aren't taking enemy fire, our battalion gets drunk and tries to forget about the hellhole we've been living in for the past few years. The only thing we're missing is women. Since no outsiders are allowed on base, it turns into a giant sausage fest. Either way, I'm not complaining. Getting drunk and hanging with the boys suits me just fine.

Trey, who has been downing tequila shots after every can of Budweiser he polishes off, is leaning on my shoulder.

"Jimmy, I wouldn't want to be in this shithole with anyone else," he says.

"Thanks, man. I'd rather be home, but if I gotta be here, I'd want to spend it with you, too," I reply.

It's hard to believe we've known each other for over ten years now. We've both promised to visit each other's hometown once we're out of here. Trey is going to take me out on his uncle's shrimp fishing boat for an all-day excursion.

When he visits me up north, I'm taking him to a Red Sox game. He's only been to one baseball game in his life, and that was a minor league game. Once he sees Fenway, he'll be hooked. Fenway Frank, loaded, and an Italian sausage with extra peppers and mushrooms sound awfully good to me right now. Heck, I'd take just the peppers. This mess hall food gets old after about a week. Trey gets me in a friendly headlock while finishing up the song.

Sweet Caroline
good times never seemed so good.
I've been inclined
to believe they never would.
But now I—
Look at the night
and it don't seem so lonely
we fill it up with only two.
And when I hurt
hurtin' runs off my shoulders
How can I hurt when holdin' you ?
warm
touchin' warm
reachin' out
touchin' me
touchin' you.
Sweet Caroline
good times never seemed so good.
I've been inclined
to believe they never would.
Oh no no.

Neil Diamond, baby, gotta love him! I can't wait to sing that song at Fenway after a big win.

"OK, let's head out to find some hotties," Trey says, slurring his words.

"I think it's too late for that, buddy. One too many tonight." I try to convince him to stay.

But Trey pushes, along with about ten other marines, who start to walk out of the tent.

I'm hesitant to leave base camp at this point, but go along anyway. Instead of following our normal protocol, which includes signing out, the guys sneak out. This leaves a knot in my stomach, but there's no turning back now.

"Guys do it all the time." Trey laughs.

He's right, but I've seen guys get caught and it ain't pretty. You basically get put back in boot camp for a week, while being humiliated in front of your buddies.

As we make our way beyond the barracks, everyone starts to raise their voices again. In total it looks like we have eleven guys including me. This is definitely the wild crew, with Trey actually tame compared to some of these guys. A bunch of guys from New York are leading the charge, not shy of bravado, that's for sure.

Then there's two guys from Southern California, who fit the stereotype perfectly. Both are sporting dark tans and Oakley sunglasses, even though it's pitch black outside.

"Which dive are we headed to tonight?" I ask.

"Off the beaten path tonight, baby. Time for some dirty women," Tony, one of the loud New Yorkers, says. By this comment, I know exactly what he means.

A few miles down, as we enter some of the ghetto regions of the city, you can find prostitutes if you know where to look. My guess is this isn't the first time this group has ventured out into these parts. I pull Trey aside.

"Buddy, maybe we should turn around and sit this one out?"

"Come on, Jimmy, for once can you tell that little voice inside you to shut it? Every once in a while it's OK to live on the edge a bit."

Man, Trey usually isn't this persistent. What happened to the polite guy from Mississippi? Well, in his defense, six tequila shots and at least that many beers is what happened.

We're forty minutes into the trek and it looks like we're finally almost there. After passing some of the cleaner establishments, we stumble across some back roads. There we see a couple of ratty metal trailers with colored lights shining out of them. That's when Tony runs up and gives a secret knock, five soft knocks and then one loud one. Almost instantly the door opens and you can hear some chatter, which includes a couple of women's voices.

Tony heads in and closes the door shut. We all start to laugh. A minute later, Tony calls out to Trey. "Mississippi Boy, you're up!"

"Wish me luck, boys!" Trey adds.

"Don't shoot a dud, Trey! Or worse, forget to unload the cannon," someone in the background yells.

"If he even can get the cannon up!"

We all cackle on the ground at that point.

For the next hour many of the guys rotate in and out of the trailer. I decide to sit this one out and keep guard. The area is definitely shady. Out of the corner of my eye I notice a light turn on in another trailer about thirty yards away. Then I see a man looking out in disgust.

Luckily, I packed a road soda to make the time go by a little faster. The Budweiser goes down real smooth.

"OK, anyone else, boys?" Tony yells.

When no one answers, Tony calls it quits.

"All right, our work is done, boys."

By this time Trey pops open the door with a huge shit-eating grin on his face.

"I needed that," he says.

Again, we all burst out in hysterics. "I need ten more bucks," Tony says.

A few of the guys scrape up the money and then we are ready to head back. I see Tony give the money to a squirmy Iraqi man and they shake hands.

"How do you know he's on our side?" I ask.

"Because we have money," Tony says confidently.

We round up all the guys and start making our way out of the slums. As we're leaving, Trey and Tony wander off towards the shed I noticed with the light on.

"I need one more." Tony laughs.

Before they reach the door, a shadow pops out of nowhere. It's a kid on a bike, probably no older than fourteen.

"You want some pooty?" he asks in broken English.

Before I can stop them, Trey and Tony run up to the bike to check out the porn material. Just as they start to open up the first magazine it happens. Boom! Bodies fly in every direction.

"Stay down! Stay down!" I yell.

Almost immediately I can hear Trey screaming in pain. "My legs, my fuckin' legs!"

I run over towards him to find total devastation. The only remnant of the bike is the steering wheel hanging from a tree above. Body parts are strewn all over the ground, mostly from the kid. I look down at Trey and do my best not to show how horrified I am.

His body has been severed from the waist on down. His shirt is soaked in blood and I can see his intestines hanging out of his stomach which look like giant spaghetti noodles. He starts to go into shock.

"I'm gonna die, Jimmy. I'm gonna die."

Even though I know he's right, I say otherwise.

"We're gonna get you home, Trey. Hang in there. You'll make it. Just stay with me."

At that point I take off my shirt and wrap it around his stomach.

"I need some tourniquets! Take off your shirts! Let's go, now!" I demand.

One of the Southern Cal guys comes over with not only a few shirts, but also some morphine.

"I always keep a little on me for good measure," he says.

I give the shot to Trey.

Several of us are working on him and it appears after fifteen minutes that the bleeding has started to slow down. However, his eyes are barely open. Just then one of our jeeps pulls up and we load Trey in there. One of the other guys must have called for help while we were treating him.

For the first time, I look to my right and that's when I notice Tony's boots on the ground, with his legs still in them, but nothing else. He was blown to pieces by this brainwashed terrorist.

Before the jeep takes off, I grab Trey by his cheeks. "You can make it, man! Hang in there. Remember, we're going fishin', buddy."

"And I want to see Fenway," he mumbles.

Tears fill my eyes at that point as I realize unless the Green Monster is in heaven, he will never experience it.

37. The Handshake

Summer 2010

Ben

I pull into the driveway of St. Paul's Catholic Church with two minutes to spare and run out of the car up to the front door.

"Man, the paper," I mumble. I sprint back to the driver's seat to fetch the Confirmation paper. Little did I know being someone's Confirmation sponsor requires the priest's approval.

As I open the front door, a polite older woman asks if she can help. "Hi, I'm Ben Chase, here to see Father McDuffy," I say softly.

"Yes, he's expecting you. He'll be right over. Please take a seat," she offers.

Looking around the rectory, I don't feel nearly as intimidated as I first imagined. Then I notice two of my fingers are bleeding. Must be from biting off those hang nails in the car. Great. Now I'll go in there and bleed on his hand. That'll make a nice first impression. Before I can even start obsessing about it, Father McDuffy appears.

"Ben?" he asks.

"Yes, Father," I respond.

"Good, come into my office," he says unassumingly. "So, what brings you here today?"

"Father, I've been asked by my wife's nephew to serve as his sponsor and need you to sign this form. When I called, the receptionist said you first want to sit down with me and ask a few questions," I finish, hoping not to sound annoyed that he can't just put his John Hancock on the form.

Sometimes I wonder why the Catholic Church needs

to make things so difficult. It's no surprise people are leaving the religion.

"Yes, Ben, the sacrament of Confirmation is a big step in a young man's life. A key ingredient of this step is having the right role models to guide young people to Christ. Do you feel you can take on this important responsibility?"

Without hesitation I respond, "Yes, Father."

However, just then so many random thoughts pop into my head, none of which are very holy. Random hookups, blackouts, binge drinking, and causing trouble to name a few.

"Very well, then, let's pray," he continues. "Father Almighty, please bless Ben and give him the strength to show his nephew John the right way to Christ. May he always remember the path to righteousness is through you. Amen."

"Amen," I follow.

I stand up, relieved, and he walks me to the lobby.

"Thank you again, Father."

"Very well, son." With one foot out the door I remember the form.

"Oops, sorry, Father. Can you please sign this as well?"

"Anytime, son. Peace be with you." We shake hands and I'm on my way.

I put the car in reverse and notice the blood from my two fingers is now smeared. "Oh great, I bled on Father. Just great!"

Do you think your open cut really made it onto his hands? If so, was it still wet enough to smear or was it dry? What if your open cut got into an open cut on his hands? Could you give him a disease, like AIDS? No, I've already been tested. What about him? What if he has AIDS and also had an open cut? Could we have shaken hands and each cut infected the other? Wait a minute, he's a priest, he's celibate and probably never even had sex in his life. Relief for a minute. *Yeah, but how about all of the cases of gay priests or child molester priests? What if he was one of those guys? Oh man, this sucks!* By now, I'm approaching the driveway home.

Before shutting off the car, I start mimicking the handshake in hopes of determining the likelihood of two cuts on the edge of fingers actually having the ability to touch one another.

Look at that. If my middle and index finger, each of which are still bleeding, touched his fingers or hands and they had a cut, we could easily spread diseases through one another. Let's say he has AIDS, how long should I wait before getting tested? Six months? Man, I just got tested last year and thought I'd never have to worry about another test again. I can't deal with this. Come on, how likely is it that a priest has AIDS? Just forget about it.

I hop on the couch and turn on ESPN. Sports Center has just started and they're recapping all of the baseball games from the night before. Sweet, the Sox are coming up. I grab the remote to skim a few other channels and my eyes focus again on my smeared blood.

If I do have AIDS, this means I have about six months before diagnosis, then another ten years max to live. That means I'll die at forty-seven. My kids will be teenagers and I will miss them so much. High school graduation, baseball games, weddings, grandkids. Why can't I just be normal and stop biting my nails to the point where I bleed on people? What a moron!

Realizing this could go on all night, I turn off the TV and walk upstairs to call it a night. Hopefully in the morning this will all just be a bad dream. Unfortunately this was the beginning of a living nightmare.

38. Sacrilegious Thoughts

Fall 2010

Ben

"Let's go, everyone, we're late again," I yell. Good thing church is only five minutes away from our house; otherwise, we'd never get there before Communion. After some fancy driving by Sarah we walk in only fifteen minutes late. Better than usual. Instead of our typical seats in the very last row, the usher holds up his hand notifying our family of a seat much closer. I actually can see the priest this time. Good, maybe his sermon will make more sense. I chuckle.

One thing I've learned about Catholic Churches over the years is that sermons can cover all ends of the spectrum. My old CCD teacher would routinely give thirty-minute sermons reprimanding the congregation on breaking church rules such as chewing gum in the sacred building. Others would dedicate the time preaching to the young parents whose little ones cried during Mass. That always made Sarah and me feel good, as we struggled to even get the kids out of the house. Occasionally, we'd enjoy a heartfelt and moving sermon from a priest. That usually happened when the priest was able to convey old-school messages in real-time language. Today, we're likely in for the gum-chewing variety, noting that Father Driscoll is presiding.

An Irish Immigrant, Father Driscoll speaks with a heavy dialect. I'm sure he's a nice guy after a few beers, but his cold demeanor rubs many people the wrong way. At no more than 5'7", clean-cut and in his mid-forties, Father Driscoll could easily pass for a neighborhood dad if he dressed down.

Ten minutes into Mass, as usual, my mind starts to wander. I notice to my left a hot blond, probably in her early twenties. A thought pops in my head. *Wow, she is hot. I wonder what she looks like naked. Big boobs. I'll bet they look great. Ben, you're in church, knock it off. Sarah would really appreciate you imagining what that girl looks like, especially in church. Do you think she is wearing a thong? Yes, definitely. What if she is wearing granny underwear, would you still be attracted to her? I think I would. Hold on, have I ever dated a chick that wore granny undies? Yes, when I was in high school. Definitely. Will you stop thinking sexual thoughts in church. What if Father Driscoll sees you? That's gotta be a sin, right?*

Just then another thought, this time an unpleasant one, pops into my head. It's Father Driscoll naked. Then it goes further. It's Father Driscoll performing oral sex on someone. *Oh my God. That's me. You are going to hell! I can't believe you would have thoughts about a priest having gay sex with you. That is just wrong at so many levels. Get that crap out of your head right now.*

I try to distract myself, but thirty seconds later it comes back. *You sick bastard. No, I don't want to have that image. Please, Lord, I'm sorry this is in my head. Lord, please forgive me and please get this nasty image out of my head. Wait, maybe this means I'm gay? How many guys have gay thoughts about their priest?*

Then an even more disturbing image pops into my head. Father Driscoll with a small boy; molesting him. *That is sick. He would never do that, would he? Oh God, why would that thought pop into my head? I would never do that, would I?* Then it hits home. An image of our son Brady being molested by Father Driscoll. *Lord, God, please protect our son Brady. Please watch over him and make sure he is never molested or violated. Oh God, please. Does this have some hidden meaning about me? Oh Lord, please no.*

This back and forth goes on not only for the rest of church, but for another twelve hours until I go to bed that night. I pack it in early because I know when I'm sleeping the OCD takes a rest. When I'm dreaming, I don't freak out about the content; at least not until the following morning.

Just like birds chirping, as an OCD sufferer, you can count on it waking you up bright and early. It's hard to describe to someone who doesn't deal with it. I guess a good analogy would be when you're hung-over and you know something happened the night before that you regret. The minute you wake up, it hits you like a ton of bricks. What did I do last night? How bad was it? Except with OCD it's more like *naked gay priests and child molestation. Yes, that is what occupied my mind all day yesterday. Then it sits there.* If you are wise, you will let it fester there and not try to fight it.

On the days I try to fight it, it's a nonstop argument inside your head. *Those awful thoughts yesterday don't mean anything. Do they? Wait, they must. They are my thoughts, no one else's. Remember that famous quote "a man is what he thinks about all day long"? Oh God, does that mean I'm attracted to gay priests who molest children? Lord, please, no. Of course it doesn't, you moron. You are married with three kids. You're not gay and you're not a child molester. Shut up now.*

Try repeating those internal arguments a few hundred times per day for a week. Good stuff! At the time I couldn't imagine my days getting much worse. Boy was I wrong.

39. Verge of Collapse

One month later

Ben

If one more person tells me how skinny I look, I'm going to flip out on them, I swear. If they only knew the crap going on in my head; instead of putting me down they'd be shocked I was even still able to function. I just wish I could just relax and stop worrying about these crazy thoughts, but I can't.

It's like a constant recording going on in my head, a broken record. And every time I go to turn it off, it gets faster and faster. Still, even though I've been pretty miserable, if this weird mental crap was only affecting me, I'd probably just continue to deal with it. But now it's starting to affect my whole family.

I can tell I'm zoning out with the kids. We used to play together in the basement and I'd get really into it. Isabella would pretend I'm the kid and she's the mommy. It never failed, within ten minutes I was always in time-out for something. This always put a smile on my face. I guess it was her way of exerting some power. If I were five and being told what to do all day every day, I'd need a little "power time" too.

While I've made a ton of mistakes in my life, I vowed to become the best husband and father that I could be. The husband piece has been going down the tubes for the past two years. Now the father goal has started to slide.

How in the world have things gotten so bad, so quickly? I used to have so many great times with Isabella and Brady. Sure, my concentration issues and ADD got in the way occasionally, but nothing like today. Back then they could count on Daddy to be with them mentally and emotionally. I would get on the floor and play dolls, cars, you name it. Now my kids are constantly reminding me to stay in the game.

Meanwhile, Sarah and I have been at each other's throats for over two years now. It probably started the day after we got home from the hospital with little Lucy. I knew three kids would be different from two. Everyone warned us that zone defense is the only option. "No man to man now," my buddies would say. Yet, we had no idea how little time we'd have for ourselves.

But I don't want to make excuses for our marriage. Yes, the kids are a handful, but Sarah and I have much bigger issues. For starters, we haven't had sex in over six months. Needless to say my hormones are raging like an eighteen-year-old on Spring Break. Except I can't do anything about it; every time I try to touch her, she moves away.

"I can't just turn it on and off like you can, Ben. I need to feel special before we start having sex. Don't you remember how things used to be? Women need positive emotions before hopping in the sack," Sarah said to me last week.

Most nights she works on the computer, putting together reports for her weekly meetings, while I usually watch sports on the couch with a bag of chips in hand. We could go full days without saying a word to each other. If things stayed at that level, I would have just dealt with it. But for the past six months, we've started to get into some pretty heated fights, a few times in front of the kids. Nothing physical; I'd never lay a hand on her. However, the verbal assaults have gotten pretty brutal. The other day we both went for the throat. Sarah compared me to my mom and I fired back playing therapist, saying all of her issues stem from her parents working too much when she was little. After that battle, I decided it was time to try couples counseling.

We've been going to this lady, Dr. Helen Pierce, who runs a tiny little office about fifteen minutes from our house. She was recommended by my insurance plan. Although it turns out they barely cover any of the costs. What a racket. Anyhow, in most of the meetings I dominate by telling her all of the things that annoy me about Sarah.

The last few meetings I've brought up the lack of sex, which clearly took me down a notch in both of their books. Sarah usually just sits there and takes it, crying sometimes. Dr. Pierce tries to engage with her, but it's like pulling teeth. I'm thinking Dr. Pierce is on my side and maybe sex is on the way when she throws me a curve ball. "Do you think you're depressed, Ben?"

I'm shocked. "Depressed?" I fire back. "Not even close. I may be a little down in the dumps right now because my job is a little stressful and the kids are a handful. But depression is for people who are weak. I will never get to that point," I conclude.

"OK, I was just asking because you seem like you're constantly looking for whatever situation you are in to be better than what you've got. I've seen that in other people and it can be really tiring. Do you feel like the life you have right now is a good one?" Dr. Pierce asks. Just by my hesitation, Sarah already knows the answer.

I honestly hadn't thought about that question, at least in that way. Deep down I know that we're lucky. We have three healthy kids, good jobs, our own health, and enough money to go on vacation every year. Yet, when you look at the day-to-day interactions in our lives, we are pretty miserable.

I leave that session pretty bummed out. Could it be me that's the problem here? All this time I've been putting the blame on Sarah and the kids. Could it actually be me that needs the help? When I get home I go online and look up the definition of "depression" on Dictionary.com.

"1. Severe despondency and dejection, typically felt over a period of time and accompanied by feelings of hopelessness and inadequacy

2. A condition of mental disturbance characterized by such feelings to a greater degree than seems warranted by the external circumstances, typically with lack of energy and difficulty in maintaining concentration or interest in life (as in clinical depression)

3. A long and severe recession in an economy or market (as in the depression in the housing market)"

Next I look up some of the symptoms listed by the National Institute of Mental Health:

• *difficulty concentrating, remembering details, and making decisions*
• *fatigue and decreased energy*
• *feelings of guilt, worthlessness, and/or helplessness*
• *feelings of hopelessness and/or pessimism*
• *insomnia, early-morning wakefulness, or excessive sleeping*
• *irritability, restlessness*
• *loss of interest in activities or hobbies once pleasurable, including sex*
• *overeating or appetite loss*
• *persistent aches or pains, headaches, cramps, or digestive problems that do not ease even with treatment*
• *persistent sad, anxious, or "empty" feelings*
• *thoughts of suicide, suicide attempts*

I go down the list. Man, according to this list, everyone I know could be diagnosed with depression. Well, except the part about headaches and cramps. Or the thoughts of suicide, suicide attempts. I'm not crazy like that. I shrug it off. I'm not going to some shrink. That's for damn sure. Can you imagine if any of my buddies got a hold of that information? Next thing you know they would tell me to take some crap like Zoloft. Then I'd be groggy all day like Ethel.

I try to be a caring person, but one thing I've never been able to get over is people that don't have the strength to work things out on their own, without medication. Once you're dependent on that stuff, it's all downhill from there.

A few days later Sarah and I have another big fight. This time I'm pretty confident it's my fault. She was on a conference call upstairs, while I was supposed to be watching the kids. I started to zone out again, this time caught up in one of my routines, and they must have slipped upstairs without me noticing. Anyhow, they started fighting and screaming while she was on the phone with some clients. She had to put the call on mute and drag the kids out of our room. Still, the client clearly heard the freak show. After her call, she came downstairs and reamed me a new one.

"Can you not pay attention for even ten minutes to help out anymore? What is wrong with you?" she screamed.

After we put the kids to bed, I crashed for the night as well. Feeling pretty down, I can sleep for hours. Turns out I did. The next morning, a Saturday, I wake up after eleven a.m. Everyone is gone, probably out doing some errands, I would think. I slept for fifteen hours. That's like my old college days. Back then I could sleep for a full twenty-four hours, especially if I were hung-over.

My first task of the day is to cancel our upcoming appointments with Dr. Pierce. While she has good intentions, it's pretty clear things are getting worse, not better. I leave her a message saying Sarah and I need to work some things out before coming back. I'm sure she's heard that a thousand times. It's probably the final sign of a divorce from her perspective.

Next, it's time for a nice, hot shower. I like having the whole place to myself. I look in the mirror before hopping in. Wow, I do look pretty frail. My face appears six inches skinnier than a few years back, my shoulders as bony as a newborn calf's. Boy, Eddie and the boys back at Omega Epsilon would be hazing the hell out of me right now. They knew me as a workout warrior during my days in college. I had a six-pack and could bench almost double my weight.

Funny thing is I probably weigh close to the same as I did back then, but my muscle is gone. It's converted to a small gut.

OK. Change the subject. On to happier things. Maybe I deserve a little centerfold action. I decide to pull out my stash of *Playboys* and toss them on the floor next to the shower. There are so many hot chicks in this magazine. The tough part is always finding just the right one to stick in my mind for as long as possible. Ah, there she is. A hot blond with C cups and a nicely trimmed down below. That works.

As I'm taking care of business, I try desperately to only think about Jenny in the magazine. But it never fails; random shit always pops into my head. Then the same two things usually ruin everything. Dudes end up popping into my head. Not any one dude. Usually I'm trying to think back to a recent porno and as I try to mentally picture the girl having sex, the dude gets in the way. Then everything goes to hell.

Am I gay? Why in the hell can't I just enjoy this for two minutes? My God, maybe I am gay. Oh man, if I really am I couldn't live with myself. Not that I'm prejudiced, but I don't want to touch dicks. I love women. I love breasts and nice asses. I love long legs and that amazing dimple in a woman's back. I love the curves of a woman's hips. And watching a woman have an orgasm drives me crazy. I could think about that all day, every day. Dude, you're not gay. You love women.

I continue to shower, giving up on pleasuring myself. The moment is clearly lost at this point. Then my family pops into my head. Suddenly I start feeling guilty for having this smut around the house. But can you really blame me? I have sex two times per year. I would never cheat on Sarah, which is a pretty big thing to say these days. Hell, everyone is cheating on each other.

Would you want someone to think of Isabella that way? Or Lucy? What if some day they get married and their husbands bring home this smut? Even worse, what if they end up in one of these magazines someday? I start to feel sick to my stomach. That thought can't escape my brain. *What if one day twenty years from now, you open up your dirty old* Playboy *and there they are. Would you look at them? Would you be attracted to them? Oh God. Please stop. I'm going to vomit. How could you be attracted to them? They are your kids. Well, how do you know you wouldn't be attracted to them? You don't know until it actually happens. Oh my God. Does that make me a some type of child perv? What if I'm attracted to my kids now? That would be awful. Please, please stop this. Hands folded together. Knock on wood three times. Lord, please God. Protect my children, Brady, Isabella, and Lucy. Please help them live long, happy healthy lives. Please protect them against evil and please don't ever let anyone treat them like I treat these magazines. Please let them have respect for themselves and to never appear in these magazines. And Lord, please help me to get these bad thoughts out of my head. I don't want to have gay thoughts or weird thoughts about the kids. Thank you, Lord. Amen. Sign of the cross five times.*

What was supposed to be a nice, relaxing ten-minute shower turns into an hour-long disturbing conversation with myself. Now I have three monsters sitting instead my head which I can't seem to get rid of. First, and the one that is now the easiest to handle, is the fear of being gay. The funny thing about this one is I have no problem with gay people. I've had several friends that are gay. Yet, somehow the fear of being gay myself freaks me out. I'm sure it's a male pride thing.

Second, the horrible thought of having people take advantage of my little babies when they are older. Then the worst one, the fear that I'm such a "perv" maybe someday I'll be attracted to my own kids. God is that sick. After getting dressed, I decide to head to the local library. I head to the self-help section and am amazed at how many books deal with mental issues.

I know I'm just going through some type of weird phase here. Ethel might want to read one of these too. Then I come across two books that catch my eye. One is on depression. It seems to cover root causes, symptoms, and a bunch of other crap. The other covers OCD. Obsessive Compulsive Disorder is definitely something I've heard of, although I can't say I've met anyone who has it.

I remember watching a show on it once. These four weirdoes were working with some quack who tried to help them overcome their fear of germs. They were literally freaking out and screaming at the thought of touching a doorknob with their bare hands. I remember howling while watching it, thinking there was no way it was real. In the end, the quack made one of the guys lick the edge of a trashcan to overcome his fear. The dude nearly passed out. Supposedly there was going to be a follow-up show in six months to see how the four OCD'ers were doing, but I missed it.

One of the back covers gets my attention: "It was like a tape recorder that wouldn't stop playing in my head, over and over again." Man, I said that once. I decide to take the two books home.

The first page of my OCD book, published in 1996 by a well-known clinical psychologist, strikes a nerve that sends panic through my entire body. It's simply the definition of Obsessive Compulsive Disorder:

"Obsessive-compulsive disorder (OCD), a type of anxiety disorder, is a potentially disabling illness that traps people in endless cycles of repetitive thoughts and behaviors. People with OCD are plagued by recurring and distressing thoughts, fears, or images (obsessions) that they cannot control. The anxiety (nervousness) produced by these thoughts leads to an urgent need to perform certain rituals or routines (compulsions). The compulsive rituals are performed in an attempt to prevent the obsessive thoughts or

make them go away.

Although the ritual may make the anxiety go away temporarily, the person must perform the ritual again when the obsessive thoughts return. This OCD cycle can progress to the point of taking up hours of the person's day and significantly interfering with normal activities. People with OCD may be aware that their obsessions and compulsions are senseless or unrealistic, but they cannot stop themselves."

Holy crap! This is me to the core. That entire definition sounds like what I've been dealing with for the past few years. Maybe longer.

"People with OCD are plagued by recurring or distressing thoughts, fears, or images (obsessions) that they cannot control."

Hello McFly. Are you there? This is you, Ben.

"The anxiety (nervousness) produced by these thoughts leads to an urgent need to perform certain rituals or routines (compulsions)."

Like praying a hundred times a day?

"People with OCD may be aware that their obsessions and compulsions are senseless or unrealistic, but they cannot stop themselves."

Yeah, like I'd ever do anything to hurt my kids. I live for my kids. I finish the entire book that night. Sarah glances over at me in bed every once in while trying to catch what I'm reading, but I've got that covered. I put the outside paper cover of my sports book, Moneyball, over it. That way she won't freak out seeing the OCD book.

At the end of the book, there is a self-help quiz. It asks all kinds of questions to try and determine if you have OCD and if so, how severe it is. Questions like: *Do you frequently worry about being hurt or having family members get hurt? Do you sometimes think about sex for long periods of time and in some cases obsess about certain sexual experiences?*

What guy doesn't do that?

Do you often perform superstitious rituals such as knocking on wood, counting, or praying?

My final score, an 8.5 out of a possible 10. In other words, I'm royally messed up and definitely have OCD. Luckily I have this book to help me out. There is no way I'm going to see a quack.

In the middle of the book it gives specific instructions for how to treat your OCD. First, you need to write out a script and memorize it by heart. Sounds easy enough. The script should talk back to your OCD and tackle it head on. Seems like I already do that sometimes, but it's not formalized.

It gives an example: *I know these thoughts are just OCD and don't represent who I really am. I'm a good person. I'm not afraid of my OCD. I know I'm not gay. I am attracted to women and happily married. I have never had sex with a man and don't plan to ever have sex with a man. This is just my OCD taking over my thoughts. Go away, OCD.*

Hmm, sounds like I could put that one in my repertoire. I guess I'm not the only nut job who's worried about being gay. When I'm finished, I have five different scripts handwritten on a small piece of paper. The book suggests carrying the scripts with you and reciting them when an OCD session takes over. It also suggests taking notes and adding to the scripts as you see fit.

I go to bed that night around three a.m. with mixed emotions. A part of me is relieved to know I've finally diagnosed what the hell is going on in my head. Yet the other side is scared to death, especially if my self-help book won't work and I actually have to go see a shrink.

The next day, feeling sorry for myself, I Google *Statistics on People with Anxiety Disorders or Depression*, hoping I'll feel better once I realize I'm not alone. I click on

www.adaa.org - Anxiety Disorders Association of America.
Wow! I start to read from the site.

Did You Know?

• *Anxiety disorders are the **most common mental illness in the U.S.**, affecting 40 million adults in the United States age 18 and older (18% of U.S. population).*
• *Anxiety disorders are highly treatable, yet only about one-third of those suffering receive treatment.*

Anxiety disorders develop from a complex set of risk factors, including genetics, brain chemistry, personality, and life events.

Facts: Anxiety and Stress-Related Disorders

Generalized Anxiety Disorder (GAD)

GAD affects 6.8 million adults or 3.1% of the U.S. population. Women are twice as likely to be affected as men.

Obsessive-Compulsive Disorder (OCD)

OCD affects 2.2 million or 1.0% of the U.S. population

Hoarding, a form of OCD, is the compulsive purchasing, acquiring, searching, and saving of items that have little or no value.

Hey, that sounds like my mom!

Posttraumatic Stress Disorder (PTSD)

PTSD affects 7.7 million or 3.5% of the U.S. Population

Women are more likely to be affected than men. Rape is the most likely trigger of PTSD: 65% of men and 45.9% of women who are raped will develop the disorder. Childhood sexual abuse is a strong predictor of lifetime likelihood for developing PTSD.

Two point two million people have OCD? Holy crap! Feeling ambitious, I start to dig around for some further information on depression as a whole. I find this one and click on it. http://trialx.com/curetalk/2011/03/depression-statistics-adults-and-teenagers-united-state/

"Depression is a common problem all over the world, not only for the adults but also for teenagers. As per the latest Statistics, almost 5.3% of the adult U.S. population is diagnosed for some kind of mental disorder every year, which comes to be approximately 17 million people. In case of teenagers, about 20% of total population gets diagnosed with serious depressed condition before they reach their adulthood."

5.3% of the U.S. population! I guess everyone really is crazy!

Depression Statistics in Teenagers
1. Teen depression is so common that almost 10-15% of teenagers experience some kind of depressive symptoms during their teen days.
2. Around 5% of teenagers have been diagnosed with major depression at some point of time.

A few things pop into my head after reading this stuff. First, if so many people are suffering from all of this crap, how come no one talks about it? Second, the stats on teenagers scare the hell out of me. God, please help Isabella, Brady, and Lucy!

40. Everything Unravels

Five Weeks Later

Ben

Five weeks have gone by and while I've made a few positive strides, overall I actually think I'm worse off. I feel like a grenade that has the pin half open. It's like I could lose it at any given moment. I can't concentrate at work. Yesterday I spent an hour rereading an email thirty times just to make sure I got it right. It was only one paragraph. I spent another two hours staring at pictures of my family and reciting my scripts.

This one I've said the most. *I know these thoughts are just OCD and don't represent who I really am. I'm a good person. I'm not afraid of my OCD. I know I'm a good father and good husband. I will be faithful to my wife. Even if I sometimes have sexual thoughts about other women, that doesn't mean I'm a cheater. And I would never, ever do anything to hurt my kids. I would rather die than hurt my kids. These weird and messed-up images that pop into my head are just OCD. Please go away, OCD.*

Thankfully, we are heading out on a family vacation to Palm Springs, Florida, for a week. Maybe this is just the break I need to get back on track.

****

Day One – Palm Springs
A Quiet Getaway
Ben

This place is amazing. Our hotel has a waterfront view and there are five huge pools. We're up on the twentieth floor. Usually I'm not the best at dealing with heights, but this balcony is incredible. I hug Brady as he walks out next to me.

"Daddy, I love this place. It's so amazing," he says.

"I know honey; we're going to have so much fun."

Then I pick him up so he can get a better look down at the pools. *What if you dropped him over the railing? He would die instantly. Hell, worse off, what if you **threw** your son over that railing? Stop it. You know you wouldn't do anything crazy like that. What a ridiculous thought. Where the hell is my script? What if you suddenly snapped into a different person and just lost it. You literally would only have to pick him up about two feet above the railing and drop him. Shut up! Shut up! I would never do anything like that! But if you did, can you imagine how horrible that would be? How would he land? What would his body look like? Stop it! Please, OCD. Just stop it. I would never do anything to hurt my kids. I would rather die than hurt my kids. Do you understand that? Stop inserting crazy shit in my head. Stop it! God, please help me!*

I step back and hug Brady as tightly as possible, my legs trembling. I'm visibly shaken as I bring him back into the hotel room with tears in my eyes, hugging him for dear life.

"Daddy, is everything OK? Are you upset?"

"I'm OK, son. Must be my allergies." I head quickly into the bathroom.

For most people who have never dealt with this kind of anxiety, it's tough to explain. Picture someone who is going through drug or alcohol withdrawals. They can't see straight, can't think straight, and look like they are about to jump off a cliff. It's as though someone else has taken over my mind. I'm not an overly religious guy, but I keep feeling like the devil has taken over my brain. He's the only one that could be this cruel.

****

Day 2 – Palm Springs
Ben

I've added a new script to my list. *I know these thoughts are just OCD and don't represent who I really am. I'm a good person. I'm not afraid of my OCD. I know I would never throw my son over the balcony. I would never do anything in the world to hurt my kids. That includes physically hurting them or sexually hurting them. Please stop putting these horrible images and thoughts in my head. I know I'm a good person and I'd rather die that have anything bad happen to my kids. This is just my OCD taking over my thoughts. I don't know why they are there, but I just want them to go away. Please go away, OCD.*

We're heading out to the north pool this morning, the biggest out of the five. I'm pumped and so are the kids. Lucy, Isabella, and Brady have been talking about this pool for the past two months, ever since we first looked up the resort online.

"It has kiddie waterslides!" Isabella says excitedly. "Daddy, can you go with us on the kiddie slide?"

"Sure I will, honey."

Lucy is only two, but she's pumped about the kiddie spray guns.

"Dadda, can we do the watta spray?"

"You bet, honey!" I say happily.

This is really going to be a great day. I know day two will be much better than yesterday. It has to be. I really need a mental break.

We find a great spot right in front of the kiddie area. Right away all of us jump in, even Sarah. The next ten minutes are probably the highlight of my trip. Each of us gets a hold of one of the spray guns and starts aiming it at one another. All of us are laughing hysterically. Even Lucy is getting the hang of it. Man, this is really amazing. Thank you, God, for giving me some peace of mind. I really needed it.

Just as I say that, I catch a beautiful blond out of the corner of my eyes. She's bending over to help her young son, when I can't help notice her amazing large breasts hanging out of her bikini. I realize she looks an awful lot like one of the Playboy chicks in my magazine. *I wonder if she looks the same as that chick naked? I'll bet she does. What did her nipples look like again? Oh yeah, pinkish. They were perfectly shaped and the size of a quarter. Will you stop it, for God's sake? You're out here with your kids having a good time and you can't stop thinking about sex for ten minutes. And this woman is here with her two-year-old son trying to enjoy the pool. Does she really deserve to have you mentally undress her? Would you want some perv doing that to Isabella or Lucy when they're older? I didn't think so.*

Then I break into script number three. *I know these thoughts are just OCD and don't represent who I really am. I'm a good person. I'm not afraid of my OCD. I know I would never cheat on my wife, Sarah, and I'm sorry for having sexual thoughts about other women. It is totally unacceptable and women don't deserve to be treated like sex objects. I would never want my girls to be treated like that when they are older nor would I want my son to treat women like that. Please stop putting these images and thoughts in my head. This is just my OCD taking over my thoughts. I don't know why they are there, but I just want them to go away. Please go away, OCD.*

For the rest of the vacation I rotate between scripts two through five for at least half of my waking hours. Such a huge amount of time! Somehow the gay fears don't come out this time. It's probably because there were too many hot women there. Even my OCD knows there's no hope with getting in the gay fears this time around.

I'll never know if my wife or kids could sense how distant I was during this trip. Hopefully, they didn't even notice, being preoccupied with so many fun things. On the flight back hope I made one of the hardest decisions of my life. I would call a quack, or therapist, on Monday morning to set up an appointment.

****

Day 2 – Palm Springs
A Quiet Getaway
Sarah

OK, Ben is really starting to freak me out now. It's like all he does the whole day now is zone out in his own world and take creepy notes on his little notepad. The other night he was reading something that he obviously didn't want me to know about. If he's cheating on me we're finished. Although I've talked to friends whose husbands were cheating and they acted more sneaky than weird.

With Ben, it's like he's here physically, but mentally far off on another planet. I can't even remember the last time we had a meaningful conversation. And sex, hah. That's a good one. He thinks I'm withholding it on purpose. Like I told Dr. Helen, I can't just turn it on and off like he can. There has to be at least some semblance of emotional attachment. Actually, if all goes well, I was thinking tonight could be our night. The hotel has a babysitting service that runs until midnight. Maybe we can drop the kids off for dinner and assuming Ben and I actually talk during the meal, we can sneak back to the room for some alone time.

Foolish of me to think a beautiful place like this could turn our relationship around. Let's face it; we've been going downhill for over two years now. It's kind of sad how all couples eventually lose their spark. I was so insistent after we got married that Ben and I would never, ever let our love fall apart. I still can vividly remember having a debate with some co-workers supporting the notion of "true soul mates." A few of these women were either recently divorced or never married and the bitterness flowed like a bag full of fresh lemons.

Is it me? I mean, I've gained a few pounds and certainly don't clean up like I used to. But who does after kids? Look at me. Is that acne? My gosh, a thirty-six-year-old overweight woman with acne, messed-up hair and saggy boobs. No wonder Ben doesn't have any romance left.

I did bring my new bikini for this trip, but it's very likely he'll never see me in it. I'll probably just stick with the granny one-piece that I've had for ages. At least that one won't reveal my saggy boobs. Now some of my friends who were adamant about never nursing their kids seem a little less crazy.

"Ben, are you almost done in there?" I yell, trying to maintain my patience. "Let's go, the kids are getting restless and it's already almost eleven-thirty. All the seats at the pool are probably gone."

What is up with him and the bathroom lately? I mean, he's always had some issues with poop, but this is getting out of hand. Is he doing drugs in there? I'm not quite sure when it started, but it seems like over the past few months he's either sleeping or in the bathroom, with an occasional break to eat. And we're invisible. OK. Enough feeling sorry for myself. Let's head to the pool and enjoy some rays.

We find a great spot right in front of the kiddie area. For at least the next few minutes Ben is back to his old self, running around in the pool shooting the kiddie water guns at all of us. I'm drenched and cold, but having a blast. Even Lucy is getting into it. Wow, do I love seeing the kids gravitate to him. This is the man I fell in love with, who has such an appreciation for the little things in life. And he's never too old to have fun.

To my left I notice a beautiful blond falling out of her bikini. She must be in her late twenties. Well, at least we had ten minutes of fun. Now this chick is going to remind me about my saggy boobs again. Oh, and look at her bending over. Can you be a little less obvious? Are those real? The sad thing is they probably are real. Although, do guys really care either way as long as they're big?

What the hell. Ben is drooling all over her. He doesn't even realize I'm watching him. Let's count and see how long he can go. One, two...five, six, seven...twelve, thirteen...twenty-one.

Are you kidding me? How embarrassing. Take a picture, it lasts longer, asshole! You just kissed your nookie goodbye for tonight.

41. Judgment Day

Two Days Later

Ben

"Our greatest glory is not in never falling, but in rising every time we fall."

Confucius - Philosopher

I head out into the lobby hallway of my work building to make the call. This time around I decide to skip the insurance recommendation and go for the best. After doing some research online that morning I found an OCD specialist who has an office ten minutes from our house. I decide to set up the meeting for tomorrow at lunch.

The first session is ninety minutes, and it costs $150. I'm a cheap bastard, but I have no choice at this point. If my boss asks, I'll tell a half truth. I went to the doctor's office.

Walking up to the office of Dr. Alvin Jenkins, I've never felt such a lack of self-confidence. As I fill out some of the paperwork, it occurs to me I've reached the low point in my life. Here I am, wasting away a perfectly good marriage, neglecting my three beautiful children, and now I'm seeing a quack. What the hell happened to me?

Dr. Jenkins has me sit down on his cushy black leather sofa and take off my coat.

"Relax," He says. "Is this your first time seeing someone?"

"Yes," I respond quickly.

"So tell me what's been going on inside your head."

Once he gives me the green light, I spend the next hour pouring it all out. I start to cry about three minutes into our meeting as I talk about the horrible thoughts that have taken over my brain, particularly those about my kids. Dr.

Jenkins just sits, listens, and takes notes. When I start to see him writing I ask, "Can we destroy those notes before I leave? I don't ever want anyone knowing I was here or heaven forbid that I'm a psycho."

He proceeds to assure me that they are strictly confidential and if I really want him to rip them up afterwards, he will. Thirty minutes later I feel like a huge weight has been lifted off my shoulders. Partly because I actually could tell someone about my OCD and all of the fears associated. Also, Dr. Jenkins has an amazingly calm aura about him that somehow radiates through me.

He doesn't look anything like what I pictured a quack to look like. I've always had the image of Doc from *Back to the Future* as a perfect quack. White hair, glasses, and big googly eyes. Dr. Jenkins looks like a regular guy, probably in his mid-to-early forties. Someone I'd hang out with for a beer if I met him in the neighborhood.

I finally take a breath with about twenty minutes left in the meeting. Dr. Jenkins looks at me and says, "OK. There is no doubt you have OCD. Just in case you were still wondering." That made us both laugh a bit.

"You are very tense and I just want you to try and calm down a bit. Everything is going to be all right. Have you told anyone else about the way you've been feeling?" he adds. I'm afraid he's going to call the cops or something.

"No," I reply, wondering where this line of questioning is going.

"Ben, you look like you are in tremendous mental pain. You also told me that your health has been affected. You aren't eating as much and you estimate losing fifteen pounds. I want to make sure you're going to be OK. I would also suggest some medication," he adds.

Here we go. I proceed to explain that while this is a big step for me to come in and see someone, I'm determined to fix this problem without meds. Dr. Jenkins hesitantly agrees to avoid the medication at this point.

"I know things seem pretty scary right now. That's OCD. It's a horrible illness. But the good news is that we can help. We've helped hundreds of other people. And while everyone's fears might be slightly different, it all still boils down to obsessions and compulsions." He sums it up eloquently.

Before he can finish his next sentence I jump in. "How do I know these thoughts won't come true? Could I hurt someone? Oh, God, could I hurt my kids? Am I gay?" I spurt out in a panic.

"Ben. Thoughts mean nothing. Actions are what matter. Rapists rape people. If someone has a thought pop in their head about raping someone, that doesn't mean anything unless they go out and physically rape someone. And if they do physically rape someone, it's because they chose to rape someone, not because a random image pops in their head. Let me give you an example. For the next five minutes, under no circumstances do I want you to think about pink bunnies. OK? If a thought or image pops in your head that has anything whatsoever do with pink bunnies, get it out. Understand?" I nod.

We continue the conversation and within about four seconds, pink bunnies pop into my head. Small ones, big ones, you name it. What the hell? I never think about pink bunnies. Get out of my head.

"Now tell me, Ben, what are you thinking about right now?" Dr. Jenkins says with a smile.

"How to get these pink bunnies out of my head." I say, laughing for the first time in a few weeks.

"It's Murphy's Law, Ben. Now take that and dial it up ten notches to negative images or thoughts that make you feel really uncomfortable and you can see how OCD takes its toll on people. No one can control their thoughts. People without OCD don't really try to control their thoughts; they just let them go without obsessing. People like you that have OCD, read into their thoughts and think they mean something," he continues.

"So my thoughts don't mean anything?" I ask, looking for reassurance.

"Sure, all thoughts probably have several underlying meanings, but you can't take them literally. Thoughts are simply thoughts. That's it. If I think about killing the President right now does that make me a murderer? Does it mean I want to kill the President? Of course not. The difference is that a person with OCD, who might be scared to death of having a thought like that, could obsess about the meaning for weeks. When the reality is those thoughts alone mean nothing.

"People have thousands of thoughts and images pop into their head every day. Most normal people don't even recognize some of the weird and crazy thoughts that pop into their head. But people with OCD have a really hard time with it," he finishes.

"Do you have weird thoughts sometimes?" I ask.

"Every day. I just laugh them off," he says.

The worst part about OCD is that it's like Groundhog Day. Your brain obsesses on the meaning of a thought or image and feeds upon the fear within you. Kind of like watching different images on a TV screen over and over, except you can't turn off your brain, so it is a horrific and repetitive cycle that can last for days, weeks, months, or years. Man, this is deep. I never thought of it that way, but it's true. This guy could be my guardian angel.

The ninety-minute session ends up lasting two hours. I show him my script pages, thinking he'd be impressed I have a head start. "I read one of the OCD books and it suggested writing down my scripts," I say proudly.

"Actually, Ben, new research over the past ten years has shown that approach doesn't work. In fact, in many cases it's counterproductive. I think your book might have been outdated."

He then goes on to explain the treatment process of

Exposure and Response Prevention (ERP). Before I leave, we set up a schedule to meet two times per week, at least in the early stages, until I settle down.

Then he has me write out my top five worst OCD thoughts and fears. Next to each, he asks me to write down a number from 1-10, signifying the amount of pain associated with each, ten being the highest. Mine are as follows:

> *Thoughts/ images involving my kids being hurt and worse by me –10*
> *Fears of my daughters being treated w/disrespect when they're older – 9*
> *Nonstop sexual thoughts of other women, disrespecting my wife – 8.5*
> *Fear of other loved ones getting hurt or dying – 8*
> *Gay thoughts – 7.5*

Man, if this list ever gets out to Mr. Browning from Omega Epsilon, I might as well chop my nuts off and hang it up. Dr. Jenkins assigns me with working on the first one. "OK. With exposure treatment, I'll put this to you in very simplified terms. We're going to reteach the brain not to worry about any thoughts that enter your head, even the most disturbing," he says. Then he goes on to explain that my scripts need to be thrown away. Between now and our session in three days all he wants me to do is simply let my thoughts be and concentrate on not fighting them.

We end with a hug and again I break down in tears. "Thank you, Dr. Jenkins. I love my family more than anything in the world and I want to get better. I need my family."

"And they need you."

As I leave, he hands me his card. "Call me on my cell if you need if you need me and good luck with your homework."

From the time I leave Dr. Jenkins office until our next

visit I call him on the cell five different times. I'm able to physically speak to him on three occasions, each time asking him to interpret the meaning of different thoughts. Dr. Jenkins is kind enough to speak with me for as long as I need. Each time we end a call, he reminds me, "You know, it would really help ease your mind a bit if you consider the medication." Of course, I reject that. Medication is for the weak.

****

Three Days Later – Second Session
Ben

During our second session, Dr. Jenkins asks me to rate my current level of anxiety and hurt, ranking it from 1-10. "Rank the last three days after our session," he says. I write down a nine.

"OK," he says. "Where do you think you were coming in on Monday?"

"Just under a ten," I say.

"So we're making progress." He laughs.

Most of our session focuses on my expectations for being able to lead a normal and happy life. I tell Dr. Jenkins that I could live with a seven on the rating scale.

"Seven?" He sounds surprised. "Ben, you deserve better than that. I'm not saying OCD will leave you entirely. It doesn't work like that. But it is very likely you could get your anxiety level down to a two. When that happens you might sometimes notice the OCD, but it very rarely affects your day-to-day activities. And the best chance of this happening is when we combine both *ERP* and medication. Are you with me?"

I resist again on the medication.

Thinking again of my mom and her struggles, I tell Dr. Jenkins that I really don't want to have to rely to artificial help. This time he's able to change my mind.

"Ben, when people have cancer, they get chemotherapy. If someone gets pneumonia, they are prescribed antibiotics. You have a clinical mental illness, Obsessive Compulsive Disorder. There are proven treatments that help reduce the anxiety levels OCD creates. As your therapist, I'm urging you to try it."

I nod. Dr. Jenkins can tell this takes some of the wind out of my sails.

"Do you know how many people just in the United States take anti-depressants? He asks.

"I have no idea," I respond.

"OK, your next homework assignment is to look up statistics on anti-depressants. Let me just put it to you this way, Ben, you are not alone."

When I get home I Google *Statistics on people taking antidepressants.* I find an article from USA Today by Liz Szabo.

http://www.usatoday.com/news/health/2009-08-03-antidepressants_N.htm

The number of Americans using antidepressants doubled in only a decade, while the number seeing psychiatrists continued to fall, a study shows.

About 10% of Americans — or 27 million people — were taking antidepressants in 2005, the last year for which data were available at the time the study was written. That's about twice the number in 1996, according to the study of nearly 50,000 children and adults in today's Archives of General Psychiatry. Yet the majority weren't being treated for depression. Half of those taking antidepressants used them for back pain, nerve pain, fatigue, sleep difficulties or other problems, the study says. Among users of antidepressants, the percentage receiving psychotherapy fell from 31.5% to less than 20%, the study says. About 80% of patients were treated by doctors other than psychiatrists.

Geez! Twenty-seven million people took antidepressants in 2005? Wow. It's got to be around forty million now.

42. Sarah's Getting Suspicious

Now I really am starting to think my husband is cheating on me. I mean, how long can a guy go without having sex? And why can I never reach him during lunch anymore? We used to talk every day at noon on the dot. Even though we didn't say much, it still gave me comfort knowing it was our daily routine. Now I keep getting his voicemail.

I haven't said anything about my suspicions to Ben yet because I don't want to come across as paranoid, but something is definitely weird. Is he hooking up with someone at work? Maybe she lives nearby and they go to her house for a quickie during their lunch break? OK. I promised myself I would let it go for at least one night.

Thank God I'm finally getting a break. I'm meeting up with a few old friends for some drinks and dancing at *Decades*. *Decades* is a new club that's quickly become the talk of the town. It's in Concord, about thirty minutes from here. They have four floors, each representing a different music genre. Seventies, eighties, nineties, and new stuff. I can't wait to let loose. Lord knows I need it. Plus, it will be good for Ben to actually spend some quality time with the kids. Hopefully they'll watch a movie together, just like old times.

It's been two weeks since we got back from our vacation and somehow Ben and I are actually more distant than before we left. If that's not a sure sign we're destined for a divorce then I don't know what is. Like my mom always said, "If you can't have fun together in paradise, it will only go downhill from there."

Now along with sneaking off into the bathroom, he's getting a bunch of calls on his cell phone and then scurrying outside to talk. He even took a call the other day in the rain. What is he hiding? I'm starting to lose my patience. The next time he gets a call and sneaks out, I'm calling him out!

Speaking of my husband, where the heck is he? "Izzy,

did Daddy tell you he was visiting a customer late tonight?" I ask, hoping he talks to my six-year-old daughter more than me.

"No, Mommy. Daddy didn't say anything to me about missing dinner."

"OK, well, our pork chops are getting cold, so eat up," I say, trying not to show the kids my emotions.

"But why isn't Dadda here, Mommy? Pork chops and apple sauce are his favorite," Brady asks with a frown.

I swear, if he makes me late for this I'm going to be really upset. I sent him the email reminder three weeks ago, so he should have it in his calendar.

"Ben, it's me again. Quarter of seven now and I'm wondering where the heck you are. Remember, I have my girls night out tonight?" I leave the message on his cell. I was supposed to meet them at seven-thirty for some appetizers before heading over to the club. I'm not skipping out this time. It's time for plan B.

"Hi Ethel, it's Sarah. Good. Good. Thank you. Listen, I need a favor. Can you watch the kids for like a couple of hours? Ben is running late and I have to be somewhere. I know it'll be your first time. You'll be fine. Oh, you can? Thank you so much, Ethel. I owe you one. Great, I'm leaving now. See you in about thirty minutes."

Now is as good a time as any to give Ethel a stab at watching the kids. She's been asking for years. Ben and I just haven't felt comfortable. I mean, can you blame us? Those pills are everywhere. Oh no, I'd better do a dry run through her house before I leave.

I carry the kids into the minivan with their PJs still on; grab some milk and the *Land Before Time* DVD. We're off. Hopefully, Ben will get my message and it will be a short stay at Grandma's house. Lucy ends up crying the entire drive, while Izzy and Brady are at each other's throats. I fly down 93 South and get to Ethel's house in twenty-seven minutes, a new record for me.

They definitely can sense the tension in our marriage right now. I feel awful about it. But tonight I just want to drown my troubles away with a few GREY GOOSE martinis. My friend Lisa Evans already told me I could crash at her place later if I need to. She lives right in downtown Concord, within walking distance to the club.

Ethel's house gets worse every time I see it. She is a classic hoarder. I can barely open the front door. She must have every single *Concord Monitor* and *Manchester Union Leader* newspaper from the past decade strewn throughout her floor. And that smell. Oh my gosh. I need to block my nose. It's a combination of must, cat urine, and dirty dishwater.

This time it smells even worse. No wonder why. There must be a week's worth of old dishes in the kitchen sink. Is that old salmon? I'm going to hurl.

I haul Lucy, who is dangling off my left arm, and plop her in the one room that has an area to walk, the dining room. Luckily my portable mini-DVD player is in the car because there is no way the kids will be able see over the stacks of clothes in her living room to the TV.

"OK, Ethel. I'm starting their movie right now. Just pour them some milk and keep an eye on them please. I'll leave a message on Ben's voicemail to come straight here to pick up the kids. Thank you so much!" I peel out of the driveway. Free at last.

"Ben, it's me for the third time. I hope you're OK. The kids are at your mom's house. It's seven twenty-five, so if you can pick them up before nine that would be great. I'll leave you a message later tonight to let you know if I'm spending the night at Lisa's place."

43. Ethel's Chance To Babysit

Ethel

"Oh my, you kiddos are getting so big. How old are you now, Francesca?"

"I'm not Francesca, Grandma, I'm Isabella. But you can call me Izzy," Isabella says.

"Oh yes, I'm so bad with names. Sorry, honey. We're going to have a lot of fun tonight, kids. Here are some pillows, you three sit down on the floor here and drink your milk. I'll go make us some popcorn. Oh, and make sure you're nice to the cats if they come by. Peaches and Snickers love kids. But don't let them drink your milk, OK?"

Where did I put that popcorn? Ah, I think I left it in my bedroom. Yes, that's right. I put the whole box there after I went to the supermarket. Hmm, I know it's in here somewhere. Wait. Didn't I just buy the kids a gift at the flea market yesterday? Where did I put that bag? *I remember now. It's a big white bag with a red flower on it. Or did it have a blue flower? Let me think. Actually, maybe it was a blue bag with a white flower on it? Or could it have been a red bag with a white flower? OK. Concentrate, Ethel. Just start digging and you'll find it. It must be close to the top of this big pile because I just bought the stuff yesterday. Uh oh. I just thought of something. Where did I put my pill container?*

****

Isabella

I wish Grandma cleaned her house more. It's really stinky. Mommy says she doesn't like to throw things away. Maybe our cleaning lady Ms. Rodriquez can come by her house too. She does such a great job with our house. I know Grandma would appreciate it.

"Grandma? Grandma? Is the popcorn almost ready?" Brady yells.

He loves the kettle corn kind. I hope that's what she has in her room. I wonder why she keeps the popcorn in her room? Don't most people keep their food in the cupboards? Lucy is getting anxious. I think she needs a diaper change. I've done it a few times before, but I'd rather let Grandma do it this time. Here comes the big orange cat that looks like Garfield. That is Peaches.

"Lucy, don't pull her tail. She'll bite you."

There isn't a lot of room for Lucy to crawl around in here.

"Stop touching that, Lucy, it will fall on your head!" I yell. "What is that in your hands? No, Lucy. That is so yucky!"

****

Finally A Night Out
Sarah

"It's about time, girl! Just for that, you're doing a shot!" Lisa laughs. Then she takes off my coat and gives me a quick back rub.

"Girl, you look tense. Tonight everything is on me!"

I take the lemon drop and down it in one smooth swig.

Lisa always has been there when I need her. It's my fault we haven't kept in touch over the past few years. I guess I haven't been in the mood to talk lately. She doesn't even know half of what's been going on with me and Ben. I prefer to keep that stuff to myself. She explains that we're meeting up with a few of her friends at La Tasca, a Spanish tapas place, before hitting the club.

I remember Julie. She's Lisa's best friend and recently went through a divorce. Since Lisa's broken-off engagement two years ago, they've become quite the man-haters. Ben doesn't really like the fact that I still keep in touch with Lisa. "She's not a good influence," he always says.

"Yeah, and like your friends are good influences! Having sex with their high school teachers! I don't think so."

The food at La Tasca is incredible. I've already had two plates of sautéed mushrooms. Julie brought along two friends, Rich and Gary. So much for man-hating. It seems like she's with Rich, but she could just be flirting. As for Gary, at first I thought he was into Lisa. But now I'm not so sure. She may not be in the best mental state to impress a guy like Gary.

OK. So he's hot. Just because I'm on a diet doesn't mean I can't look at the menu, isn't that how the old cliché' goes? He's tall, about six foot two, with broad shoulders and a runner's build. Those blue eyes are what make him tough to resist. All right, enough already, Sarah. Don't get carried away.

As the night goes on Gary insists on doing a shot every hour on the hour. At least he lets us do some "Fu Fu shots," as Ben calls them. The last few fruity shots I've ordered have been blueberry and strawberry. But don't let the taste fool you. I'm definitely feeling it. Decades is pretty amazing. There must be a couple thousand people here.

My shirt is drenched from sweat. We've made the seventies room our home for the past two hours. I think they've played "Oh What a Night" three times now. Lisa met some guy and they've been making out in the corner for the past three songs straight. I haven't seen Rick and Julie for a while. So that leaves me and Gary. Boy, if I was single I'd have a hard time resisting him. Heck, if I wasn't faithful I'd have a hard time resisting him. The last song I think I felt his hand on my left butt cheek, but it could just be the alcohol talking. And to think Ben might be out there cheating on me as we speak. I doubt he had any regrets. Maybe I should give him a taste of his own medicine.

****

Ben On His Way Home

Can I get one night where she doesn't pester me so much? Do you really want me to call you and say, "Hi honey, I'm coming home late tonight because my shrink had to push back our appointment time to seven o' clock?" Aren't I dealing with enough crap right now? I mean, Dr. Jenkins has been available for me at a moment's notice ever since I starting seeing him. I could have waited until lunchtime tomorrow, but I have to get a few things off my chest.

I wonder what his normal hours are. Or, should I say, his normal hours before he met me? Hopefully, I'm not the only nut job that's made him miss the family dinners.

Time to check my messages. Oh man! I totally forgot about Sarah's night out. I'm losing it. Message number two. Great. She's getting pissed. What? She let my mom watch the kids? Wow, she must have really needed to get out of the house. I'm on my way.

****

Babysitting Continued
Ethel

Well, I haven't found their gifts from yesterday, but I did find my checkbook that's been missing for two months now. Oh, what a nice surprise. Fifty dollars! Yes. I love finding money.

Yuck, what is this gooey stuff on my checks? Oh, I remember, the carrot cake that Mrs. Edmonds baked for me on my birthday. I guess I'd better throw it away now. Look, there's still two pieces left. Should I eat them? I hate wasting things. Well, I don't know. When does cake go bad? Let's see, my birthday was how many weeks ago? Oh, that's right, just under four months. Hmmm…it might be OK. I'll just try one piece to make sure. No mold. Not bad. Well, it does taste a little funny now that I think of it. I didn't even notice that. Oh well, a few bugs never killed anyone.

"Grandma! Grandma! Lucy's eating Peaches' poop!" Izzy shouts.

"OK, I'll be right there honey," I respond.

Wait, wasn't I supposed to be getting something in my room for the kids?

"Grandma. It smells in here!"

"OK. I'm coming, dear. Hold on one second. I just need to go to the bathroom."

A few minutes later I make my way over to Lucy. "Put that down now. You know better than that! That is so naughty!" I yell. "Peaches, come here! You're a naughty girl too! Now let's get you two cleaned up."

****

Picking Up The Kids
Ben

Wow. Mom really needs to find a landscaper. Hah. First she needs to clean out the thousand pounds of trash in her house. Then she can worry about pruning the yard. Funny, her house feels like my brain. Full of clutter and chaos.

"Hi kiddos. Daddy's here!" I shout, hoping for a nice welcome.

"Daddy! Daddy! Lucy smells! Peaches poopoo! Peaches poopy!" Brady shouts, greeting me at the door.

"She smells like Peaches, huh?" Yes, my little sweetie pie smells like Peaches and roses.

I missed you guys so much!" Just as I finish, the putrid smell hits me. "Crap!" Mom! What the hell is going on in here?"

Lucy is covered in fresh wet cat feces. She somehow

managed to smear it all over her Dora PJs and it's gnarled into her beautiful hair. I'm going to vomit.

"Dadda! Here Dadda!" Lucy says, reeking worse than my mother's house. Are you kidding me?

"Mom, where are you?" Seconds later she comes around the corner.

"I found it, kids. Here's the popcorn. Who is ready for some yummy kettle corn?"

"Me!" Brady and Izzy yell at the same time. I pick all three of them up, each hanging on a different limb. Then I grab the DVD player and their milk containers, storm out of the house, and drop the kids in the car.

She drives me crazy. This is the last straw. I don't care how many anxiety disorders she's been diagnosed with, if you mess with my kids, it's over.

I march back into the pigsty.

"Mom, that was completely irresponsible. Do you realize Lucy had fecal matter all over her? She's going to get sick. Thank God they didn't stay long enough to get into your pills! It's not safe around you anymore. Right now I think it's best if we stay far away from us each other." My blood continues to boil. "Why can't you be like a normal grandparent? Please just leave us alone!"

****

Sarah's Night Comes To An End

Last call. Oh man. I'm ready for an after-party.

"Why don't we party at my place? I have a hot tub," Gary says.

"Sounds like a plan to me." Lisa jumps in before I even have time to think about the implications.

"I didn't bring my bathing suit," I say, not realizing how funny that sounds at one-thirty in the morning.

"Who said anything about bathing suits?" Gary laughs, and then reaches for my hand. This time I let it sit for a few seconds before brushing it aside.

Then instinctively I look down at my wedding ring. Ben saved up for three months to get this ring. I've been thinking about an upgrade now that we're doing better financially. I know it sounds kind of petty, but a quarter carat these days isn't much.

The six of us squeeze in the cab. Lisa is locking lips again with her new man and Julie and Rick are feeling each other up in the front seat. I'm on Gary's lap, but where else can I sit? There's no room.

Wow, his hot tub is pretty sweet. They're on the tenth floor of a new high rise condo in the city. The hot tub overlooks downtown Concord. Right away Julie takes her clothes off and hops in. Rick quickly follows. That's the first penis besides Ben's that I've seen in over ten years.

Eeuh, it's not circumcised. Kind of looks like a turtle hiding in there. Weird, if you ask me. But I'm sure Julie won't care. After Lisa and her man get buck naked, Gary drops his drawers. Wow, what an ass! And a six-pack. He looks like Tom Cruise in *Top Gun*. I haven't felt this riled up in years.

"Come on, Sarah. Have fun. Ben never has to know." Lisa laughs.

"OK. I'll be right back. Where's the bathroom?" I make my way to the restroom and start to take my panties off.

Are you an idiot? You want to ruin everything just for one night of fun? An image of Izzy's face suddenly appears. I throw my clothes back on, walk out the side door, and head towards downtown. I sleep the entire cab ride home back to Bristol. After I pay the cab driver it hits me - home never looked so good.

44. The Green "Monstah"

Spring 2011

Jimmy

What a day for a baseball game. Usually I'm still wearing a winter coat the second week of April, but we've lucked out today. The weather forecast shows sixty-five and sunny at game time. Perfect!

What a treat to watch batting practice. I'm glad Trey insisted on getting to Fenway no later than eleven o'clock. "Two hours before the first pitch," he insisted. He's been talking about this moment since the first day we met back in boot camp in the mid-nineties. Man that was a long time ago.

We watch Big Papi, or David Ortiz, for anyone who's been living in a hole for the past five years, hit about ten bombs into the right field seats. He even hits one the other way over the Monster! Standing over thirty-seven feet in height, "the *Monstah*," as Bostonians so eloquently put it, is the tallest fence in all of baseball.

Every time Trey tries to imitate the accent, it gets me howling. One thing a boy from Mississippi can't do is imitate a Boston accent. Sounds more like a wounded alley cat.

Youkilis is up next. Man, I love his crazy swing. He's actually Trey's favorite player. The way he times the bat to slide down his hands perfectly before crushing the ball is amazing. It's reminiscent of a pool shark sliding his stick before putting the eight ball in the corner pocket.

As a line drive hitter, Youk's not as much fun to watch in BP, but boy are those balls coming off his bat hard. He almost nails one of the kids running around in shallow center.

Our seats are pretty sweet; ten rows off the third base line and even with the bag. Trey brought his glove and swears he isn't boarding the plane home unless a live game ball comes with him.

I haven't seen that kid smile this much in my whole life. I'm still amazed he even knows the rules of baseball based on where he grew up. Surprisingly, he got hooked on the Sox back in eighty-six, when we lost the heartbreaker to the Mets.

Like most southerners, his passion is college football. Yet, like the rest of us poor New Englanders, he stuck with the Sox even though Buckner let the ball go through his legs that fateful day in eighty-six.

Actually, to be fair to Billy Buckner, most fans forget what really happened that day. Prior to the infamous play there was Bob Stanley's wild pitch and Calvin Schiraldi's inability to throw a strike. Even worse, no one remembers that we still had game seven left to make up for the debacle of game six.

By the time the National Anthem is played, Trey and I have already wolfed down two Fenway Franks each, along with four icy cold draft beers. We're saving our appetite for the spicy Italian sausages loaded with onions and peppers.

My favorite pitcher, Josh Beckett, is pitching today. I love his intensity on the mound. Trey's favorite is Jon Lester, mostly because they're both lefties. As the anthem ends, Trey and I both have tears running down our faces, taking it all in.

The giant red, white, and blue flag covers the outfield, topped off by three fighter jets blazing overhead. Trey looks so proud. He thanks me again for the hundredth time.

"Semper Fi," I reply back.

Beckett starts off strong, striking out the first two Twins hitters. Then big Joe Mauer, their All-Star catcher, comes to the plate. After taking the first pitch, Beckett fires a ninety-five mph fastball by him to make the count quickly 0-2.

As is the tradition with two outs and two strikes, the

crowd stands in unison and encourages Beckett to get the strikeout. Mauer makes solid contact and drills the ball our way. It scorches right towards us, so fast we both forget to put our gloves up in the air.

Then everything turns black. I can hear people talking around me but I can't see anything. Slowly my sight comes back and I'm greeted by a familiar face. It's Trey.

"Trey, Trey, you OK?" I say concerned, grabbing the bloody baseball rolling by our legs. He's lying on his back in between the Fenway seats. As I look closer, I'm horrified. His lower extremities are missing and all I can see are his intestines coming out of his stomach, while he screams in agony.

"What the hell is going on?" I yell. "Somebody Help! Help us!"

It feels like the entire Fenway crowd is staring down at us. Trey turns to me.

"It's all your fault. Why didn't you just let me get kicked out of boot camp, man? Look at me. Look at me! I'm useless!"

Then I hear a loud barking sound. The neighbors never have been able to control that dog. My T-shirt is drenched with sweat. I look at my alarm clock; four-thirty a.m. I already want this day to be over. I can't take this shit anymore.

45. Giving Up my Man Card

Ben

I'm not as nervous visiting Dr. Allen as I was during my first appointment with Dr. Jenkins. I guess you could say I'm a pro now when it comes to seeing therapists. Although this is the first psychiatrist I've seen.

Apparently there's a difference between psychiatrists and psychologists. Most people are probably fortunate enough not to have to worry about learning this distinction. I found out the hard way, when Dr. Jenkins informed me he couldn't prescribe medication as a psychologist. Pretty dumb if you ask me, but regardless, here I am.

Dr. Allen was referred by our family counselor Dr. Helen, even before I found Dr. Jenkins. I kept his information handy just in case things didn't work out with Dr. Jenkins. Now it looks like I'm going to have to work with both, since I'm not leaving Dr. Jenkins.

Hopefully Dr. Allen can just write me up a quick prescription and let me out of there. I've already divulged every embarrassing detail of the horrible images and thoughts that have taken over my life. Do I really need to do it again just to get some drugs? If I really have to pay the full ninety minutes just to get his John Hancock on a little note, I'm going to be pissed off.

His office is much bigger than Dr. Jenkins'. Of course, he also has the black leather couch. Must be in the quack handbook.

But the first impression he makes is much colder. Unlike Dr. Jenkins' calm and caring demeanor, Dr. Allen comes across pretty arrogant. He's a lot older too, probably in his late fifties. His short white hair meshes nicely with his black, thin-rimmed glasses. I couldn't see myself hanging out with him after hours; that's for sure.

He opens up by telling me he's spoken with Dr.

Jenkins. Good, hopefully he told him all of the messed-up crap going on in my head so I don't have to embarrass myself again.

Unfortunately, that's not quite the case. Dr. Allen asks me to explain which thoughts and images bother me the most. After I do, he reiterates what Dr. Jenkins told me, that the most damaging thoughts always target the most sensitive topics to the person with OCD. Usually it involves the people or subjects that are most important to the individual.

"I understand sexual thoughts are something you are struggling with," Dr. Allen says.

I nod yes, feeling even more uncomfortable now. He goes on to tell me that most people with OCD have distressful thoughts involving sex in some way, shape, or form.

"As Freud would say, sexual thoughts can dominate a person's subconscious mind." Dr. Jenkins must have told him about my strong feelings against medication because he came right out and asked me about it. "So, I understand you think it's weak to take medication?"

"No offense to your patients, but yes, I've always thought if people were strong enough, they wouldn't need artificial influences."

"Do you know what happens to the brain of people who suffer from OCD?" Dr. Allen asks.

I confess that I've really never thought about any of the biological reasons for OCD. I just assumed it's something I'm stuck with and that I likely I inherited this mental disorder from my parents.

He goes on to describe some of the brain imaging research his team has been involved in. Holding a model of the brain, he explains, "Our research has revealed a link between OCD and insufficient levels of the brain chemical serotonin. Serotonin is one of the brain's chemical messengers that transmit signals between brain cells. Serotonin plays a role in the regulation of mood, aggression, impulse control, sleep, appetite, body temperature, and pain." This catches my attention.

"So the OCD isn't my fault or some consequence of my mom's warped parenting techniques?" He laughs and then explains that while behavioral experiences contribute to the levels of OCD a person experiences, he believes the root cause is biological. "That's where the medication comes into play. I'm going to prescribe Lexapro. This is one of the newest medicines used to treat OCD by raising the levels of serotonin available to transmit messages," he says.

"What if I can cope OK with just the behavioral therapy from Dr. Jenkins?" I ask, still resisting the inevitable.

"Would you rather cope or return to a happy life? I've seen so many families and marriages ruined because people suffering from anxiety disorders like OCD didn't get help. How is your marriage?" That's a low blow.

"It needs work," I say, putting my head down.

"Then let's give this a shot. You can always wean off the medication later, but I have a feeling you're going to want to stay on it because it will dramatically improve your life."

We wrap up twenty minutes early. The visit will still be expensive, but at least I won't pay the full amount.

Just then he hands me the invoice for $350. Holy shit! Dr. Jenkins charges $80 per visit. I do a double-take and ask him to sign it.

As I'm walking out the door, I thank him and then feel compelled to say something. "Shouldn't I be charged a little less since we ended twenty minutes early?"

He stares me down.

"All initial visits are $350. Good luck, Ben."

Even though I'm feeling annoyed, I decide not to press the issue.

Luckily, it sounds like I can transfer the prescription to my primary physician after a few months. The car ride home is full of mixed emotions. Relief knowing I can finally stop worrying about the meds and just suck it up. A slight burden has also been lifted after learning about the biological causes of OCD.

But the feeling of getting ripped off takes front and center - $350 for ninety minutes! That is bullshit! Actually, seventy minutes. Here I am trying to get help and I get raped instead. All so this asshole can write up a prescription for me.

I don't care if he suggests that I come back in next month for a follow-up, this is the last damn time I am going here. I'll convince my primary physician to renew the prescription from here.

How in the hell do people with real problems afford to get help? No wonder nobody trusts these Quacks!

Just forget about it. It's over. You can afford it. I turn on the radio hoping to refocus my thoughts. Commercials, that sucks. *Didn't the receptionist tell me a different rate on the phone?* I pull over to the side of the road and look at my contact notes in the BlackBerry.

Luckily, I save everything and specifically wrote down notes in the contact record. Here it is, $175/hour. *Wait a minute that means I should have only paid about $260. He conned me out of $90.*

I pick up the phone and dial Dr. Allen's office. "Hi, is Dr. Allen in?"

"He's with a patient, is there something I can help you with?" his receptionist responds.

"Well, you might be able to help. I just met with him and I have a question about my bill." I try to remain calm.

"Sure, I can try to help," she adds.

"When we set up the meeting you told me he charges $175 per hour, so he must have overcharged me. We met for seventy minutes and he charged me $350." My voice gradually rises as I mention the amount.

"That sounds like something he needs to handle; can he call you back after his appointment?"

"Sure, have him call my cell." I'm disappointed the

issue now must drag on.

I should at least get back $90. Sure it's still expensive, $250, but getting some cash back will help. This situation is starting to cost way too much money. I set a goal to only pay $1,500/year total to fix it and I just spent 20 percent of it in one meeting. Do I even need medication? Maybe I should have just skipped the meeting with him and continued going for the behavioral sessions. If this guy wants me to meet again in six months, is he going to charge another $175 or more? What a nightmare. Why can't I just fix this on my own?"

The phone rings; it's him. "Hi, Dr. Allen. Did your assistant tell you why I called?"

He confirms.

"OK, I think you must have made a mistake on the bill, we met from 3-4:30pm, but I was charged for two full hours. That means I was overcharged $90."

I stop, proud of myself for staying calm.

"My first diagnosis sessions are always charged on two hours, even if we finish up a little early. That is why you were charged $350. I told you that when you left. It's standard practice for this area." He sounds pretty annoyed.

"Yeah, but the receptionist didn't tell me that over the phone when we booked the appointment. She told me it would be based on how long I stayed," I reply.

"Ben, if you want to nickel and dime me over your mental well-being, perhaps I'm not the right doctor for you. There are cheaper options out there, but you will be dealing with public facilities. Is that the kind of care you want?" He stops abruptly.

"Doctor Allen, sorry, I'm not trying to offend you, I just thought you could help out by knocking some money off the bill. Any chance you can make it $275 and cut me back a check for $75?" I'm pretty good at negotiating.

"Ben, clearly this is your OCD taking over. Think about what you are asking. You are haggling with me over a few dollars when it regards your well-being. Do you really think it's worth it? I'm not in the business of haggling with patients. Maybe we should part ways. You can still use the prescription, but you will have to transfer it over to your personal doctor after a few months," He says adamantly.

We hang up. *Is that what you wanted? Now he's probably going back to Dr. J and will tell him I was difficult to work with. Still, $75 is a lot of money. I wish this would all go away. Maybe I don't really need the help. I've dealt with this for thirty-five years, why do I need help now? Besides, medication is for the weak.*

I pull the car back onto the road and make my way home through some back roads to avoid traffic. *Do you know what you could do with $75? That's three meals out, heck, that's like fifteen lunches. And on top of it, I pissed off the shrink. Maybe I should just apologize? Or, did I already? I forget. Wait, I did say I was sorry for questioning him, didn't I? No, no. I said I was sorry for offending him, but that's not the same as saying I didn't mean to disrespect his services. I know he's been doing this a long time and was recommended to me. I need to call him back. But what if he gets more annoyed? Wait, he probably left for the night anyway. Oh, I have his cell phone. Just wait to let this settle and call tomorrow if you want to.*

I pull up to the house, but decide to make one more call before walking in.

"Hi, Dr. Allen, sorry to bother you again. This is Ben; we just spoke a few minutes ago. You gave me your cell; I hope you don't mind that I called it."

I pause. Dead silence on the other end.

"Well, I want to apologize for coming across as not appreciating your help. I do appreciate your help. I just was obsessing about the $350."

"It's OK, Ben; this is why you need help. This is all OCD taking over. Take the medication and let's meet up again in a month. Oh, and please only use my cell phone for emergencies. Goodbye."

When I get home, I type in "Biological Causes of OCD" on Google. He was right.

I click on the link:

http://www.anxietycare.org.uk/docs/ocdcauses.asp

Chemical and brain dysfunction

One cause that is gaining ground concerns the probability that there is a level of brain dysfunction in many OCD sufferers. This does not mean that people with this problem have damaged brains or that their reasoning functions are inferior to those who do not have OCD.

The chemical messenger, Serotonin seems to be heavily involved. Serotonin is a chemical called a neurotransmitter that allows nerve cells to communicate with each other by working in the space between nerve cells, called the synaptic cleft. According to research, Serotonin is involved with biological processes such as mood, aggression, sleep, appetite and pain. It also seems that Serotonin is capable of connecting to nerve cells in the brain in many different ways and so can cause many different responses. It is not even fully established if it is all or part of the Serotonin chemical or another chemical entirely acting on it; or a malfunction in one or more of the receptors in the brain that Serotonin attaches to that causes the OCD problems.

Brain scans have also shown that people with OCD often have abnormalities within the brain, particularly in the orbital cortex (the part of the brain above the eyes) and in deeper structures such as the Basal Ganglia and Thalamus. This research suggests that the communication between these parts of the brain is not functioning correctly. Basically, when anxiety rises in the OCD sufferer, a circuit of inappropriate response happens between these parts of the brain.

"Whoa! Ain't that the truth!" I continue reading.

So, with the Thalamus sending messages that makes this person very (probably very uncomfortably) aware of everything around him or her and the Caudate Nucleus opening the floodgates to intrusive thoughts, the Cortex is perceiving major problems that feed in to the 'fight or flight', or major danger response. The Cingulate Gyrus then demands that compulsions are carried out to relieve the terrible anxiety feelings.

Some research points to the likelihood that OCD sufferers will have a family member with the problem or with one of the other 'OCD –Spectrum' of disorders.

I continue on.....

One American study suggested that up to 30 percent of teenagers with OCD had a member of the immediate family with the problem or with obsessive symptoms. I wonder if my sisters have it? Oh no, my kids. God, no. Please spare them from this shit!

I read on....

Other studies tend to suggest that if a sufferer's OCD began in adulthood there is less chance of this person's offspring contracting it than if the problem was contracted in childhood, specifically if the latter is the type of OCD that tends to start in childhood (if there are different types).

Other research suggests that if one parent has OCD the chances of the child having it are between 2% and 8%. Here again, if the parent has family members with the problem, the chances of the child contracting it increase and if the parent has no family history of OCD, they decrease. A point to bear in mind concerning children is that OCD can involve increased stress and poor eating habits, particularly if the problem relates to food. Children with OCD might then not do too well physically and be prone to stress related problems like headache and upset stomach.

OK. Two to eight percent isn't that bad. Hopefully my kids will fall into the ninety-plus percent category and not get this crap. I move onto the next link.

http://understanding_ocd.tripod.com/ocd_possiblecau ses.html

The old belief that OCD was the result of life experiences has been weakened before the growing evidence that biological factors are a primary contributor to the disorder. The fact that OCD patients respond well to specific medications that affect the neurotransmitter serotonin suggests the disorder has a neurobiological basis. For that reason, OCD is no longer attributed only to attitudes a patient learned in childhood--for example, an inordinate emphasis on cleanliness, or a belief that certain thoughts are dangerous or unacceptable. Instead, the search for causes now focuses on the interaction of neurobiological factors and environmental influences, as well as cognitive processes.

OCD is sometimes accompanied by depression, eating disorders, substance abuse disorder, a personality disorder, attention deficit disorder, or another of the anxiety disorders. Co-existing disorders can make OCD more difficult both to diagnose and to treat.

Oh joy, more than one disorder. Sounds like Ethel to me.

"When OCD is successfully treated with drugs or therapy, the activity in this area of the brain usually decreases. This shows that both drugs and a change in "thinking" can alter the physical functioning of the brain."

Maybe there is some hope here.

46. Isabella's Big Performance

2010

Isabella

"You look spectacular, sweetie pie," Mommy says.

I'm so excited about my first big show. My ballet teacher, Mrs. Kropchoff, says I'm going to be first in line.

I've been doing ballet now for three years, so I'm pretty much an expert now.

"Mommy, can we get there early so you and daddy have a seat in the front row?"

"We'll do our best, Isabella. Daddy was supposed to leave work on time tonight. I'm not sure where he is right now. He may have to just meet us there."

Daddy used to always be on time for everything. But now he's late a lot. I hope I didn't do anything to make him upset.

Me and Brady got into trouble this morning while daddy wasn't paying attention. It was his day to get us ready for school, but he was resting on the couch. That's when we took the new crayons and wrote all over our bedroom wall.

I know we're not supposed to use real crayons on the walls, but Mommy said these ones were washable. My friend Allie drew nice pictures all over her wall, so we thought it was OK. I tried to ask Daddy, but he wouldn't answer. He was just lying there like he normally does, snoring even.

My favorite part of the performance is when we get to put on our purple princess dresses. I love the tiara. Mrs. Kropchoff says it makes me look like Belle.

"Why isn't Daddy here yet, Mommy? The show starts at five-thirty. Is it five-thirty yet?"

"He still has five minutes, honey. Don't worry, he's probably just running late. I already left him two messages on his cell phone. He'll be here. You just do your best and concentrate." Mommy always tries to make me feel better.

"But Mommy, the best part is at the beginning. He'll miss me wearing my purple princess dress."

"I'll take a picture, sweetie," Mommy says.

"But I don't want a picture taken. I want Daddy to see the whole thing. He doesn't love me anymore."

****

Sarah

"Ben, this is me again, pick up please. Where are you? Please tell me you didn't forget about Isabella's ballet performance tonight? We're at the Laconia Ballet Academy on First and Broad Street. The show started ten minutes ago. At least text me to let me know you're OK."

I want to keep talking, but his damn voice mail only allows for twenty seconds. I'm getting so sick of this. I can handle disappointment. It's been going on for a few years now. But the kids shouldn't be subjected to this crap.

Last week he missed Brady's pre-school graduation. I still haven't been given an explanation as to where he went. Now he's missing Izzy's big day. The day she's been talking about for two months!

What is his problem? This is NOT the man I married and fell in love with. That is for damn sure!

As the performance comes to an end, I'm so proud of my sweetie pie. She's put in so many hours and it's really showing on stage. Mrs. Kropkoff is recommending her for the "Advanced Ballet Group" this fall, which is comprised of nine- and ten-year-olds. Izzy had the biggest smile on her face once she found out. Now that smile is completely wiped out because of my slacker husband.

I know my daughter. She put up a fake smile on stage, but I can see the tears welling up. Her eyes were constantly scoping the crowd looking for her missing Dad.

That's it. I need a break. I'm not saying a separation yet. Maybe just a long weekend to get out of the house and clear my head. If he's cheating on me, it's over.

47. One Week On The Drugs

Ben

The first few days of taking the medication didn't seem to have much of an impact. However, after a full week, I've to notice something different. The pain I used to feel when trying to combat the negative thoughts is lessening. It's like the images have moved from right in front of my face to my rearview mirror.

It's still not easy dealing with them, but I will admit it's more bearable. Meanwhile, I've seen some major progress with the Exposure therapy.

There were a few moments when I wanted to revert back to the scripts, but I resisted. My time obsessing has gone from about 60 percent of my day to 30 percent. Even though 30 percent still sounds high, the times when I've felt extreme levels of anxiety is much less frequent.

I still have the occasional panic episode, but overall Dr. Jenkins' recommendations are working. Within the first few weeks of my initial visit, I had an hour-long battle with OCD that centered around my kids. It started with the balcony again and peaked after changing Lucy's diaper.

The OCD tried to convince me that because I wiped her ass, that meant I was somehow feeling up my two-year-old daughter. How sick is that? But, with the help of Dr. Jenkins, I battled through it.

It's now week three and Dr. Jenkins asks if I'm ready to step up it up a notch. "You bet. I was born ready." My confidence, which was completely stripped away from me by this horrible mental illness, is actually starting to show signs of life.

Dr. Jenkins explains the next chapter in our therapy sessions. Not only do I have to let the thoughts be and sit there, but this time I actually have to wish for more horrible thoughts.

"I want you to beg for the most heinous thoughts and images you can imagine and then let them fester in your head without doing a damn thing about it," he says.

Wow, this sounds like it's going to suck. Luckily, this time around we start with the low numbers on my list and work our way up.

First step, embracing heinous gay thoughts and images. Great. I can't wait. Dr. Jenkins suggests that I take thirty to sixty minutes a day by myself, without any distractions, to fester in these horrible thoughts and images. I decide to amp it up a notch and do at least two hours.

That night I sit down in the basement, with the TV off, and try to picture the gayest images I could possibly conjure up. Wow, this is weird.

I picture hooking up with random dudes and having raunchy gay sex. It's repulsive, but I stick with it. Just when it appears I'm going to make it through without any major harm done, suddenly an old memory sticks.

I was young, maybe ten or eleven years old, having a sleepover with one of my friends, Blaine Rogers. We used to cause all kinds of trouble. This particular night we were crank calling people and saying they won $500 from a local radio station. They just had to answer three trivia questions.

At first we made the questions so hard that no one could possibly get all three right. Then we dialed the meanness up a notch and made the questions easier, but on the third question, regardless of the answer, we insisted they were wrong.

I can still to this day remember one lady who started yelling at the top of her lungs when we insisted the capital of Alaska was Anchorage and not Juneau. At the end of our call, before she hung up, she started bawling. I wish that was the worst memory of that night.

Later on, Blaine wanted to play truth or dare. I had never seen a girl naked. Hell, I was afraid of girls at this age. So it never dawned on me that it was a little weird for two ten-year-old boys to play truth or dare. Either way, we played.

Things started off pretty harmless. We each revealed that we'd never made it to second base with a girl. Then we confessed to some pretty mean things we'd done to our siblings.

An hour later, we're playing a mixed version of strip poker and truth or dare. I'm sure I thought this was weird, but as a ten-year-old, realizing you have hair on your nuts is kind of funny.

Next thing you know Blaine dares me to touch his nut sack. Showing that I'm not a coward, I take two quick steps to my left, reach out my pinky and barely make contact with his sack. Then I run back to my spot.

That was the worst part of the night. I don't even think it dawned on me that those two seconds of nut touching would ever come back to haunt me. I still remained friends with Blaine, but we gradually drifted apart. He had no interest in sports while they consumed my whole life. Then we moved out of the neighborhood two years later and I haven't spoken with him since. Years later I found out that Blaine came out of the closet. I wasn't surprised at all, but the news kind of shook me up. Did I have a gay encounter with that kid?

As I'm finishing up my exposure session, Blaine pops into my head. Then the image of that little naïve boy running over and touching his hairy nuts, as if that moment from twenty-five years ago happened yesterday.

I try to let the image sit, but it's unbearable. *You really are gay, aren't you? If you say you're not, how come you touched another guy's nut sack? That must mean you're gay. No, I'm not gay. I have never had sex with a guy. I'm not attracted to dudes. I love women. I love breasts. I'm married with kids, for God's sake!*

At this point I remember Dr. Jenkins gave me his cell phone for emergencies. I dial him. "Hi, Dr. Jenkins. Sorry to disturb you. I want to make you aware of something that just happened during my Exposure Session. Do you have a minute?"

I go on to explain the story about me touching Blaine's hairy nut sack when I was ten years old.

"Does that mean I'm gay, Dr. Jenkins?"

He laughs. "Ben, calm down. You probably don't realize it, but this is your OCD again. Let me ask you a few questions. Have you ever had sex with a man?"

"No," I reply. "Well, unless you count touching Blaine's nut sack?"

"That isn't sex, Ben; it's just two kids curious about their bodies. Or maybe one." I can hear the smirk in his voice.

"Question two; do you want to have sex with other men?"

"I don't think so, Dr. Jenkins. But how do I really know for sure?" I say hesitantly.

"OK. Let me rephrase the question. Do you seek out men at gay bars or other places in order to have a future sexual relationship?"

I laugh. "No, I don't go to gay bars."

"Ben, gay men have sex with other gay men. They do things that other gay men do. You don't. You're not gay. This is your OCD," He concludes.

I hang up feeling much better. Two days later I go back in for another session and Dr. Jenkins asks why I decided to call his cell phone. "You told me if it was an emergency that I could call," I say, trying not to sound defensive.

"I'm not upset that you called, Ben. I'm merely asking because one of the rituals that people with OCD practice to make themselves feel better is confessing their thoughts to other people with the hopes of getting approval or positive reinforcement to help overcome their fears. In other words, you called me to confirm you aren't gay. Do you really think you need me to tell you that you aren't gay? Or can you figure that out on your own by your actions in everyday life?"

He asks me to try and refrain from calling his cell, so that he won't hurt me more by providing affirmation over the phone.

"Remember, Ben, let the thoughts sit there. You don't need me, your wife, or anyone else to affirm who you are as a person." At the time I never realized how right he was about this rule.

****

Sarah Finds Out

So I've spent the last five nights crying myself to sleep. What's pathetic is my husband hasn't even noticed. Why? Oh, he decides to fall asleep on the couch downstairs while watching that stupid television.

I'm sorry. Normally I don't talk in such a negative tone, but I've had enough. Six years ago, if you would have asked my feelings on divorce, forget it. I would have lectured you for an hour. Oh, and if kids were in the picture? Now we're talking a mortal sin.

Wow, are my eyes wide open now. I've already done a little reading at the library about divorce and it seem like the kids could still be fine if we handle things cordially. He can visit every other weekend. Assuming, of course, he even wants to. I doubt he'd have the time to pay attention to them. Lord knows what he's been doing.

OK. So I know this isn't right, but I can't help it. You see, Ben got this letter in the mail yesterday and I'm dying to open it. It's totally not who I am. I realize opening my husband's mail is a complete breach of trust. But this one seems weird. It's from Dr. Michael Allen. The only doctor Ben has gone to for the past twenty years is Dr. Finch. So what gives?

Maybe I can open it with that steam trick and put the letter back in there without him ever noticing. Yes, that's what I'll do.

I've only tried the steam trick once and it failed miserably. Maybe this time I'll get it right. OK. Yes. It's open. Nice. No tearing. I think it worked.

Initial Psychological Consultation
90 minutes
$350.00
*Please remit payment in 30 days.

What the heck is this? Psychological consultation? Oh my gosh. Is Ben OK? This is getting really weird. Why did you open this, Sarah? How could you betray his trust like this? Now you have to tell him. You just have to. No way. He'll never forgive me.

Wait. This still doesn't explain anything. Maybe it's a mistake. Oh, here's a phone number. Just call.

I dial the number.

"Hi, I have a question about a bill. Sure. Invoice number 122141. Thank you."

Will they really tell me any details about it? It's worth a shot.

"OK. My question is, can you explain what *Initial Psychological Consultation* means?"

"Oh, that's our standard bill for someone's first visit with us. Each one after that is billed at $150 an hour. Does your insurance cover it?" the billing contact responds so matter-of-factly.

This is my husband, lady. This is our life! Oh my gosh. Insurance? Three hundred fifty dollars? My gosh. Ben. What is going on?

48. Three Weeks On The Drugs

Ben

Three weeks later, when dealing with fear numbers one and two, I had unbearable thoughts and images. My goal was to finish up with Dr. Jenkins in the next three weeks. That would mean I've spent about three months with him. Longer than I wanted to, but much shorter than what it sounds like other patients have done.

I really hate spending our hard-earned money on therapy, but I have no other options if I want to save my family.

"This is going to be really hard and uncomfortable for you, Ben, but it's the only way you're going to overcome your fears and hopefully get back to a happy and peaceful life," said Dr. Jenkins. "I want you to spend an hour or two each day for the next two weeks imagining the worst possible things that could ever happen to your kids. I'm talking stuff so bad it wouldn't even make a movie. This includes you hurting them, your wife, and complete strangers. If you need to take it slow, go for it. Try your best not to call me."

The first week is so horrifying I wouldn't wish it upon my worst enemy. As a father, dealing with these horrendous thoughts and images makes me feel worthless. I won't go into the details, but let's just say I take Dr. Jenkins' advice to the max and let every horrific thought and image enter my mind. Many times I do it while sitting near my kids, for extra effect. It works.

During the first two days I weep like a baby several times by myself in the bathroom. The kids just think Daddy had to go number two.

I weigh 142 pounds at this point, my lowest weight since my freshman year in college. But that was when I could barely bench press 100 pounds. Truth be told, I look like a cancer patient, just with hair.

My eyes have huge bags under them and virtually everyone I come in contact with asks if I've started running or if I'm trying to lose weight. The lowest point comes when my four-year-old daughter Isabella wants to sit on my lap while watching her favorite TV show, *Dora the Explorer*.

I start to sit with her then a horrible thought enters into my head. I let it sit and the horrific thoughts are excruciating. So bad, I have to get up off the couch. She watches the rest of the show alone while I cry in the bathroom.

Maybe I should talk with Sarah about this so I'm not doing it alone. Yeah right, I'm not sure what will happen first; divorce or she may just pack up the kids and leave my crazy ass! There's just no easy way to explain this shit. It sucks.

At least if I had a physical ailment like a broken arm or some type of disease, I could talk about it with my wife. She'd probably be there at my side with some chicken noodle soup and maybe a nice massage. Instead, I'm moping around on my own while she's pissed off at me. Boy, isn't my life great?

While at work the next day, I randomly decide to check our home voicemail. It's odd because I usually couldn't care less who leaves a message at home. For some reason today I decided to check. There's a message from Dr. Allen's office.

What the hell! Why are they calling my house? I thought this stuff was confidential, for God's sake!

"Hello, Mr. Chase. It's Loretta from Dr. Allen's office. I'm following up on your billing questions from the other day. Can you please give us a call at …"

OK. This is complete bullshit. I'll bet Sarah has already listened to this message and if she's called the number, she'll easily figure out I've been going to a quack for the past few weeks and that she married a nut job. Just great. Exactly what I need right now.

****

Contemplating
Sarah

These past twenty-four hours have been pure hell for me. Why? Well, I completely violated my husband's trust by opening that letter. Yes, he'll probably never know. But I know. And that's all that matters.

I just need to say something to him tonight and admit what I did. It's the only way I can redeem myself.

Maybe he hasn't been cheating on me this whole time? Well, I don't know anything yet. Not until I put all the pieces together. The only thing I do know right now is that we spent $350 on some psychological analysis and my husband was too embarrassed to tell me about it.

Wow. And to think a few years ago my friends were jealous about the level of trust Ben and I shared in our marriage. That fell apart awfully quickly.

****

Ben and Sarah Finally Talk
Ben

It's probably time to fess up. I mean, she already knows anyway. That stupid lady at Dr. Allen's office let the cat out of the bag. Now I have to say something.

Well, I guess I don't really have to. I mean, can things get any more awkward than they've been for the past three months? I know she thinks I'm cheating on her. But I'd rather have that than say, "Honey, I'm going to the *shrink* again and will be home late for dinner. Can you please save me some pork chops?" No. I'll take the speculation about getting laid, thank you.

I walk through the front door and Sarah's face gives it all away. "Ben, there's something I have to talk with you about. Can we go upstairs in our room?" We walk upstairs.

Before she can open her mouth I jump in. "I know you found out about my problem, Sarah. It's OK. I couldn't hide it from you forever. I'm going to a psychologist. Actually two to be exact. I've been diagnosed with a pretty bad case of Obsessive Compulsive Disorder, or OCD. It's a form of depression."

I pause for a second as Sarah's face gets bright red and she starts to bawl.

"I'm going to be OK. Dr. Jenkins has already been making great progress with me. I don't feel depressed, but it is all starting to make sense now."

She holds my hand. I notice her hands are shaking. She looks stunned and doesn't say anything.

"Can you tell me what you're thinking right now? If you want to leave me, I understand. But please, I have to see the kids regularly. I just won't be able to live without my kids." I start crying uncontrollably.

We spend the entire night talking. It's the most I've talked to Sarah in one night since the first month we started dating. How do you explain to someone who is normal the hell your brain can put you through when you have OCD? I try my best.

"Picture the worst nightmare you've ever had. Then imagine that you can't get those thoughts and images out of your head. The more you try, the more they show up. Then your brain starts to convince yourself that the nightmares are real and every image that enters your head must be true. Even the sickest, most vulgar thoughts and images you could ever concoct. That's been my life for the past year."

I even explain some of the crazy crap about the kids. She takes it surprisingly well. Hell, most women would have packed up their bags in the middle of the night, changed their name, and moved to Mexico. Sarah stuck by me. For that I'll be eternally grateful.

"Why can't you just ignore those thoughts? I know

you, Ben, and you're a good man. Don't let that stuff bother you," she says, showing the compassion I fell in love with over twenty years ago.

"I wish it were that easy, honey. There actually have been biological studies showing a chemical imbalance. But that's where Dr. Allen's drugs come in. Between the sessions with Dr. Jenkins and the drugs, hopefully we can all start living a more peaceful life soon."

"So you're not cheating on me?" she asks as the sun rises.

"Not unless you count a black leather sofa in the quack's office," I respond, proud of myself for showing a sense of humor.

****

The Next Day
Sarah

Could I feel any crappier right now? After I woke up and Ben left for work, I did ten Hail Marys apologizing for my insensitivity this past year. My husband's been suffering and here I was assuming he was sleeping with other women.

Oh my gosh. Gary. I saw other guys naked and almost cheated on Ben. I saw his penis! What is wrong with me?

I even turned my kids against him. Oh, poor Ben. I'll never claim to understand anxiety disorders or OCD, but I did some reading on it last night after he fell asleep. It sounds horrible.

Like many other people, I just thought it was people who hoarded a bunch of stuff or were freaked out about dirt like the movie *What About Bob*. I had no idea people could suffer so much on the inside.

There's definitely nothing funny about it. When he first told me it was a form of depression, things really started to make sense. He sleeps late all the time and is so moody.

So many ups and downs. It's like we can never coast at a normal level. We either have an incredibly fun day or a really crappy day. No gray area.

Well, now that the puzzle pieces have come together. I know my role. *To love and honor. For better or for worse.* He needs me now more than ever and our family needs Ben to get better.

****

Making Progress
Ben

The second week of battling my largest demons goes much better. At this point I've seen it all in my head. Every possible negative image or thought has already been there, so it's really all downhill from here.

I actually got to a point where I was wishing for more negative thoughts, defiantly battling back against my OCD. "Come on, you bastard! Is that all you got?"

The confidence is back! Yes, Ben. You can do it! And having Sarah by my side makes such a huge difference.

A month later, Dr. Jenkins is surprised when I tell him I want to take a break and try to apply what I've learned on my own for a little while. He feels we have more work to do, at least on some of the potential underlying reasons for my OCD. He also suggests there may be some other rituals which I'm not even aware of that I partake in.

I couldn't disagree with him, but I really feel like he's provided me with the ammunition to conquer the rest of this horrible illness on my own; at least for now. I'm sure plenty of patients have said the same thing, only to come crawling back to him with a heavy relapse a week later.

It makes me feel really good when he acknowledges how far I've come in such a short time. "Three months ago, Ben, it looked like you were on the verge of a nervous breakdown. Hell, you may have been in the middle of one.

Here you are now dealing with your OCD head on. I'm really proud of you."

While I realize my OCD will always be there, if I continue to let things just sit rather than obsess about changing my thoughts or images, I can live a normal life. Well, at least normal in relative terms. I'll probably still be slinging poop at my friends. That's normal, right?

I give Dr. Jenkins a huge man hug as I leave and can't help but to let the tears flow.

"You changed my life. Thank you for saving me and my family."

He hugs me tighter. "I was honored to help you."

I close the door to his office with a huge smile on my face. Then a random thought pops in my head. *Did you brush against his penis when you hugged him?* This time I laugh out loud.

49. On The Verge Of Collapse

Summary 2011

Jimmy

"Olé, olé, olé, olé, ooooolé, oooolé!"

There must be forty thousand fans in the stadium tonight. What a sight! Fans of all ages rocking the building back and forth with undying support as they try to will us to victory.

It's the first round of the World Cup, being hosted in Frankfurt, Germany. As I take everything in from the sidelines, I think back to my old high school coach, Mr. Mirsky. Who would have thought a small town boy from Bristol, New Hampshire, would be representing the U.S. on this stage? Especially a guy whose favorite sport is American football. Unreal.

Now all of those sprints and foot-fires Mirsky forced us to do seem well worth it. Even though I'm the fourth man off the bench, it still feels like an amazing accomplishment.

We're playing Iraq tonight, who we're favored to beat. But they're a feisty group and we find ourselves trailing 1-0 late in the game.

I look up at the clock: "87:00." Wow, we probably have no more than five minutes left, counting the extra two minutes of injury time.

Then I hear coach. "Ref, sub!"

He turns to me.

"Jimmy, get in there. We need your wheels to make something happen. Let's not lose to these towel heads."

I run onto the field, proudly wearing my number twenty, hoping my quickness can turn the game around. The ball stays down at the opposing end for nearly two minutes, as they fire a shot over the head of Freddy, our stud goalie.

Corner kick. The ball flies over their striker and is headed by Johnny, our sweeper. Larry takes it and yells to me, "Jimmy. Coming to you buddy!" He lays into one that travels deep down the right sideline. I sprint towards it and start dribbling just the outside of the box.

It's just me and the goalie. I take a few steps and just as I'm about to shoot, I notice something weird with the ball. Actually, it's no longer a soccer ball, but rather a tin-can ball similar to the one Amir and the other kids played with back in Iraq.

As I go to kick it, the goalie slides in front of me. Except, instead of a man, its Amir's face, with a large chunk of his head missing.

"Brotha, why didn't you see me there?" he says painfully.

I scream at the top of my lungs, so loud it wakes me up. Two-thirty a.m. on the clock and I'm sweating profusely. *I CAN'T TAKE THIS SHIT ANYMORE! WHY DIDN'T I TAKE A SECOND LOOK BEFORE FIRING THAT ROUND? I'M A CHILD KILLER. NO CHILD KILLER DESERVES TO LIVE.*

50. Isabella's Party

Present Day July 2011

Ben

"OK, kiddos. We have all morning to play together before we have to get ready for Isabella's special day. Mommy is doing some errands before the party starts, so it's just the four of us. Let's see. What would you like to do? Any ideas?" I say.

"Park, Daddy, park!" Brady says.

He is growing up so fast. Just yesterday it seemed like he could barely walk; now he resembles a little man.

"OK. One vote for the park. What do you think, Isabella?"

Whenever she concentrates she looks identical to her mother. What a beautiful little girl. And such compassion for such a little kid. It's like she can feel the hurt from someone else inside her heart.

"I know, Daddy, what about Play-Doh?"

"OK. One vote for Play-Doh and one vote for park. Looks like you're the tiebreaker, Lucy. Park or Play-Doh?"

I laugh, not expecting a response from my two-year-old. She catches me off guard with "Pahk, Dadda, pahk!"

Lucy is such a delight. Our little angel. To think we almost lost her at birth makes me even more appreciative of every waking moment I have with her. Actually, with all of my children.

Back in our planning days, when Sarah and I looked at life through rose-colored glasses, our vision was no less than five kids. We wanted three boys and two girls. That way Izzy could have a girl playmate of her own and the boys could grow up together in a pack.

That was before Sarah's complications. Before my

kidney disease. Now the last thing on my mind is feeling sorry for myself just because we only have three beautiful kids instead of five. Wow, looking back, we were so selfish.

"OK, Lucy made the call. Pahk it is! Don't worry, Izzy, you'll have all afternoon to have your choice of activities. Especially with the chocolate cake and ice cream!" She licks her lips.

"Daddy, can we stop by the store to have popsicles on the way home from the park?" the birthday girl asks.

"Honey, don't you want to save some room for cake and ice cream later? I think we'll have to pass this time."

Usually I'm a pushover, but I've seen what happens to our kids if they binge on sweets.

We enjoy an amazing morning at the local park. I spend half the time playing with the kids and the other half just sitting back on a bench and taking it all in.

Adults can learn so much from kids. Nonstop laughs and smiles, my kids didn't have a worry in the world. That's the way life should be for all kids.

Sarah and I have done a decent job of hiding my illness from them. Although Izzy is starting to get more curious about Daddy's appearance.

What will they do if I'm gone? Will there still be days like this at the park? Will Sarah take them? I can't handle it. I can feel myself starting to lose it, so I quickly walk towards the woods, hands covering my face. I cry, but do it softly. My insides take the brunt of it.

Reality has started to set in. I may not be here in six months. No more birthday parties, visits to the park, sports. No weddings. Oh my God. Who will walk Isabella and Lucy down the aisle?

What about the man-to-man talks Brady will need as he becomes a teenager? Who will intimidate the high school boys as they take out Lucy and Isabella on their first dates?

And Sarah, Oh, my love, Sarah. How will she hold up? Will she remarry? Would I want her to? Yes, whatever makes her happy.

One of the saddest things I've come to realize is that just because you might be sick and dying, living your last days, it doesn't mean the world stops. It doesn't even stop for a nanosecond. As a matter of fact, it probably goes even faster, just to rub it in your face.

Now I wonder how many people I came across during my life were also living out their last days. They were busy thinking about their legacy and worrying about their loved ones who would be left behind, while I was probably honking or yelling at them to get the hell out of the way. Maybe I'm getting what I deserve.

On the way home, I give in and buy the kiddos their popsicles. What can I say, I'm a sucker.

Since Sarah is now home, I quickly drop the kids off at the house then run out to pick up Jimmy. I'm actually kind of surprised he took me up on the offer to pick him up. Not that I'm complaining. The fact that he accepted our invitation almost floored me.

Jimmy isn't exactly a family guy. I can't even remember ever seeing him around small children. Jeez, come to think of it, he's never even met my kids.

I wonder what's gotten into him. He did seem a little out of it at the bar. Maybe he's going through some type of mid-life crisis or something. Either way, I'm glad he's opening up a bit.

He's lived a tough life and as a result can block out just about anything from his memory. I'm sure that's helped him get though the hell in combat, but it's also severely hindered his ability to maintain any semblance of a steady relationship. I don't think he's even dated a chick seriously since high school.

I pull up to the address he provided. Unlike the well-organized Jimmy I've known my whole life; he's not sitting on the front step. I beep.

Five minutes later still no sign of Jimmy. I get out

and bang on the front door.

"Hurry up, you woman!" Surely that will get his butt off the couch.

How long does it take to put on some work boots, an old camo t-shirt, and jeans? Hell, he probably didn't even shower.

A few more minutes go by. I bang on the front door again, but no answer. I decide to walk around to the garage door. The light in the garage appears to be on, so I bang on the glass. Again nothing.

Is that Jimmy on the ground? I see some old work boots protruding from under his car. Then I see him walking out the side door. "You had me scared there for a minute Jimmy."

He's neatly dressed in a polo shirt, which is pretty rare for Jimmy. Of course, I make a snide remark as we get in the car.

He does have a different look about him. Maybe he's trying to make a positive change and become more open. Jimmy immediately knocks back a full beer in about ten seconds. Or maybe not, I laugh to myself.

I play the song for Jimmy which has been tearing at my heart ever since I heard it a few weeks ago, "Father and Son" by Cat Stevens.

During the song I use every last ounce of toughness to avoid the tears. Jimmy would have no respect for me if I bawl in the car listening to a Cat Stevens song.

On the flip side, he seems to not even pay attention to the words. Before I get too hard on him, I remember memories of his dad aren't exactly inspiring ones.

The main reason this song gets to me now is because of the kids. I never could have imagined how much love I could have for a human being until my kids were born.

Sure, I love Sarah with all my heart. But I think anyone with kids will tell you that the love you share for your kids is different than any other in the world. It's like I look at them and see angels. Living angels that actually were created by me and Sarah. How amazing is that?

I want to live through their experiences. I want to feel the sadness, enjoy the laughter, all of the moments. I want to embrace them.

As a father, those words have new meaning to me. Like an awakening of sorts. I can only pray that God blesses me so I can experience a man-to-man conversation with Brady in twenty years.

Jimmy is pumped when he gets to the house and realizes I have a cold case of Heineken in the fridge. We always said if we ever got out of the poorhouse that would be our beer of choice.

The party doesn't start until four p.m., so I thought Jimmy and I could catch up on old times and have a few cold ones. He's pretty content just pounding beers, so I try to break the ice.

"So what do you think of us setting you up with that chick, you know, Casey Hollister?"

"Are my blue balls bulging out of my jeans?" Jimmy replies. "I mean, we all know I'm hard up, but right now I'm focused on just having a few beers with an old buddy. Is that cool?"

At this point I feel guilty. Guilty for assuming he needs a woman to be happy. And even more guilty knowing Casey will be arriving at our house for a surprise birthday party visit. Sarah's idea, of course. She's always loved playing matchmaker.

Unfortunately, or perhaps fortunately, depending upon what the outcome of their meeting would have been, Jimmy passes out well before she arrives. The only conversation they have is when she walks by him while he's face flat on the couch and he snores back at her.

That's when Sarah finally comments on Jimmy's drinking. "That's not normal, Ben. Finishing almost the whole case by himself at a six-year-old's birthday party is a sign of some major issues. We need to talk to him and see if he'll get some help."

Once again Sarah is dead on. I've never had an issue opening my big mouth. So the awkwardness of it all doesn't scare me in the least. In fact, I tend to seek out confrontational moments like this all of my life.

Later on, the irony of it all would finally hit me. This might be the one time that I don't open my big mouth fast enough.

51. Isabella's Party

Jimmy

What in the world do I get a six-year-old for her birthday? So many choices. Wow, I had GI Joes and a Big Wheel. Maybe a few Lego's. There's five aisles just for kids Isabella's age.

Finally a teenage girl hooks me up.

"You can never go wrong with Barbie," she says.

I agree. Just to play it safe, I'll get her the "Spring Break Barbie". I highly doubt she has that one.

Is it me or are these dolls revealing more and more? And with curves that could kill too. Jeez, please don't remind me I haven't had sex in a few months.

The real Spring Break Barbie would be in a wet T-shirt contest, but that probably wouldn't sit too well with Ben and Sarah. Hah. Sometimes I crack myself up.

Isabella will never know she was the reason I lived an extra four days. What can I say? I can't resist hanging out with Ben, especially seeing him and Sarah as parents. Sure, I saw Ben a few times since high school, but I never did meet the kids.

He definitely invited me, but in typical Jimmy fashion, I preferred to meet up at the bars. Fewer reminders of the life I never got to live. I know, weird hearing a rough and tough marine say that. But if I could do it all over again, I'd settle for the white picket fence, a pencil pusher job, and five kids living out on the farm somewhere.

Screw my dad if he wouldn't respect me for it. My whole life I've tried to live up to his expectations and look where that's gotten me.

One more stop. I'd better make it snappy if I want to still catch a ride with Ben. He's picking me up at one o'clock on the dot. Funny, my designated driver for a six-year-old's party is her dad. I guess he can't get too hammered; he's got to take pictures, right?

As I walk into the men's department store, it hits me that I haven't bought a nice piece of clothing for myself, ever. Hell, when did I ever need anything nice? Growing up, my family never went to church and we definitely didn't dress up for special occasions. Uncle Sam provided me with all of the dress-up clothes that I ever needed.

Now it's time to treat myself for once. I owe it to Isabella to wear a nice polo shirt. I've always wanted one, just been too damn cheap to get it.

Turns out the clearance aisle has the perfect one. A bright-red, short-sleeve polo. It will match real well with my jeans. Regular price $39.99, on sale for $19.99. My mom would be proud. Is red the right color to wear for the casket?

Yeah, red is perfect. I'll get hammered all day at Ben's, he'll drop me off later tonight, and I'll sleep until whenever I feel like it tomorrow. Then, after I wake up, I'll fulfill the original plan.

I get home with about thirty-nine minutes to spare. Just enough time for a nice hot shower, shave, and if I'm lucky a nice dump. I turn on the radio to my favorite country station. The water hits my face in a flurry. "Jesus! This piece of garbage!" I yell.

That old lady never did listen to my requests about fixing this damn thing. I guess I'll save her twenty bucks by never asking her again. Man, is there anything I can be positive about these days?

What will I really miss about life? Hmmm, I think hard. Not much. I'll miss the Rueben's at Bob & Edith's. I'll miss sex, although I haven't had nearly enough the past few years. What else? Drinking. Yes, definitely drinking.

Wouldn't you know it, one of my favorites songs come on. "American Soldier" by Toby Keith. I sing, knowing it's the last time I'd ever belt that tune.

I don't do it for the money, there's bills that I can't pay,
I don't do it for the glory, I just do it anyway,

And I will always do my duty, no matter what the price,
I've counted up the cost, I know the sacrifice,
Oh, and I don't want to die for you,
But if dying's asked of me,
I'll bear that cross with an honor,
'Cause freedom don't come free.
I'm an American Soldier, an American,

Man, that song really does it for me. You want to see a grown man cry, have him watch two thousand marines sing that song the night after one of their buddies dies. Tears every time, it never fails. "I'm out here on the front lines, so sleep in peace tonight." Amen! That sums it all up right there!

If I can just leave the world with that memory, all will be good. But, of course, the story of my life, I can't enjoy the positive for more than thirty seconds. The negative crap pops into my head. I definitely won't miss that aspect of my life.

Will you miss thinking about how you were responsible for the deaths of so many people? If you would have never helped Trey in boot camp, he'd be alive right now. If you had watched his back, he wouldn't have been blown to pieces. Why couldn't I have been the one who died? Now I'm throwing in the towel on life. Meanwhile, these other guys, the unlucky ones that did make it back, are sitting in wheelchairs. Many are severely disfigured. They would give anything to trade places with my ass. I'm healthy, still young, could pick up chicks if I actually went out of the house. Have a job. I have it made compared to those sorry asses. Guys like Joey Brawn had half their intestines removed. He eats through a fucking straw. Meanwhile, I'm bitching about my showerhead. Stop feeling sorry for yourself, you asshole. You did this to yourself. No one else did. If you would have just paid more attention. You know the biggest regret you have. Killing that young kid. Dad always said you were a scatterbrain. He was right.

So much for the relaxing shower. Ben's horn sounds as I'm stuck battling my inner demons. No longer any time for my dump and a shave. One "S" will have to do.

"Hurry up, you woman!" Ben yells as he bangs on the front door. Ten minutes later I run out, grabbing Isabella's neatly wrapped gift and, of course, two beers for the ride over. That should still leave me plenty to do the deed tomorrow. It's only a five-minute ride.

"Look at you all dressed up, my man! Isabella will be impressed!" Ben says, laughing. "I don't think I've ever seen you in anything other than camos or a t-shirt."

"What can I say? I decided to clean myself up for the night." I chuckle, downing a large gulp of my beer. "Want some?"

"I think I can wait the two point five miles until we get back to our place. But don't worry; I bought a case for the guys to drink AFTER the party."

Then he says to me, "With my illness and all I've really started to think more about life. You know, I mean really think about what's important."

His eyes were watering up and full of purpose. A look I hadn't witnessed from Ben during our high school days. "Check out this song. My kids. My life is all about my kids. They are my everything." Then he pops in the CD. Cat Stevens' Greatest Hits. The song "Father and Son."

Father
It's not time to make a change,
Just relax, take it easy.
You're still young, that's your fault,
There's so much you have to know.
Find a girl, settle down,
If you want you can marry.
Look at me, I am old, but I'm happy.
I was once like you are now, and I know that it's not easy,
To be calm when you've found something going on.

But take your time, think a lot,
Why, think of everything you've got.
For you will still be here tomorrow, but your dreams may
not.

Son
How can I try to explain, when I do he turns away again.
It's always been the same, same old story.
From the moment I could talk I was ordered to listen.
Now there's a way and I know that I have to go away.
I know I have to go.

Father
It's not time to make a change,
Just sit down, take it slowly.
You're still young, that's your fault,
There's so much you have to go through.
Find a girl, settle down,
If you want you can marry.
Look at me, I am old, but I'm happy.
(Son-- Away Away Away, I know I have to
Make this decision alone - no)

Son
All the times that I cried, keeping all the things I knew inside,
It's hard, but it's harder to ignore it.
If they were right, I'd agree, but it's them they know not me.
Now there's a way and I know that I have to go away.
I know I have to go.
(Father-- Stay Stay Stay, Why must you go and
Make this decision alone?)

This song especially reminds me of Brady. It makes me both happy and sad. Sad because the boy in this song is hurt by his dad never listening to his side of the story. Kind of how we both feel about our dads. In a different way, you

256

also empathize with the dad as he tries to share his experiences with his kid. He knows he hasn't been the perfect dad. Probably not even an average dad. Yet he desperately wants to share his wisdom before it's too late," Ben explains poetically.

I pause, at first shocked by both how much of a man Ben has become and at how right he is about the analogy with our fathers. "That's deep stuff, man. Way too deep for me right now," I say, shrugging off reality. I desperately want to open up to Ben about the horror in my head, about the severe depression and soon to be suicide. Now is my chance.

But I play tough guy again, the story of my life. Instead I say, "You mind if I have your beer?" Ben nods, laughing both at me and with me, I would suspect.

"You'll never change, Jimmy. Gotta love you for it. Take my beer, bro." And with that I knock it back in one gulp. Those two are just an appetizer for the rest of my afternoon.

I blacked out at around five p.m., right at the heart of Isabella's party. From what Ben tells me, I missed the singing by a hair. At that point I was passed out on the living room couch, snoring like a wounded dog. At least that's how Sarah described it.

All I remember is one brief but overwhelming scene of a dream while I was comatose on the couch. It was "Judgment Day", I was in the car with the engine on and the garage door closed. I had polished off two-thirds of the case and was feeling nice and relaxed. The carbon dioxide was really starting to kick in. Just as I started to close my eyes, a figure appeared on the dashboard. It was my father. Then the radio turned on and Cat Stevens' "Father and Son" came on by itself.

Father
It's not time to make a change,

Just sit down, take it slowly.
You're still young, that's your fault,
There's so much you have to go through.
Find a girl, settle down,
If you want you can marry.
Look at me, I am old, but I'm happy.
(Son-- Away Away Away, I know I have to
Make this decision alone - no)

Son
All the times that I cried, keeping all the things I knew inside,
It's hard, but it's harder to ignore it.
If they were right, I'd agree, but it's them They know not me.
Now there's a way and I know that I have to go away.
I know I have to go.
(Father-- Stay Stay Stay, Why must you go and
Make this decision alone?)

Throughout the section where Cat performed as the dad, my father was holding his hands together in prayer formation, tears streaming down his eyes. Yet, as a thirty-seven-year-old bitter ex-Marine, I simply closed my eyes and let the fumes overtake my lungs. Peace at last.

52. Isabella's Party

Sarah

I can't believe my little girl is six years old. No time to cry right now though, I have too much to get done today. Plus, I've shed enough tears since we found out about Ben's kidneys to last a lifetime.

I would do anything to have type O blood. Funny, if someone asked me a year ago, I wouldn't have even known my own blood type. Now, because of Ben's kidney failure, I could teach a class at the local college about blood compatibility. Ben has O negative and I have B positive. The weird thing I learned during this whole ordeal is that even though O blood type is the most common, people who have it can only accept donations from other type O's.

Murphy's Law, I suppose. I would give both kidneys to my husband if it means my beautiful children wouldn't have to lose him so early in life. When Dr. Kayle at the hospital first broke the news about the severity of Ben's condition, I immediately felt a sense of calm when moments later he mentioned that if we found our own living donor, we didn't have to wait in line.

Since I didn't know my blood type, we had to call my OB Gyn's office to wait for the confirmation. Kind of embarrassing that I didn't know it off-hand, but a working mom with three kids has bigger priorities.

Ben isn't close enough with the rest of his family to even bring up the subject. He'd probably be too proud even if they were close, now that I think about it.

I went to both of my brothers the night I found out. Ray was willing to do it. He even had type O. If only he didn't have diabetes. The doctors said it would be too risky.

Ben wasn't surprised in the least about Ray's willingness to give up his kidney.

"Your family is so special. I can only pray that our

kids are that close with one another when they get older."

I think Isabella knows something is wrong. We've done our best to keep it from all of the kids, but she's six going on sixteen. Her questions are getting more and more Columbo-like.

Just yesterday she asked Ben why his face looks so skinny. When he replied, "It must just be my haircut," she quickly fired back, "But why are your clothes falling off of you, Daddy? And why are you tired all the time?" I had to leave the room after that exchange and barely made it upstairs in time before I started to wail in the towel.

I keep praying to God that we'll be blessed with a kidney before it's too late. I think about it nonstop. It's gotten so bad that I look in the obituary section daily now and try to scope out people under fifty with the hopes they took the time to fill out that stupid form on the back of their license.

I don't mean to get snappy, but this is really starting to take its toll on me. I want Ben to get better, but I really don't want to wish for other people to get hurt so he can take their kidney.

I have just a few short errands this morning. Pick up the cake, get the balloons, and then order the pizza. That will give Ben some precious time with the kids. I can't wait to see the look on Isabella's face when the Dora ice cream cake comes out of the freezer.

Oh, one more stop, Casey Hollister's house. She seemed open to being set up with Jimmy when we spoke the other day, but now I have to convince her to stop by the birthday party.

Ben thinks I get a little obsessive about matchmaking. What can I say, I like to try and make people happy. If two people, both attractive, are lonely, then why not spend some time together? Ben always laughs when I make it sound that easy. "You should quit your day job and join Dr. Phil," he sometimes jokes.

Ben drops the kids off just in time for Brady and

Lucy to take naps before the party. Isabella will help me decorate.

The first thing I notice when he walks in with Jimmy is the case of beer. Since Ben has a shot kidney, he can't have more than one. Who is planning to drink the rest? Well, maybe my dad can have a couple, but I hope Jimmy behaves himself. I don't need any chaos at my kid's sixth birthday party. Especially one that could be her dad's last.

****

The party was a big hit. Isabella loved her Dora cake, as witnessed by the several great pictures we got with blue ice cream covering half of her face. We had over twenty people at the house, including my family.

Casey did manage to make a brief appearance, just in time for cake. Unfortunately, Jimmy was passed out on the couch by then. I can't say with complete accuracy that he finished the whole case by himself. However, I can tell you that I never saw anyone else at the party with a beer in hand. A few of the girls had a glass of white wine and Ben drank water.

That kid has some real demons inside. I can just look at him and tell. Jimmy never had it easy growing up. I know that from his days in high school. But his eyes have a sadness about them that's new.

The next morning I wake up bright and early at six-fifteen a.m., motivated to finish the dishes and clean up a bit. I can't stand a messy kitchen. Walking down the stairs with my robe on, I hear the water running. It's Jimmy.

"Oh, hi Sarah. I was just grabbing a glass of water before I head out."

"Head out? Don't you need a ride?" I offer.

"No, it's only a few miles. After last night I could use the exercise," he says, right before gulping down his water and starting to rush out.

Jimmy definitely has a new awkwardness about him

that was never there back in high school. It's like he's running from something.

"Why don't you stay for a few minutes and drink some coffee with me? I make a great brew. Non-alcoholic though." I smile.

"Well, I suppose that would be a nice start to cure my massive headache. Thank you." He sits down at the far end of the table, keeping his distance.

I can tell it's only his polite manners keeping him here. An awkward silence takes over the room while we both look up at the coffee maker. I'm not sure what I can talk about and what might be off-limits with Jimmy. His family? Better not touch that subject. For all I know his brothers could be in jail. Job? I'm not even sure what he does for a living. His buddies back in the military? Not touching that one with a ten-foot pole.

"Your kids are so cute. And I'm shocked at how you and Ben have become such great parents. Well, that didn't come out right. Not that I didn't think you guys could do it, but I guess I'm impressed with how well you two have adapted."

Surprised by the seriousness of his tone, I thank him. He then goes on describing how Isabella looks at Ben and how he sees a look in Ben's eyes that has never been there before.

"Full of life. Like he's on top of the world," Jimmy praises.

"He really has become a great dad," I say proudly.

"How is he doing with the treatments and all?" Jimmy changes the subject. I explain the dialysis treatments and how they're taking their toll on the family.

"How many more people have to die before he gets a new kidney?" Jimmy says, trying to lighten the mood.

"Still over three hundred, but they're dropping like flies." I try to smile, but suddenly lose it.

I spend the next thirty minutes in his arms. In

between sobs I list all of the things I'm most fearful of if we lose Ben. The kids at graduation without their father, weddings, the list goes on.

"What about when Brady needs someone to play ball with? Or when he comes home after being bullied in school? Moms can't fill in for dads the same way."

I notice Jimmy starting to tear up as well. Before I can say anything, he looks towards the stairs and motions for me to look over. Isabella is sitting there in the dark, taking it all in. I get up and walk over towards her.

It's too much for Jimmy to handle. He puts on his sneakers and heads out of the house. Little do I know this might be the last time I see him.

53. The Jog Back Home

Jimmy

I had to get the hell out of there. Such a weird thing, feelings. I've just never been good with them. Numbness is much easier to handle. I can walk into a firefight with AK47s being fired at me in all directions, outmanned tenfold, and not even feel an ounce of fear. But put me in front of a little kid whose daddy is dying and I lose it.

Why can't that be me? Wait, maybe I can write a note on top of the car and request for my kidney to go to Ben, while it's still warm even. Yeah, that's what I can do. Then I would at least have lived for something.

With renewed purpose, I sprint through the center of downtown Bristol; passing the old volunteer fire house I make it home without seeing a single person on the streets. Better that way. I don't want anything to interfere with my plans later today.

It's bad enough I pushed this off four days. That's why I didn't open my mouth to tell Sarah I'm type O-positive. When I get into my apartment, I start looking for a piece of paper to write out my wish for Ben to have my kidney. Hell, he can have every organ in my body. He's a much more deserving man than I am.

Wait a second, maybe I should check with someone to make sure this is legit. It just seems too easy to write a half-baked note. I decide to call my Aunt Shirley. She's been a nurse in Wilmington, Massachusetts, for over thirty years.

Even though we haven't talked in over a year, she's always pestering me to keep in touch. Now's my chance. I catch her on the cell and try to make casual conversation before getting at the real reason for my call. Of course, I don't plan on giving her all of the details. But there's no harm in telling her about Ben's situation.

Turns out one of her best friends, Leyla Johnson, has

been working on the dialysis floor for the past five years. They eat lunch together every day. Shirley usually bitches about how arrogant the surgeons are in the operating room, while Leyla shares the latest sob story from her area.

I try to slip in the question about someone who dies with a wish to give their organs to someone else. "Too bad it ain't that simply, honey. They need a pricey lawyer to make sure the will spells it out just right. Even then, it could take months. I've seen so many good people die waiting for a donor. Such a shame."

She goes on to share her frustrations. "If people would just take a few minutes out of their days to go to the DMV and sign up for organ donation, this travesty wouldn't be happening. And you know the sickest part of all? Even the ones who do fill out the card, half of them don't tell their loved ones, which means they get buried without ever donating."

Great. More good news. I thank Aunt Shirley then rush her off the phone. After we hang up I realize she will be the last human being that I've ever spoken with.

54. Executing the Plan

Jimmy

So much for Bob & Edith's succulent Reuben sandwich being my last meal. That was before I decided to delay my fate a few extra days. Now I'm settling for a few slices of ham dipped in mayo.

I realize the original plan had called for my last breaths to take place at night; who gives a crap. No one is coming by to check on me. Plus, I already have a good amount of alcohol in my system from last night. Hopefully that means I'll get buzzed quicker. I grab the checklist:

Case of Natty Lite
Car Jack
Full tank of gas
Oil-stained rag
Almost new muffler – 98 Pontiac Sunfire
Boston Red Sox boxer shorts

Oh great, my boxers are dirty. What's more important, being found in clean boxers or getting buried with the BoSox? I decide on the BoSox and put on the crusty pair. If anyone wants to check down there, that's their fault.

After getting dressed, I pop open my first Natty Light. Ahhh, tastes pretty good at seven-thirty a.m. Only the best for a former Marine. Semper Fi.

After beer three, I set the jack up under the car, to fool even the savviest of mechanics. Beer five is a shotgun. One of my few talents. Four seconds, a near record.

Beer eight is when I finally feel a little buzzed. I let out a gut-wrenching belch, which my brothers would be proud of. I wonder how they'll react to this whole thing?

I'll probably be talked about like a saint when I'm gone. That's usually how it goes in my family. When the person is alive, people could give a rat's ass about them. But the minute they're dead, it's like they were Mother Teresa.

For beers nine, ten, and eleven I decide to spice it up and play anchor man. Guess who's the anchor man every time? Oh, and guess who is up first and second as well?

For fun, I set a time limit of one minute. I set my fictitious teams as The Pats and Jets. Pats end up winning three to two. Brady sinks a bomb to end the game. Now I'm feeling nice and relaxed.

My second game of anchor man takes me through beers twelve through fourteen. This time the Jets kick ass, winning in a shutout three to zilch. I pound the pitcher without ever letting my lips off the frosty beverage.

Puke burp. Nice! Tastes like the Buffalo wings we had at Isabella's party. That was before I passed out. What a useless person I am. Passing out at a six-year-old's birthday party. I would be the drunken uncle, except we're not related. I guess I'm just the drunk vet back home from the war. Good enough.

For beers sixteen and seventeen I decide to do something a little more interesting. I shotgun both at the same time. I'd seen one guy do it back at basic training. He must have had more practice because I get sloppy. The second beer sprays all over my shirt. Some of it makes it up my nose.

OK. I'm feeling it now. Time to start up the car. Nice. I finished sixteen and a half beers and it's only nine-thirty. Two hours, not bad. What is that, over eight an hour? My old math teacher would be proud.

I sit in the car, radio on. Wouldn't you know it, *American Soldier* again. This time, I turn it off. No need for getting sentimental right now. There's nothing proud about what I'm doing.

After sipping on beer eighteen, I start to doze off. It's getting a little tougher to breathe in the car, but it's manageable. Then I'm out. Or am I?

I'm no longer in the car, but instead sitting in the waiting room of the hospital. Some kids are sitting next to me, coloring. It's Ben's kids. Where is Sarah? Oh God, she must be having another one. Wait a minute, is it Ben's?

I look back at the kids. Isabella doesn't appear much older than when I saw her today. Brady and Lucy look about the same too.

Then a doctor rushes over to us.

"Kids, is anyone here for your mommy? How did she get here today?"

"We took a taxicab," Isabella responds.

The doctor turns back and started digging through a folder. I get up to see what's going on. As I peer through the glass window, Sarah is lying on her back. Her eyes are closed and a nurse is hooking up an oxygen mask to her. Then I hear the baby cry.

Where the hell is Ben? I cover all angles of the room and he's nowhere to be found. I guess the only good news is that another guy isn't taking his place.

Oh no! Is Ben dead already? And what about Sarah? The doctor runs back to Isabella.

"Honey, listen to me. This is very important. Who does Mommy call when she needs a babysitter?"

"Grandma and Grandpa!" Isabella responds.

As the doctor figures out the remaining pieces from Isabella, I feel the most incredible sadness.

Then, flashes of scenes hit me. First it's Isabella graduating from high school, then Brady on the pitcher's mound. Finally, Lucy walking down the aisle. Something is missing with all of these.

In each scene, the kids are crying as they plead for mommy and daddy. I come to and start gagging. Jesus! That was a dream. I slam open the car door and head inside. Don't let those kids down.

55. Feeling Alive Again

Jimmy

"He stands erect by bending over the fallen. He rises by lifting others."

Robert G. Ingersoll - Orator, Attorney, Politician

In about thirty minutes I'll have my insides opened up and will have one less kidney, yet I feel more alive right now than I ever have in my entire life. Knowing that my sacrifice will give Ben another ten or twenty years with his kids is something I'll be able to take to my grave proudly.

Sure, I wasn't able to pull the plug on my life as planned, but there's always time for that after the operation. I'd do no good to Ben six feet under right now. Besides, maybe this feeling of euphoria will stay with me for a while.

I don't want to get my hopes up. The odds are I'll be back to the same old messed-up Jimmy in a month after I recover, but so what? No one can take away the feeling I have right now. Not even the demons from the desert.

Sarah and Ben have been trying to talk me out of this ever since I brought up the idea three weeks ago. She's convinced that somehow our morning coffee sold me on the idea. Ben keeps asking me what led to my decision and I respond the same way every time: "It's the right thing to do for an old friend."

That statement certainly is true. Seeing Ben play with Isabella, Brady, and Lucy made me realize there are in fact good parents out there. The thought of them having to bury their dad gave me the chills.

But the real reason I'm doing it will be for me to know and no one else to ever find out. This decision is as much for me as it is for their family. I can never bring Trey or Amir back; that I know.

No matter how much I cry at night or pray to God, I

can never undo the events which led to their deaths. But maybe helping out a friend by giving my organ can make up for a small portion of the horror which I inflicted on others.

I now realize the only time I'm happy is when I'm sacrificing myself for others. That's just who I am. If I die on the operating table even better. God had just better make sure my kidney is out first.

56. Renewed Hope

Ben

I've been dreaming about this day the minute we left the doctor's office eight months ago with the horrible news that I had STAGE 4 KIDNEY DISEASE. Weird how I'm not nervous in the least bit. It probably helps knowing that Jimmy will be sharing a room with me during our recovery period.

We've already worked out a plan for sharing the TV remote. I have the odd days, he has the even ones. They just upgraded to ESPN 2 a few weeks ago. As Jimmy said, "Good timing."

When people ask me how I got kidney disease, I still don't really have a good answer. Sarah is convinced my four Tylenol every weekend after pounding a case or two is the leading cause.

The doctor didn't disagree, but pointed out that the disease may not have anything to do with my excessive partying. Although I'm sure vomiting every weekend didn't help either. It could even be partially hereditary.

I've tried not to focus on the causes, since it does no good for me now. All I know is that I started to piss like four times in the middle of every night. This combined with losing about twenty-five pounds was enough to have Sarah force me to go see a doctor.

I'm just eternally grateful that Jimmy stepped up to the plate and became the most important pinch hitter of my life. And he's going to hit a home run today, I just know.

The docs say the chance of my body rejecting his kidney is less than 15 percent, given all of the preliminary tests done so far. Sounds like pretty good odds to me.

I'm just so blessed to have a guy like Jimmy in my life. And to think a few weeks ago Sarah and I were really worried about him after Isabella's party. He comes out of nowhere and is willing to risk his life for me. Sure, we were close back in the day, but really I've only seen his sorry ass a handful of times in the past decade.

He's been out killing bad guys while I've been living the "American Dream" with my family and white picket fence. I just wish that guy would get a break every once in a while too.

57. Mixed Emotions

Sarah

What can I say? I have so many mixed emotions today. My soul mate has a second chance at life. How could I not be happy? But I feel responsible for Jimmy's decision.

When he held me in his arms that morning I took advantage of him. He's been through so much crap in his life; the last thing he needs is more drama.

Ben says that Jimmy has only told him stories about killing guys when he's been really drunk. Otherwise, he prefers never to mention anything. But from the little he has shared, he's an emotional wreck.

And subconsciously I must have known he was weak and preyed on him. The kids think I've been crying so much because I'm happy for daddy's new kidney. Which I am. But really I'm feeling so guilty. And heaven forbid if something doesn't go right during the operation. I'll never forgive myself.

Weird how I've been crying myself to sleep every night for the past two hundred days praying for an angel like Jimmy to arrive. Now that he's here, I cry because I feel guilty. I could use a break from the tears.

Our family has been trying to come up with the perfect thank-you gift for Jimmy. So far Isabella had the best idea, season's tickets to the Patriots. Sure, they're not cheap, but Ben has been doing really well the last few years. Of course, he's in favor of the idea because we're getting a pair of tickets, not just one. That means plenty of trips to Foxboro for him, unless a girl comes into the equation.

Ever since we heard the news about Ben's kidney nearly eight months ago, I've started going to church a lot more. I feel really selfish since I only came to God because we want help. But our priest says that doesn't matter. What does matter is that I've come back.

I promised God that when all of this is over, I'll commit myself to getting Ben back to church too. It's always been something I've felt was missing from our marriage. Sure, we go to church about once a month not including Easter and Christmas, but that's not enough. Maybe as a bonus thank you to God I'll even get Jimmy to attend a Mass.

58. You're Not Alone

Jimmy

The first two weeks after the surgery were pretty cool. It's nice to have company. Ben and I relived so many old high school stories I feel like they happened yesterday. Hell, a few of them were so distant I hadn't thought about them for about fifteen years. But they're all classics.

My body feels fine. Sure, I'm still a little sore and I've lost about twenty pounds because my appetite hasn't been the same, but that's about it. And according to the docs, my kidney has taken a real liking to Ben's body. He was up walking around day three. There he goes again trying to show me up.

Emotionally, I still feel at peace about my decision. I just wish my brain could be fixed. During the first two weeks of recovery I guess there were too many distractions to mess with my mind. Then things got back to normal last night.

I'm pretty sure I scared the crap out of Ben when I jumped up and screamed during a nightmare. This time it involved both Trey and Amir. Usually it's a pick 'em, one or the other. Now I'm getting a double dose just for good measure.

I just wish I could get this craziness out of my head! Why can't I just think about normal stuff like everyone else? I pray over and over again but it doesn't seem to make a difference. It's like just when I feel even an ounce of happiness; a bad thought comes by to ruin it.

The thoughts always seem to include someone whom I've betrayed. The more I try to get rid of the images, the worse they get.

"Roommate, what was that all about last night?" Ben says to me.

I play dumb. "What was what all about?" I respond.

"That scream woke up half the damn floor, man. You

sounded like you were getting stalked!"

I brush him off. "Just a stupid nightmare, man. Won't happen again."

The next night it happens again. This time I start sleepwalking and wake up screaming while flailing on the ground. I'm trying to help Trey heal from his wounds. The nurse had to practically pry me off the floor.

Ben acted like he was sleeping, but I'm sure he was awake. Who could sleep through that?

The next morning Ben asks me to go for a walk with him outside. The hospital has a really nice common area out back with benches to sit on. I've been making a daily trek out there to my favorite bench every morning after breakfast.

I've started to take a liking to a couple of cardinals who've built a nest in one of the large trees outside. There's a male and a female. Two weeks ago the male donned beautiful bright red feathers. Now something weird is happening with his head because he's completely bald. His head looks more like a chicken now.

Meanwhile the female, an orange color, hasn't lost any feathers. Yesterday it hit me this is a pretty good analogy for Ben and me.

I'm the one all messed up; losing my mind just like the male is losing all of his beauty. Meanwhile, Ben has life by the balls, just like the female. No pun intended.

Ben sits me down on my favorite bench and starts acting all serious.

"There's something I want to tell you."

"Oh great, what now? The last time I heard big news from you it was because you were dying. What now? You're not gay, are you, man? Not that I wouldn't still be your buddy, man. It might just be a little weird at first, you know?" I laugh.

"No dude, I'm not gay."

He then goes on to tell me that even though on the surface he appears to have it all together, things aren't always as they appear.

For the next hour he tells me intimate details about his OCD and the mental horrors he's lived through for the past several years. He continues to reveal his deepest secrets. The loneliness which once occupied my soul like a huge boulder starts to slowly break apart.

He even reveals things got to a point where he wasn't sure if he and Sarah would make it. The mental battle he faced was pulling him further and further away from his kids and his wife. Everything he loved.

By the end of our conversation we're both in tears. I don't have to tell Ben anything about the hell I've been going through. He already knows.

Before we get up, he asks me to keep one promise for him, now that we share an organ. He makes me promise that I will get help for my PTSD. I give him my word that I will make an appointment the first day we get out of the hospital.

59. Izzy shows signs

Izzy

I'm so scared for my daddy. I know he's getting better. But seeing him in the hospital made me so sad. If he dies, I know he's never coming back.

Mommy used to try and trick me saying that people who die go up to Heaven and are everywhere. But when our dogs died they never came back. And they aren't watching me either. I know. I'll say another prayer for daddy. *Lord, we thank you, Lord, we thank you for our food. For our food. And our many blessings. And our many blessings. Amen. Ahhhmen. God, please pray for mommy, daddy, Brady, Lucy, and everyone else. Please, please, please protect daddy's kidney. Oh, and Jimmy's kidney too. I think he only has one now. Bless us this our Lord, amen.*

I know it's weird praying for food when I'm not eating, but that's how I say my prayers now. It makes me feel better. *Wait. I forgot to ask God to pray for daddy to be able to play with me again. God, please help my daddy get better so he can play with me. Wait; please help him get better so he can play with Brady too. Oh, and Lucy. Amen. Wait. I forgot to say the first part. Lord, we thank you, Lord we thank you. For our food. For our food. And our many blessings. And our many blessings. Amen. Ahhhmen. There, that's better.*

Tonight I'm having a hard time sleeping. I wish I could stop thinking about monsters, but I can't. Every time I close my eyes another one pops in my head.

And my covers are bothering me. *Why can't these covers stay straight? Stay right here. Stop it! I don't want the covers to crinkle up. I want them straight. Please. Please. I can't sleep when my covers aren't straight. Oh no. There's the really mean monster. He's the big hairy one with long teeth. OK. Close your eyes like mommy says and it will go away. Now a deep breath and count to five. One, two, three, four, five. Open up. Ah. Better. Wait, there he is again. Get away. Get out of my thoughts.* "Mommy! Mommy!"

60. A Soldier Calls for Help

Jimmy

"The best day of your life is the one on which you decide your life is your own. No apologies or excuses. No one to lean on, rely on, or blame. The gift of life is yours; it is an amazing journey; and you alone are responsible for the quality of it."

Dan Zadra – Businessman, Inspirational writer

Luckily Ben's psychologist, Dr. Jenkins, has a good friend from college that specializes in treating PTSD. The thought of going to the VA scared the hell out of me.

As a gift of appreciation for my sacrifice, Ben offered to pick up any difference in cost for seeing a top doctor. I've heard some horror stories from other vets who tried to get help at the VA. Let's just say that Medicaid doesn't exactly attract top-of-the-line treatment.

Before making the appointment, I take Ben's advice and do a little research on PTSD. I Google *"PTSD Stats"* and come up with the following:

PTSD General Stats

• *70 % of adults in the U.S have experienced some type of traumatic event, at least once in their lifetimes. That's 223.4 million people.*
• *Up to 20% of these people go on to develop PTSD. As of today, that's 31.3 million people who have had or are struggling with PTSD.*
• *An estimated 1 out of 10 women develops PTSD; women are about twice as likely as men.*
Combat PTSD
• *Lifetime occurrence (prevalence) in combat veterans 10-30%.*

*• In the past year alone the number of diagnosed cases in the military jumped **50%-** and that's just diagnosed cases.*
*• Studies estimate that **1 in every 5** military personnel returning from Iraq and Afghanistan has PTSD.*
*• **20 %** of the soldiers who have been deployed in the past 6 years have PTSD. That's over **300,000.***
*• **17%** of combat troops are women; **71%** of female military personnel develop PTSD due to sexual assault within the ranks.*

A few reactions. Wow, I knew some guys were messed up from serving, but 300,000? Second, I've always thought of PTSD as being related to the military, but I totally forgot about all the people out there suffering from other messed-up experiences. Especially women.

My first visit with Dr. Julia Andrews goes much better than I expect. Like Ben, I've always viewed people who go to shrinks as weak. To compound the issue, my military background has added a few additional quarts of testosterone.

Her office is pretty basic. Just a desk, large black couch, a few plants, and a small running waterfall which plugs into the wall. I have to admit, the sound of water does relax me.

She's not at all what I envisioned. Actually she's very fit; tall and slender, with curly black hair and really white teeth. Boy, if I were ten years older. Heck, I'd do it now.

Dr. Andrews is probably in her late forties or early fifties. I love the thin black glasses she wears. Midway through the session I have to remind myself to stop trying to get in her pants and focus on why I'm here. Although I'll take that kind of fantasy any day over the horrible nightmares I've had to deal with.

It seems like Dr. Andrews is taking it easy on me the first session. All she does is ask me to talk about myself and to share a little about my experience in the Marines.

We only cover my nightmares for ten minutes; she says we'll have plenty of time to get to it in other sessions. I give her the "Cliffs Notes" version of my horror. I want to make sure she isn't freaked out by me in our first session. That way I would at least be eligible for one more.

Dr. Andrews suggests meeting two times per week for at least the first two months. Then we can re-evaluate at that point to see how much we've progressed.

I arrive fifteen minutes early for my next session on the following Tuesday. Her door is closed so I sit down and start reading the outdated *Sports Illustrated* magazine. Why can't these doctors have at least one updated subscription?

I keep looking up, curious about the patient in her office. Is he suffering from PTSD too? Maybe he just got out of the mental hospital down the street? Just then the door pops open and out walks a true hottie. A brunette with a booming body and beautiful face pokes her head in. She looks about my age too, maybe a few years younger.

She gives me a little smile as she walks past me. Then I come back to earth, realizing I'm about to meet again with my shrink. Yeah, probably not the best place to pick up chicks.

Dr. Andrews spends the first half of the session having me relive my worst nightmares. She asks me to close my eyes and narrate for her in detail what went on. I start with the ones about Amir and finish up with the Fenway Park story and Trey.

Surprisingly, she doesn't even flinch. Then she asks me to explain the real-life story behind Trey and Amir. She's the only human being in the world that has heard me admit my guilt.

"Why do you feel responsible for Trey dying?"

"Because if it wasn't for me, he would have never been in Iraq. I bailed him out so many times during boot camp, when all he really wanted to do was go home."

Instead of debating with me she simply nods.

"OK. What about Amir? Why do you feel responsible for his death?"

I couldn't help but to mockingly laugh.

"Because I put two bullets in him! Why else?" I quickly apologize for the tone of my voice.

"No need to apologize. I want you to be open and honest with me."

In just our short time together I already feel like I can tell her anything.

"Did you know it was Amir when you shot him?"

"Of course not, I thought it was that bastard sniper who took out a bunch of my men."

She doesn't react and continues to take notes. A few minutes later she reassures me these are all classic signs of PTSD, and tells me that no one deserves to suffer from these nightmares.

"When these nightmares happen, what do you want to say to them?"

"I want to say leave me the 'F' alone!" I fire back.

She smiles. I'm starting to wonder if she's coming on to me a bit. That lasts about five seconds. Then she proceeds to tell me that we're going to do the opposite.

"For the next several weeks we're going to wish for even worse nightmares. I want you to pray to God to plant the most horrific thoughts and images in your head for the next two weeks."

Is this lady crazy? I came to her to stop the nightmares, not ask for more. She may be hot, but she needs to go see a shrink. "Say what?"

"I know it sounds counterintuitive, but we're training your brain to stop fighting these nightmares."

She goes on to explain *Cognitive Behavioral Therapy and Exposure Treatment*. The last part of our treatment will involve *EMDR*, or *Eye Movement Desensitization and Reprocessing*. I don't follow everything she says, but it has something to do with my eyes blinking a lot when I'm stressed out.

She finishes by suggesting I take Zoloft.

"I'll do the crazy nightmares and even the blinking BS, but I'm not taking any antidepressants."

Instead of trying to convince me she simply lets it go.

"Everything we do here must be decided on together. So if you don't feel comfortable taking medication, we won't do it. Oh, and your first homework assignment is to read up on *EMDR*. It will help you as we dive into it more next week."

I agree and surprisingly feel really good about this session and can't wait for the next one. I think she even notices a slight twinkle coming back in my eyes. I'm sure she's attracted to me. Hopefully she can keep this to a strictly professional relationship.

As I get up to shake her hand, I notice some of the pictures on her desk. One must be her whole family. It's her, some dude with gray hair, a guy about my age, and a hottie.

Wait, that's the girl. The girl I saw coming out of her office. Holy crap! That's Dr. Andrews' daughter. I guess I'm showing up early for the next session.

61. Ben Checking In

Jimmy

"How did it go? Are you crazy?" Ben asks.

"No more than your crazy OCD ass, brother!" I fire back.

"Low blow," Ben says, laughing. "So what's the next step?"

"She wants me to check into Walter Reed Hospital down in DC in the psych ward." I try to keep a straight face.

No reaction; silence.

"OK." Ben hesitates.

"Hah, gotcha sucker. I'm going back next week to start our sessions. We'll be meeting twice a week for as long as it takes, buddy."

While I'm joking around, I have to admit the first session was a little nerve-racking. I didn't want anyone to see me in there, that's for sure. Especially talking about all of the messed-up stuff in my head, that's not fun. Plus the real life-things that I've done make it worse.

I go on to tell Ben about some of the stats on PTSD.

"How about if you stay with us for the next couple of weeks? We have a pullout in the basement. You'll even get your own TV. Just no smut. Deal?" Ben offers.

"Let me think about it."

I'm used to handling things on my own.

****

Jimmy Letting It All Sink In

So Dr. Andrews says I need to just let it all sit there and enjoy the images. Yeah, how about if she tries that and I just sit back and watch how she reacts.

I tried it last night, I wished for some of the worst

285

thoughts ever. And guess what? They came with a vengeance. I mean nonstop nightmares.

I must have only slept about two hours last night. My bed is drenched with sweat and I look like Saddam when we pulled his scared ass out of that rat hole.

Maybe I will take Ben up on his offer. How bad can that pullout be?

****

The Next Night
Jimmy

"OK, Sarah, no more telling me how proud you are, all right?" I say sarcastically.

She can probably sense I'm only half joking.

"I know, Jimmy. It's just great to see you confronting this stuff head on."

Enough patronizing already.

"Has anyone ever suggested you could be an inspirational speaker?" I continue with the sarcasm.

This time she gets the hint. I wonder what their kids think about Daddy's drunken friend Jimmy. I guess we'll find out over the next few weeks. One thing about kids, you can always count on is gut-wrenching honesty. Which I could use right about now.

"I'm going to crash downstairs with you tonight. You cool with that?" Ben says.

At first I want to give him a hard time, but then realize now's probably a good time to get serious.

Joking has always been my way of deflecting the pain. It's my mask. But like Sarah said, head on is the best way to handle this crap.

"Sure, man. I could use the support. I appreciate it," I respond.

Wow, it feels weird but also kind of nice to say something without any hint of sarcasm. Heck, if it wasn't for

Ben, I'd be dealing with this nightmare by myself. Can you imagine if I called Al and asked for his help? He'd probably laugh so hard he'd hang up the phone on me. "PTS what?"

After watching a few *Seinfeld* reruns, I'm down for the count. It doesn't take long for the nightmares to make their mark. This time it's me and Ben. Kind of weird, he's never been in my dreams before. Thank God.

Where are we? Oh. I recognize this place. It's the makeshift hospital tent in Fallujah. Where Trey passed away. I'm walking over to Trey, who's perfectly healthy. I feel proud introducing him to Ben. They shake hands. My two best buds.

Then, out of the blue, Trey pulls an AK47 from behind his back and fires at Ben. I jump in front of the bullets, trying to save my friend. Yet the bullets pass right through my body. I can see holes in my chest from the trajectory of the bullets, but I'm unaffected.

Meanwhile, Ben is on the ground screaming in pain. Then Trey rushes over and points the gun at my head.

"You killed me, you bastard. Don't trust this guy, Ben. I'm putting you out of your misery." Trey fires the gun at Ben's head. I wake up screaming.

I spend the next hour recanting my horrific nightmare with Ben. He seems to take it in stride. I guess he can't be too freaked out considering all of the wacky nonsense that goes on inside his head.

Nonetheless, I don't know how anyone can live with these nightmares and have any semblance of a normal life. And Dr. Andrews wants me to ask for more. Are you kidding me?

"I'm no therapist, Jimmy, but maybe these dreams bother you so much because you're afraid they mean something."

He has a point.

"They do mean something. I killed a lot of people, man. And even though I didn't pull the trigger with Trey, he did die under my watch," I add shamefully.

Jimmy, I've known you for how long now? Twenty years? You've never done anything without giving every ounce of your heart. I know your service in the Marines wasn't any different. You need to stop being so hard on yourself, man. Stop trying to please your father. You're a great man; my idol. If Brady has half the honor and courage you have, I'll be the proudest dad alive."

It didn't come from my father; it came from my best friend. A guy who is now standing my by side when I'm in need. Even better.

Semper Fi.

62. Grandpa's Party

Nine Months Later

Ben

"I can't believe your grandfather is turning eighty today. Wow! If I live to seventy, I'll be ecstatic," I say, pulling into the long VFW driveway.

"Honey, you'd better not die at seventy, or I'll have to scour the town looking for some young sixty-year-old to take me home." Sarah laughs.

"So what are some of the activities planned for today?" I'm curious.

"What would you do if you were eighty, Ben?" she fires back.

"I have no idea. Probably sit on the couch and veg."

"Well, old Grandpy Collins has different plans. There's gambling, bingo, volleyball. I think there's even a pie-eating contest," Sarah says.

"Pie-eating contest? What is this, *Stand by Me?*" My attempt at humor fails miserably.

"OK, kiddos, remember your manners. When we get in there I want you to wish Grandpy a big happy eightieth birthday. Got it?"

"Yes, Dad!" They all reply in unison.

I smile. We finally have them trained.

The banquet hall is packed. Sarah and I are probably the youngest adults in there by about forty-five years easily.

"So where is the rest of your family?" She gives me an elbow to the gut. "I'm sure they're here. Besides, you have plenty in common with these old folks. Just talk about some of your poop stories. I'm sure they can relate."

"Funny. Very funny," I fire back.

A Korean War and World War II vet, Grandpy

Collins is quite the character. I've seen pictures of him in his prime and he was quite dapper. Now he's carrying around an extra person. I'll bet he's five four and weighs in at two-fifty easily. But, the scary thing is he's outweighed by nearly two-thirds of the seniors here.

I feel like we're at a *Cocoon III* preview.

All right, that's enough. Lighten up on the guy, will you? He's turning eighty, for Christ's sake.

I know, maybe I'll try to win a little money and charm the old ladies at the bingo table. Sarah's grandmother, Mrs. Ruth Collins, or Ruthie, is the MC.

Ruthie looks as healthy as she did when I first met her a dozen years ago. I'll bet she's in her early eighties, but could easily pass for sixty. Heck, if I was a little older and single, I'd probably hit on her.

She looks like a cross between Katharine Hepburn and Jackie O. Except I'm almost positive she's not a Democrat.

Ruthie sees me and points to an open spot right in the front.

"Hi, Ben. Glad you could make it. Please, sit next to my friend Agnes. But watch out, she can get feisty." I start to laugh just as I feel my butt being pinched from behind.

Agnes outweighs Grandpy Collins by a hundred pounds easily. She's got cellulite coming out of every conceivable place on her body and luckily for us she's wearing a skin-tight tank top.

I turn and smile, prying her hand off my buns. *Would you hook up with her if you were hammered? I wonder what she looks like naked?* OK. This isn't good. Not now.

But, of course, the images come at me like a ton of meatloaf. *Do you think she's wearing a thong? What color? I'll bet she shops at Victoria's Secret. You know what Jimmy always used to say. The heavy ones are the best in bed because they never know if it might be their last time.*

"B3," Ruthie calls out.

I try not to make any more contact with Agnes, hoping these beautiful images will go away. Remember what Dr. Jenkins said. Just let it all sink in. OK. That's all you got? I've dealt with much worse than this.

Just then I notice Agnes adjusting her dentures. *I'll bet she gives a mean one, baby. No teeth.* And just like that not only does the entire video frame of Agnes doing the nasty pop into my head, but now all of the women sitting down in front of me appear naked. And they're all doing the nasty. I can't help but to laugh. And let me tell you, it is nasty.

These thoughts would make most grown men limp lying in bed with a naked Elle MacPherson. OK. I think I've had enough bingo. Volleyball is calling my name.

They have two volleyball nets placed next to each other outside. I can't believe some of these older men are actually active, especially given their size. There's Sarah's uncle, Frankie. His claim to fame is his amazing ability to balance full beer mugs on his belly without dropping an ounce. In this group he's actually skinny. Well, I should say his legs and arms are skinny. His gut is like a full keg.

Oh pleasant, he's decided to take his shirt off during the game. His full keg belly is completely hairless, a nice contrast to the rest of his apelike body. The belly hangs a full six inches below his trouser line, which means we're one long volley away from getting a pretty horrific peep show.

"Ben, we need one more. Come on, buddy. Can you hang with us?" Frankie says.

I nod and take my spot. As he hugs me, the odor is unbearable. It's like I put my nose straight up his sphincter.

I wonder what his sphincter looks like? God, it must be nasty. Wait. Are you fantasizing about this hairy dude's asshole? What are you, gay? Hey, you think his wife has seen it? The image is now all consuming. But instead of puking, I actually let out one of those uncontrollable laughs. When I try to hold it in, it shoots out and gets louder.

"What's so funny, Ben?" Frankie asks.

"Oh nothing. Nothing. Whose serve is it?" I try to change the subject.

Boy, I'll bet old Frankie can let out a mean dump! Man, can you imagine the smell? Here we go. It always has to come down to poop, doesn't it? Sarah did say I would have something in common with these guys. You know, I might as well let it ride and have fun with this stuff.

For the rest of the afternoon my brain continues to one-up the previous thoughts or images. From old hairy balls to ninety-two-year-old camel toes, I get it all.

Oh and when you mix the images with the live volleyball action, it gets good. Let's just say I'll never think of volleyball the same way again.

If I could use a video projector and display all of the images and thoughts that fill my brain during Grandpy Collins' eightieth birthday party, it would be the nastiest yet funniest film ever made. And I get to watch it for free. Lucky me.

On the drive home I take it all in. All joking aside, I'm proud of myself for coming so far. A year ago this day would have haunted me for weeks. I'll never take for granted how fragile a man's state of mind can be. Thank God I met Dr. Jenkins.

I email him every so often with an update on my progress just so he knows his hard work paid off. I'm still hoping to get together with him for a beer sometime as friends. Maybe when the time is right I'll bring it up. Hopefully, there's a statute of limitations for the patient-doctor relationship rule.

Everything in my life is starting to come together now. I'm even running. Not bad for a guy who just got a new kidney ten months ago. My job couldn't be better and Sarah and I have rekindled our romance. There's only one empty bucket I need to fill.

63. Making up with Ethel

It's been well over a year since I blew up on my mom and essentially told her to get out of our lives. Sixteen months to be exact. While this isn't the longest stretch we've gone without talking, it's definitely my most guilt-ridden one.

I'm not even sure what the right term is for my dysfunctional relationship with my mom. Love-hate isn't accurate because neither depicts the way I feel inside. It's more like, I'm crazy with her and painstakingly guilty without her. Lose/lose, I guess.

But I've done a lot of thinking, especially now that my mind is back on track. Regardless of how much my mom irritates me, she's the only one I've got. And more importantly, my kids shouldn't be penalized for their dad's issues.

Every time we'd watch a movie and make popcorn, Brady would ask when they're going back to Grandma Ethel's house. I would just act like I didn't hear him. But is that really setting the right example? At least they were in the car when I freaked out on her.

Sarah was pretty pissed off about the whole cat feces incident as well. But even so, she thinks my punishment was too harsh. I stood firm, believing strongly that even though other people witnessed my mom's irresponsible and erratic behavior first hand, they tended to let it slide.

Now I've come to terms with some cold, hard facts. Yes, my mom is extremely difficult to be around due to her severe anxiety disorders. However, a part of me continues to blame her for my mental demons. Was it subconscious? Sometimes yes. Sometimes I was fully aware of the resentment.

Each time I'd witness one of her panic episodes, a part of me would flinch, realizing I inherited her DNA. When I was at my weakest moments with the OCD, deep down I blamed Ethel.

Was it fair? At the time I would have vehemently said yes. After all, people who suffer from OCD contract it genetically.

Now that I'm on the right track I realize how selfish and unfair I've been to my mom. She's a victim just like me. The difference is she's much older and never had the luxury of meeting someone like Dr. Jenkins.

I've made up my mind. It's time to be the better man and make amends with my anxiety-ridden mom. Just one rule, no more babysitting.

64. The Surprise

Ben

"When I started counting my blessings, my whole life turned around."

Willie Nelson – Singer, Songwriter, Poet

"Daddy, don't forget Grammy's flowers!" Lucy kindly reminds me.

"Thank you, sweetheart. Mommy picked out some really pretty ones, didn't she?"

"Don't you think you should call first, Ben? What if she's out and about?" Sarah does have a point. But I want to surprise my mom.

I have it all planned out. I'll knock on the door; then lay the flowers on the doormat while I hide. That way I'll get to see her expression before I jump out and surprise her with a big hug.

"Sarah, don't forget to make the dinner reservation at *Bishop's* for six."

My mom loves seafood and you won't find better lobster than at Bishop's.

The ride over to Concord is nice and relaxing. Much better driving down 93 on the weekend, that's for sure. I turn the radio to my favorite country station. Just in time. This song from Tim McGraw has special meaning. *Live Like You Were Dying.*

He said, I went skydiving
I went Rocky Mountain climbing.....
And he said some day I hope you get the chance
To live like you were dyin'............................

What a song! Wow, I loved it before all my issues. Now it should be my anthem. People can learn so much from this song!

As I make the turn onto my mom's street, an unsettling feeling hits my gut. Who is that? I see a woman running frantically down my mom's front steps.

It's my mom's next door neighbor, Susan Harris. She's been dropping off the local paper, the *Concord Monitor*, along with my mom's favorite Dunkin' Donuts coffee, every Sunday for years.

I hop out of the car and sprint towards her. "Susan, is everything OK?"

It takes me a few seconds, but I finally make out what she's saying. "Oh no, Ethel! Oh God, no, Ethel! Pills! Pills! Too many pills!"

"Call 911!" I manage to say before rushing towards my mother's house. I rush through the wide open front door searching frantically for my mom.

Why didn't you ask Susan where she is, you idiot? After covering the downstairs, I make my way up towards her bedroom. That image will haunt me for the rest of my life.

My mom's lifeless body is sprawled out on her bedroom floor like a deer that just got clipped trying to cross the highway. On the floor next to her curled-up hand is that damn pill container. The same one my kids almost got a hold of when she babysat them.

I check for a pulse. Nothing. The guilt drowns me like a tidal wave. Is this what Jimmy felt like watching Trey get carried away without his legs?

If only I could have been there ten minutes earlier. How did she forget to take the right dosage of pills? She does it every day, for God's sake.

****

Later That Night
Ben

My mom's official time of death was seven-twenty a.m., five minutes before Susan rang her doorbell. If I had just skipped making my coffee I likely could have prevented this tragedy.

Sarah is holding it together for our family right now. I'm in a state of shock. She suggested it might be good for me to take a drive and let out some steam. That's when I decide to call Jimmy.

"I'm sorry, man. That is so horrible. Are you hanging in there?" my best friend asks.

I nod, trying to keep my composure, but he can see right through me.

"It's my fault. If I was a little earlier this wouldn't have happened. What a horrible son I've been. Who goes over a year without talking to their mom? My kids will never see their grandmother again."

Jimmy pulls me into his grasp and I let it all out. I cry like a baby for what seems like hours.

THE END